THE COUNTDOWN

Also by Kimberly Derting

THE BODY FINDER
DESIRES OF THE DEAD
THE LAST ECHO
DEAD SILENCE

THE TAKING
THE REPLACED

KIMBERLY DERTING

THE COUNTDOWN

An Imprint of HarperCollinsPublishers

To everyone who's ever felt like they don't belong.

You can still be the hero of your own story.

HarperTeen is an imprint of HarperCollins Publishers.

The Countdown

For information address HarperCollins Children's Books, a division of HarperCollins Publishers, 195 Broadway, New York, NY 10007.
www.epicreads.com

Library of Congress Control Number: 2015956262
ISBN 978-0-06-229366-4 (trade bdg.)

Typography by Andrea Vandergrift
16 17 18 19 20 PC/RRDH 10 9 8 7 6 5 4 3 2 1

❖

First Edition

PART ONE

The surface of the Earth is the shore of the cosmic ocean . . .
— Carl Edward Sagan

Boy, you're an alien
Your touch so foreign
It's supernatural
Extraterrestrial
—Katy Perry, "E.T."

CHAPTER ONE

Day Thirty-Five
(Three Days After the NSA Attack on Blackwater Ranch)
Somewhere in Northern Colorado

BEING AN ALIEN, OR A REPLACED MADE ENTIRELY from alien DNA . . . or whatever the heck I was supposed to be was giving me a serious complex. Five years ago I was the star pitcher on my high school softball team, headed for college, loving life. Then I was abducted by aliens. And ever since coming back just over a month ago, I'd been blindsided by one nasty surprise about myself after another. I'd gone from total hero to utter zero in the (cosmic) blink of an eye.

Not that I'd tell my dad I felt that way. He'd just pull out one of his inspirational quotes, something along the lines of: "Hang in there, baby!" or "If life hands you lemons . . ."

You get the idea; my life was sort of a mess.

Here's the thing, though, it was *my* mess. I might not have understood that at first, but the message was definitely starting to sink in now that we were on the run, my dad and Tyler and me.

Still, this wasn't the playground. There were no do-overs. No take-backsies. I didn't get to call a time-out so I could catch my breath. It was time to pull up my big-girl panties and play the hand I'd been dealt.

That old life of mine was done. Finished. *Finito.*

I was on a new trajectory now, and even though it usually felt more like a derailment—a hurtling-out-of-control-train-wreck of a thing—I figured I might as well embrace it.

Grin and bear it, as my dad would say.

That didn't mean I didn't miss some of those things from my old life. If I said otherwise, I'd be straight-up lying. This new life meant I'd never get the chance to stand on a stage with my classmates and accept a diploma—not from high school or college. My days of playing ball with the teammates I'd known most of my life were a thing of the past. And I'd never have the luxury of doing regular girl things like staying up all night and sharing secrets with the best friend I'd grown up with, because that best friend . . . she'd deserted me . . . thrown me over for my ex, Austin.

Even my own mother had disowned me as far as I knew. Pretty much replacing me with a new family. So it was just me and Dad now. Don't get me wrong—I was grateful to have him back—but to be fair he was almost as messed up as this new life of mine. And just because he'd turned out to be right about the whole alien thing, that didn't make him any less weird.

Now, instead of trying to convince everyone I'd been abducted by little green men, he was focusing his obsessive nature on keeping Tyler and me safe. While we fled from campground to campground, he constantly worried we were being spied on, whether by satellites or park rangers . . . or maybe even undercover bears. Who knew?

And sometimes I couldn't help wondering if that paranoia of his didn't extend to me as well.

Sometimes, when he thought I wasn't looking, I'd catch him watching me out of the corner of his eye, giving me these super long glances. Like he was checking to see if I might still be in here—the old Kyra.

I would have come out and asked him what was going on inside his head, but I was worried about what he might say and the questions he might ask, which was all kinds of wrong since my dad and I used to talk about just about everything.

When I was little, it had always been my dad I'd gone to whenever I'd had a problem, even before my mom. He'd been the one to clean up a scraped knee when I fell off my bike. He'd taught me long division when all the other kids seemed to understand it before I did.

But now there was this inexplicable barrier between us that had never been there before, not even when I'd thought he was crazy.

No, this was different. . . .

But I did mention that different was the new normal, right? And just because things were somehow *off* between me and my dad didn't mean I wasn't happy to be back with him. Or that he didn't feel the exact same way. I knew because of his hug.

It was that simple—the way he hugged me when we were finally reunited. Simon had driven Tyler and me out to meet him from Blackwater Ranch, the secret camp where we'd been staying, after it had been attacked by Agent Truman and his Daylight Division—the NSA's not-so-nice branch that hunted down us abductees. The second my dad had laid eyes on me, he'd nearly smothered me in his flannel embrace. And he hadn't stopped ever since. Even though he looked at me strangely sometimes, he was always touching me—my hand, my shoulder, sometimes my cheek—asking me if I was okay or if I needed anything. Like he was silently reassuring himself I was still there.

He never asked questions about the things that made me different, even though we both knew those questions were there, right beneath the surface. He had to be curious; it was in his nature . . . his conspiracy-theory, we're-not-alone, tinfoil-hat-wearing nature.

And I couldn't entirely blame him, because I was thinking the same things, wondering whether being made entirely from alien DNA somehow canceled out my human memories and personality. I was curious about the things I could do—my abilities, my strengths, the dangers I posed, even though I *100 percent* felt the same. Even though I looked and acted exactly like my old self.

I wanted to tell him to cut it out with the weird looks, because . . . *not cool*, but every time I started to say something, my throat closed tighter than Fort Knox and I ended up pretending I hadn't noticed.

Inside, though . . . inside, the idea that my dad—*my own dad*—couldn't figure out what to make of me, made me want to vanish again. One more chink in my already tarnished armor.

Nice.

I wondered what he'd do if my stomach ripped apart and some alien baby popped out, grinding and gnashing its acid-dripping teeth while it screeched its alien battle cry.

Maybe that's what he expected. That any second I'd be torn apart by whatever was inside me, waiting to break free the way it happened in the movies.

Aliens versus humans.

Us versus them.

In real life, though, Alien Kyra was super boring. Plainer even than Old Kyra, with far fewer friends and a lot more empty time on her hands.

Just thinking about it made me miss the other Returned Tyler and I had left behind at Blackwater because at least they had a clue what we were going through—Simon, Jett, Willow, Natty.

They'd taken me in when I'd had no place else to go, back when Agent Truman had first discovered I existed and set his sights on me. When my mom had decided I was too dangerous to be around, which turned out wasn't so far from the truth.

Like me, the Returned had also been abducted by aliens and sent back after being *altered.* Only they'd been less changed than I was.

Half alien and half human, they considered themselves hybrids. Like me, they could heal faster and needed less food and sleep than our human counterparts. We also aged slower; making them . . . making all of *us* look like teenagers indefinitely.

But I'd give anything to have the one thing they had—the half-human part they still could lay claim to.

Like I said, I'd been taken too, but I'd come back different from the Returned. Different from almost everyone, except Tyler.

Tyler, who was exactly like me.

Well . . . almost. He was as close to me as anyone in the world.

We weren't Returned, we were the Replaced. The difference being that when we'd been abducted, it wasn't only segments of our genetic coding the aliens had messed with, it was everything. All of it. Our entire bodies had been replicated.

Replaced. So that Tyler and I now shared full-on alien DNA, leaving only our faces and our memories to remind us who we used to be. Although even in that I was alone, since Tyler had a gap in his memories—he was missing the time we'd spent together before he was taken. Which was the one memory I wanted him to have most: the part where the two of us had fallen in love.

That was a biggie.

Without it, we were just *friends*, like Old Kyra and Old Tyler, which maybe could've been enough, once upon a time.

There should have been a song in there somewhere . . . an angsty, twangy country song filled with lyrics about love lost and found again. But I couldn't wrangle enough of my former smart-alecky self to think up a single line.

Maybe *spunky* had been part of Old Kyra's DNA. Maybe Alien Kyra had no game. She was straitlaced and boring. She was into bubblegum pop. Or worse, church hymnals. She was the kind of girl who colored inside the lines and wore pink. Crazy amounts of pink.

Alien Kyra was already on my nerves.

Of course it was good to have New Tyler back. He was the one person I'd been fixated on from the moment we'd been separated. I mean, my dad too. But Tyler . . .

It was Tyler I'd spent hours single-mindedly focused on. Picturing in my head. Daydreaming of.

I'd driven Simon and the others crazy for weeks on end, talking incessantly about Tyler after he was taken and wondering why he hadn't been sent back yet.

I should have been satisfied to have them both—Tyler *and* my dad. Even though we had to lay low, we were together, the three of us.

Yet I couldn't help thinking there was something wrong. With me . . . and with Tyler.

With this whole screwed-up situation we were in.

Like I said, my life was a mess.

"You look beautiful." Tyler stood above me as I sat on a log covered in coarse moss, combing my fingers through the knots in my tangled hair.

My hair. It was the last thing I should be thinking about, considering all the other, way more important things we had to deal with.

"Shut up," I insisted, but already blood was rushing to my cheeks.

It had been like that for days. Three, to be exact. Three awkward days with Tyler giving me these long, deliberate looks, like he was searching for something he couldn't quite put his finger on and me wishing he'd hurry up and figure it out already—the memories of who we'd once been together—so I could stop thinking about that other thing.

Because for three days it had been eating me up inside, and even though I'd been unwilling to face it head-on, I couldn't drop it either: What had Tyler meant that night in the desert when he'd said those chilling words: *The Returned must die*?

Now I stared up at him, blushing like a schoolgirl just because he'd said I was beautiful.

"I found something," he told me with that earnest expression I couldn't get enough of, his green eyes overly intense—one of the side effects of being a Returned or a

Replaced, the change to our eye color. He kept his voice low; we both did, not wanting to wake my dad, who was stuffed inside his miniature-sized tent with his not-so-miniature-sized dog, Nancy.

He didn't have to invite me twice. I forgot all about my hair and followed him as he disappeared into the thick forest. I reminded myself for the hundred-millionth time that it didn't matter what he'd said the other night. It didn't mean anything because he'd been sleepwalking, and sleepwalking didn't count, right?

If only he'd said something else.

The Returned must die.

Had that really only been three nights ago? It seemed like another lifetime. Three nights since I'd found him, standing in front of a sheer rock wall in the Utah desert, drawing strange symbols and chanting in that strange mumbo-jumbo language I'd never heard before.

To be fair, no one had probably ever heard it before because it was nonsense.

And when he'd finally looked at me, his expression had kinda-sorta cleared, and he'd said: "*Ochmeel abayal dai.*"

Then, plain as day: "The Returned must die."

At first, I thought he'd have some logical explanation for what I'd just heard. That he'd just *blink* and be magically awake, losing that blanked-out expression he'd been wearing and he'd ask me what we were doing there because it was weird to be out there in the middle of the night like that.

But that wasn't how it happened. And when he didn't

explain, it became this *thing* . . . this strange unspoken weirdness between us.

I'd been stuck like that ever since. Wishing I could find the right words and the right time to just . . . *ask him*, because that's what people did, they asked each other things. But I never quite got around to it because the timing was always . . . off.

So three days had gone by. And every time I tried to ask, the words just died on my lips. Where would I even start, other than *What the hell, Tyler?* and that wasn't much of an icebreaker when what I really-*really* wanted to ask was, *Do you remember anything . . .*

. . . about me?

About us?

About what I did to you?

That last one was the one that made my stomach twist. Somehow, I had to find a way to tell him, to explain before the memory came back to him on its own. Because what if he only got back pieces and they were jumbled, and he didn't understand it had all been a giant-terrible-*horrific* mistake? That I hadn't realized my blood had been toxic to him . . . to all humans? What if he didn't understand that sending him with them—the aliens—that night up at Devil's Hole was the only way I knew to save him from dying?

I never would have risked letting him be changed if I'd had another choice.

Again, I totally would have talked to my dad about it, if my dad had been acting like my dad. I would have told him about the strange words Tyler had said in the desert, and confessed about the guilt I felt over my decision to let Tyler be taken in the first place.

I might even have mentioned the thing where Simon had kissed me when he'd dropped Tyler and me off to meet my dad. The day he'd decided being "friends" wasn't enough for him.

I could've used a dad for that one.

I wished he could help me out with other things too, questions I still had. Like what exactly had happened to him that night up at Devil's Hole when Tyler had been taken? Agent Truman had held my dad hostage, using him as leverage to make me turn myself in. And I would have, if the fireflies hadn't come and made them both disappear—my dad and Agent Truman—at the same time they'd taken Tyler.

So if he'd been taken like the rest of us, why had my dad come back without having been changed at all?

The whole thing was all so strange . . .

And then there was this thing with the mornings. Every dawn came with an unbearable gut-wrenching pain that wasn't getting any easier to deal with. Most mornings it doubled me in half, to the point I had to bite my own tongue to keep myself from crying out.

My dad hadn't noticed it, but Tyler most definitely had.

Even stranger, each morning a number ticked off in my head. I couldn't explain it, but whatever the number was, it became my obsession of the day. And suddenly I'd see that number everywhere we went.

Today's number was seventeen, and so far I'd seen it in the newspaper my dad had found at one of the campsites, on a mile marker we'd passed, and I'd lost count of how many times I'd happened to check my watch at the exact moment the minute hand landed on the seventeen mark.

It was eerie.

The crippling pain I felt each morning combined with my increasing obsession with numbers and time was making me start to think I might be dying. That my body—this new alien body—was rejecting me . . . rejecting *this world*, and I would eventually just . . . vanish again.

Only this time I wouldn't come back.

Maybe that was what kept me from going to my dad. My fear that my time here was limited. If that was the case, I didn't want to waste a single second by worrying him, especially if Tyler's nonsense mutterings turned out to be nothing. Just the mumbo-jumbo ramblings of a sleepwalker awakened too soon.

Die . . .

The Returned must die.

Still, I couldn't shake the guilt over what I'd done to Tyler. I needed to come clean to him about how . . . why . . . he was taken.

"Up ahead. Through here . . . ," Tyler said, but I'd been following so close that when he finally stopped, I ran into him from behind. Not that it was a bad place to be—I'd always appreciated that side of him.

Flustered, I jumped back. "Oh, crap . . . sorry."

Laughing, he at least pretended not to notice that my hands had just been all over him. "There," he said, sweeping a large cluster of branches out of our way.

Ahead of us was a pond. And flowing away from the pond was a stream. For three days we'd been climbing toward higher elevation, leaving the desert far behind. My dad never said exactly where he was taking us, only that we had to put distance between us and Blackwater Ranch, which really meant getting far away from Agent Truman and the rest of the No-Suchers, the agency's nickname because of its extreme secrecy.

To me, it meant leaving behind Simon, Jett, Willow, Natty, and all the other Returned, including Griffin, who'd risked their lives so Tyler and I could escape the secret camp when Agent Truman and his goons had attacked it. The idea that we were putting more miles between us each and every day made me more desperate for word from them—news that they'd survived. Information about where they were now. Anything.

"It's warm . . . the water . . . ," Tyler breathed, leading me closer. "Hot, even. Some kind of natural spring."

"Nuh-uh. Are you for real right now?" He didn't have to tell me what that meant, I was already peeling off my shoes and socks.

The last time we'd seen water clear enough to wash in was two days ago and it had been bitterly cold—mountain runoff, my dad had called it. I'd only been able to stay in long enough to rinse off the thinnest layer of grime before my skin had been rigid with gooseflesh. I'd shivered the rest of the day, despite the campfire my dad had reluctantly let us build.

Our new life on the run had come with strict rules, and fires could only be lit when they were absolutely crucial. Fires made us conspicuous, my dad had warned, and conspicuous was the last thing we wanted to be. Our plan was to set camp at dusk, and break it again by dawn, never staying in one place long enough to be noticed. Never giving anyone the chance to recognize us.

Tyler had made the case that preventing hypothermia was cause enough to break my dad's no-fire rule, and for that, I was sure I owed him some sort of life debt.

But now . . .

Now he was presenting me with an even better gift than fire: a heated pool.

When I reached for the hem of my shirt and started stripping it over my head, Tyler whipped his head in the opposite direction, acting like I'd just thrown acid in his face. "Whoa . . . *hey* . . . do you want me to leave or something?"

I laughed over his sudden inhibitions and tossed my shirt on top of my shoes, making a pile beneath the bushes at my feet. I planned to keep my bra on, and in another second or two it would be just that and my underwear remaining. "How is this any different from a swimsuit?"

He dared a peek, uncovering his eyes with exaggerated hesitation. "I mean, I guess so . . ." But even his skepticism was beginning to sound suspect. We might not have any human DNA left in us, but that didn't mean his memories weren't completely and totally red-blooded . . . and what all-American teenaged boy didn't want to look at a half-naked girl?

Without waiting for his verdict, I lowered myself into the blissfully steamy water. It was seriously luxurious, better even than the hot tub Cat and I had snuck into that one time at her uncle's country club when we were fourteen.

"You should get your butt in here," I called to Tyler. "You have no idea what you're missing . . ." I sighed as the water reached the back of my neck, and then holding my breath, I submerged myself completely.

The water became a filter then, dulling all my senses. Vaguely, from somewhere above me, I heard Tyler say something back to me, and it sounded an awful lot like, "If you insist . . ." But I stopped caring as I raised my toes off the rocks beneath me and let the water cradle me.

Slowly, I eased away from the edge.

Below me something warm surged toward my feet. It felt like a current, and I guessed it was the source of the spring's heat . . . maybe of the spring itself. I kicked my legs, relishing the feel between my toes.

I sank lower into the water . . . diving . . . plunging closer to the heat . . .

Opening my eyes, I realized my strange ability to see in the dark worked just as well down here. I released a breath and watched the bubbles swell toward the water's surface.

Around me, I could make out the rocky walls and ridges of the pool's edge. I traced them, following them lower; to where they reached depths I could no longer see.

I wondered just how far down the pond went.

Deciding to explore, I spun myself in that direction and propelled myself with my hands, letting my super-vision lead the way. Eventually I saw tiny, almost microscopic bubbles seeping toward me. As I kept going the bubbles grew denser, making it harder to see through them.

I had to be nearing the source.

"Kyra!" The sound—my name—was muffled by both the water and distance. Then it came again, and I felt it more than understood it . . . *him*. "*Kyra!*"

From way above, near the surface, Tyler was shouting for me.

I rolled onto my back so I could find him, and even from all the way down here, I could make out his form, bare except for his boxer shorts. I could see his expression, distorted as it was. There was something there as he searched for me. What was it? Worry? Fear?

Anxiety percolated in my chest, bubbling like the spring beneath as I realized I needed to reach him. I kicked my legs hard behind me. When I was close enough, the drawn line of his mouth and his pinched brow became crystal clear.

It wasn't just worry on his face, it was stark panic.

His fingers pinched my arm as he dragged me the rest of the way to the top. When we broke through the surface, he choked out, "Kyra . . . what the . . . *What the hell?*" His feet caught the rocks beneath him finding his balance, and I couldn't tell if he was stammering because he was frustrated or because he was breathless.

When his green eyes probed mine there was hot accusation in them.

I shot him a mute frown as I tried to unravel what I'd missed during the time I'd been down there.

His grip intensified. "I thought . . ." He scowled back at me, and I saw the way his gaze swept over me then. "You were down there too long."

Then realization hit home: Tyler didn't remember.

I shook my head, my whole body unwinding. I reached up and pressed my thumb to the bridge of his nose, where his eyebrows were practically fused together. "It's okay," I explained, willing him to understand. "I didn't need to breathe . . . down there. I can hold my breath for so, *so* long." It sounded strange to say it again, especially to Tyler, but even without seeing the proof on his face I could sense him collecting himself.

And then he released a strangled sigh. "God, that too? *How long?*"

I shrugged. "I never really tested it. A long time though." I dared a quick smile, thinking of the first time Tyler had seen that little trick of mine in action, when it wasn't a trick at all but because my leg had been trapped beneath a fallen log in a rushing river. Agent Truman had been chasing us and we'd had no choice but to jump into the raging waters.

That was nothing at all like now. Here.

"*Really* long," I finally answered.

Tyler might be like me in the sense that we could heal faster than the Returned, which was already pretty darned impressive, but I had a few other new talents he didn't. Maybe because the aliens had taken me for five years versus Tyler's five days. I could see in the dark and hold my breath for forever. I could also throw crazy hard—something Agent Truman had discovered when he'd been on the receiving end of my new killer fastball and ended up with a broken hand.

And sometimes, when I concentrated just right, I could even move things with my mind. Even I had to admit that last thing was pretty freaking cool.

I lowered my hand to his jaw. He didn't move, and our eyes stayed locked while my stomach flipped. I swallowed nervously.

"Your eyes," Tyler said, his voice thick now. Low too. "They're doing that thing again."

I studied his eyes back, only slightly brighter than they'd been before, but definitely greener. Then I blinked deliberately, intentionally casting a long slow shadow over his face.

Another of my freaky new talents.

"They always remind me of fireflies, when we're in the dark like this." He spoke softly, his eyes fastened to mine.

I shuddered. That word, *fireflies*, raked up my guilt all over again.

I tried to shrug it off. There were so many things I wanted . . . *needed* to tell him. So many things I needed to confess, starting with Devil's Hole—the night I'd let him be taken.

For me, it may as well have happened yesterday. There wasn't enough bleach in the world to scrub the memory of those bugs, all those prickly firefly legs swarming over my skin, tangling in my hair, and finding their way up my nose right before Tyler vanished. I'd felt choked by them, smothered.

He was right about my eyes, though. Denial didn't make the truth any less real. There were times, especially at night, when my eyes flared like strange glowing orbs—impossibly-ridiculously-*comically* bright.

So, not only could I see in the dark, but if the moment was right, I could also *be* seen. I'd become a human beacon.

Tyler ran his finger along my cheekbone. "If it makes you feel any better, it's not really your eyes I'm thinking about." This time, I didn't blink to get a reaction from him; it was strictly knee-jerk. But the glow from my eyes, which was too intense for the kind of blackness out here in the dense woods, flashed over his face all the same—once, then twice, and then a third time, while my breath faltered.

Simon had the worst timing and chose that moment to pop into my head, all grinning and smug-like. *Typical.*

"You know, if we have to be going through all this, I'm glad we're in it together." Tyler's gaze shifted, moving to my lips.

My stomach dropped as I tried to blot Simon from my mind's eye. He was a serious mood killer.

A week ago, I'd have begged Tyler to look at me like that. For his lips to find mine.

But that was a week ago, before I realized he wouldn't remember who we were to each other, and what we'd been through. And before Simon had planted that stupid, stupid, *stupid* kiss on me at the last minute, right before he'd left me and Tyler with my dad.

Now . . .

Maybe it would do me some good to kiss Tyler . . . to rid myself of Simon once and for all.

So why didn't I then? Why couldn't I just let things go back to the way they were . . . the way I wanted them to be between us? Clearly Tyler had feelings for me. I mean, he was standing here ready and willing to kiss me, wasn't he?

But was that really enough? Could I really pretend nothing had changed, when *everything* had?

That's the thing. I couldn't because this wasn't about Simon.

It wasn't enough for Tyler and me to share the same DNA—to be part of the same species—because even if he never remembered who we'd been, there was no way we could move forward until he at least knew the truth about what I'd done to him. About my part in his abduction.

As much as I wanted him to love me the way he used to, if I didn't come clean, anything we started would all be built on lies.

"I need to tell you something," I said.

"I need to tell you something too," he answered. But the

way he was looking at me, his gaze flicking back and forth between my mouth and my eyes made it all too clear we were not on the same page.

Please don't kiss me . . . I thought achingly, wondering if I'd even find the will to stop him if he did.

Oblivious to my psychic petitions, he lowered his head, and my heart stumbled hard as it tried to wedge its way into my throat.

I tasted his breath and his lips ever-so-lightly feathered across mine. And just as my mind was screaming at me to pull away, he stopped moving . . . going inexplicably-unnaturally-*morbidly* still.

And then, before I had a chance to process what was happening, Tyler grabbed me by the arms and hauled me deep, *deep* beneath the water.

CHAPTER TWO

TOO LONG. THAT'S HOW LONG WE'D BEEN DOWN there, for *way too long.*

Not for me, of course, I could hold my breath for ages.

But for Tyler . . .

I struggled in his arms, against his grip that was stronger than I'd imagined it would be. But he kept me pinned where we were . . . far below the water.

Far too deep, for far too long.

Shooting a questioning, and probably panicked look at him, I begged to know, *Why? Why are you doing this?*

But Tyler just shook his head and pointed a single

determined finger toward the surface.

Somehow I understood what he was trying to tell me—something or someone was up there. I don't know how he knew that. I hadn't seen anyone, but that wasn't important.

He was convinced. And he was freaked out by it. Enough so that he had no intention of going back up there anytime soon.

So what then? Did that mean he was willing to die because of it?

He kept his lips . . . lips that had nearly been on mine just minutes earlier, pressed tightly closed as he harnessed his air reserves. But he couldn't hold his breath forever and he'd have to let it out soon.

Then he'd have no choice but to inhale.

His body wasn't like mine.

Mine . . .

My lungs were fine. I had more than enough breath remaining . . . more than enough time.

An idea sparked. Something I'd seen once, probably on TV, which made the whole thing seem more than a little bogus. But maybe . . . just maybe, if there was even an ounce of validity to the concept I could buy Tyler an extra minute or two.

I closed the small gap between us, not completely unaware of how undressed both of us were as our bare skin pressed together. But more than anything, I prayed he'd go along with me. Hoping, if there was anything to this, I could get it right.

Blood rushed noisily past my ears as I strained to reach his mouth, and suddenly the feel of his lips on mine was no longer just a memory. It was achingly real.

Unfortunately, there was no time to savor it.

It took Tyler a second to realize my intention, but when he did, his eyes went wide and he flinched slightly in surprise. Only, now *I* was the one gripping *him* and I wasn't about to let him go. I ordered him with my crumpled brow to *Be still!*

I had to concentrate, to be careful. Mindful. There couldn't be any space between our lips, not a single gap or opening, or else water would bleed through. The seal would literally have to be airtight, or else I would be breathing water directly into Tyler's mouth and I would drown him. I was already worried I wouldn't be breathing any actual oxygen into his lungs, that all that was left in me was carbon dioxide—a little tidbit I remembered from tenth grade Life Science—and this whole effort would be futile to begin with because carbon dioxide was useless to him . . . just waste matter his body couldn't process.

But I thought when I'd seen this on TV, they'd said there was some oxygen leftover when someone exhaled, and right now *some oxygen* was better than *no oxygen,* wasn't it?

When I was as sure as I could be that my mouth was secured over his, I slowly . . . so very, *very* slowly, and very, *very* firmly began parting my lips. With my deliberate actions, I directed Tyler to do exactly as I did, at exactly the same rate. I tried to ignore how soft his mouth was, and the way I could feel his pulse beating where my fingertips pressed against his neck.

So far, so good, I told myself, trying to remain clinical about this despite my own rising pulse.

I blinked at him, trying to instruct him about timing, and as if reading my thoughts, as if we'd done this a thousand times before, Tyler blinked back. I ignored my doubts, the part where I knew that the tiniest wince or gasp could ruin everything. I tried *not* to imagine the worst.

When there was enough of an opening, or what I hoped was enough, I'd intended to exhale, giving Tyler a much-needed boost to his depleted oxygen supply.

But what I hadn't counted on was that he would have to exhale first. He'd been holding his breath for so long that he had no choice but to expel it before he could take in any more.

When he did, he filled my mouth with air. But even worse . . . far, far worse, the seal had just been broken, and it was my fault because I'd dropped my head to keep from choking. And the whole time all I could think was, *This is it. I've killed him. He can't make it any longer. I can't save him again. . . .*

My eyes squeezed shut as my body struggled not to inhale—to swallow huge mouthfuls of water, even though I probably deserved to die down here.

When I felt Tyler's fingers gently grip my arms, I reluctantly opened my eyes. He was there . . . alive. And not just alive, but grinning back at me.

Grinning!

I had to blink several times to make sense of it. To put the pieces together. Then he held up his hand and gave me the thumbs-up. As if I'd done this. As if I had anything at all to do with whatever was happening.

I was slow, but eventually I got it: Tyler hadn't needed me to be his human oxygen tank. He'd never needed me because *he* could hold his breath too, same as me. He just hadn't realized it until we were down here.

Beneath my palms, which were now flat against the bare skin of his chest, I could feel his heart pounding. I spread my fingers wide, letting them explore his muscles as the look on his face told me everything I needed to know: Tyler was okay. We were okay.

Then, just when I finally felt my body easing, just the slightest bit, his lips drifted toward mine and I thought maybe I'd been mistaken. Maybe I'd misread the pounding of his heart and he *did* need me to breathe for him after all.

But when his lips landed on mine, it wasn't for any practical purposes—he didn't need me to save his life or anything. It was just a kiss. An abrupt, waterlogged peck that was over as quickly as it had begun.

I wasn't sure if I should take it as a sign of things to come—the kiss I'd been anticipating right before he'd tossed me into the pool. Or if he'd just been swept up in the moment over his newfound skill and gotten carried away.

Either way, my lips were buzzing long after the kiss ended.

★ ★ ★

When we broke the surface again, Tyler kept his hand closed protectively around my wrist. My heart was still crashing wildly as I waited for Tyler to give the *all clear,* although it could just as easily have been the underwater kiss that caused the banging.

"It's okay," he exhaled, his grip loosening. "They're gone."

"They? How many of them were there?" I asked, opening my eyes at last. Before we'd emerged from the water, Tyler had signaled for me to shut them, and as I saw the shards of light flaring back at us from the ripples, I knew why—the glow from my eyes.

At that moment, they'd become a liability, so I'd put my sight in Tyler's hands, letting him guide me to the edge of the pool. I wouldn't admit it, but I'd preferred it that way. My skin tightened everywhere his fingers skimmed my body as he'd eased me onto the rocks. It had been hard to breathe, almost impossible, when I'd slid across him wearing almost nothing.

I watched now as he pulled himself out of the water and crouched on the bank. I'd seen Tyler without his shirt before. A few times. But with his bare chest glistening beneath the moonlight . . . well that was a whole 'nother story. One I wanted to burn into my memory.

He glanced back at me, confusion clear in his eyes. "Two, maybe? You didn't hear them?"

I tried to remember if there'd been anything, but I shook my head.

"You're kidding? It was so clear. They were so . . ." He reached down to help me out. "We have to get back and warn your dad."

I let him haul me up and shivered as the cold night air blasted me. Water dripped in rivulets down my bare skin, puddling at my feet. "Why? Who were they?"

His green eyes were feverish as he shot nervous glances past me, in the direction of the woods beyond the steaming water of the hot spring. He yanked his jeans from the tangle of our clothes pile and then passed me my shirt. "I don't know. But there was something . . . *strange* about them."

"Strange, how?"

"Strange, like—" He frowned. "I'm not sure how to explain—this is gonna sound crazy—but they were talking in static. Like they were talking over some sort of radio frequency."

I'd just started toweling off with my shirt when his words hit me. "How do you know you weren't hearing a radio?" I thought of the way Tyler's voice had sounded that night in the desert. Would I have called it static-y?

"I told you it was crazy. I just *knew*." He threw my jeans at me and then wriggled into his, not an easy task when you were still dripping wet. "We need to get out of here in case they come back."

"Wait," I prodded, wanting him to explain. "Like how *exactly*? Obviously it freaked you out enough that you thought you needed to risk drowning us. Tell me what you heard." I crossed my arms defiantly, refusing to get dressed until he answered my question.

He glared back at me, but I could tell from the set of his jaw he'd already given in. "God, you're stubborn. Has anyone ever told you that?" I bit back a grin because I desperately wished he could remember the first time *he'd* told me that—that I was stubborn—back when he'd begged me to admit I had feelings for him. My heart had been pounding for a completely different reason then. "I can't explain *exactly*," he exhaled, clearly annoyed. "But it was like I *sensed* them before I ever heard them. Like I . . ." He shifted, and his hand kneaded the back of his neck. "Like I *felt* their footsteps coming. Then I heard this strange vibrating sound, or, I don't know, maybe I felt that too. But it was like they were speaking in code or something. Like they were communicating in sound waves." He pursed his lips, looking at me like he was saying, *I told you it was crazy.*

And it was, but it wasn't the most far-fetched thing I'd heard, not by a long shot. Especially considering that Tyler and I were no longer human and had just held our breath for who knew how long.

"Do you know what they said?"

He shook his head. "Something about the Returned maybe? But that was when I pulled you under the water."

My stomach plunged, even as I found my voice. "What about the Returned?"

"Kyra, we don't have time—"

I caught hold of his arm. "Just guess."

He looked at me, his eyes drilling into me when he said

the words that turned my skin to ice and made my heart stop: "I know how it sounds, but I might've heard: 'The Returned must die.'"

A sour taste filled the back of my throat and the ground tilted beneath me. I shook my head.

The Returned must die.

No way was that a coincidence.

Tyler froze beneath my fingertips. "What is it?" I started to ask, but he was already dragging me backward. My chest tingled in anticipation. "Are they back? Do you hear them again?"

"No," he answered distractedly. Then vaguely added, "I don't know."

When I finally heard something, it was faint—the snapping of a branch maybe. It was far away.

I might have see-in-the-dark super-vision, but we'd just learned that Tyler's hearing was vastly superior to mine.

The underbrush shuddered then, the bushes shaking more violently. Someone was in there. Chills raced along my spine. I wanted to run but my feet were rooted in place.

Nancy exploded out at us, bursting from the foliage with leaves and twigs all matted in her fur. I nearly had a heart attack. Branches snagged and pulled at her, but didn't slow her at all as she barreled forward, looking every bit an animal on the run.

Every nerve fiber in my body was on high alert. She shouldn't be here. She should be back at camp . . . with my dad.

She came skittering to a stop at the edge of the warm spring, her nails clattering against the rocky embankment. Then she turned toward us, and her body went utterly and totally still.

It was me, I realized. Me, she'd fixated on as she lowered her front haunches, her teeth bared.

I felt it in my gut, the wrongness of the situation. The not-Nancyness of her behavior.

She was confused, I tried to reason, she had to be. This was Nancy and I was me.

But seeing her hackles rise, and hearing her breath as it shifted from a heavy pant to a deep and guttural growl, caused the skin at the back of my neck to prickle.

What if I was wrong?

"It's okay, girl," I whispered, but my voice wavered. Nancy just showed even more of her teeth and her growl deepened.

"What's wrong with her?" I wanted to know.

Tyler's voice was unshakable. "Get dressed. We need to go." His hand on my shoulder steered me back a step and then another. "Easy now," he guided. "Slow." After I'd shimmied into my jeans, he pressed my shoes into my hands and without missing a beat, I slipped them on, not bothering to tie them.

We'd barely managed to get three steps from Nancy before a beam of light flickered out from the trees at our backs. It was bobbing crazily and my first thought was: they'd come back. Nancy had led them right to us, and we had nowhere to run.

But it was my dad's voice I heard. He was breathless and yelling for us from between the brush.

"Go," Tyler mumbled absently. And then, with more conviction, "*Go.*"

Then I could make out my dad shouting the same thing Tyler had just said, "Go!"

"*Go?* Dad, what—?" I shoved away from Tyler to reach my dad now. To get a glimpse of him.

And when I did, when I finally spotted him, he was running, or rather staggering. Moving as hard and fast as he could manage.

His shaggy hair was damp, and his plain white undershirt clung to his belly.

"Get to the truck, Kyra! *Run.*" His last word came out on a wheeze, but his panic-stricken expression melted into relief once he spotted me and my glow-in-the-dark eyes. He paused only for a second as he clutched his chest, his fist curled around his trademark flannel. He gasped for air like an asthmatic, but then forced himself to keep going, his long strides tearing at the brush.

Tyler sprang into action. "Let's go." His voice rumbled against my ear as he tugged me toward our camp.

Panic gripped my throat, Darth Vader–style.

We should've been unfindable. My dad had taken extreme measures to ensure no one, not even Simon and the others, would know where we were.

But what if it was them? What if they'd somehow tracked us down and were here . . . now, Agent Truman and the rest of his creepy Daylight Division? They'd like nothing more than to pin Tyler and me down, like dried-out butterflies in their collection.

Oddities to be marveled at.

Without thinking, I started to reach for Nancy's collar as I passed her, but she snarled at me and I recoiled, torn somewhere between fear and rejection.

So we left her. My dad would have to deal with her.

When we reached camp, my dad wasn't far behind. To say I was impressed by his stamina would have been an understatement. Still, he was more than a little winded when he appeared in the small clearing, his breath coming in hard, heaving gasps. He waved the flashlight around at our tent and all our stuff, which was scattered around the dead remains of what had once been a campfire. "Leave . . . it. All . . . of it," he wheezed. He fumbled in the pocket of his jeans and, probably because I'd never passed my driver's test, he tossed the keys to Tyler. "You . . . drive."

Oblivious to the fact that it was me who'd set Nancy on edge, my dad half dragged the unwilling dog and shoved her in the backseat of the truck before climbing in after her. She was still growling, but it was lower now, coming out in breathy woofs. But the awareness that she didn't want to be anywhere near me crawled over my skin like a million fireflies . . . unpleasant and unwanted.

I took shotgun as Tyler fired up the ancient pickup truck. If my dad had somehow lost whoever he'd been running from in the woods, there'd be no fooling them now—the engine was big and old, and crazy loud. It rumbled as Tyler slammed the truck into gear, the transmission grinding before it caught, and then we were bouncing over backwoods gravel roads that were riddled with potholes, hills, and ruts.

"All right, we need to sort out what just happened back there," I managed, finally able to breathe normally as my dad gave up his stakeout and swung around to face us.

For the first hour or so after we'd slammed out of the campsite, my dad refused to say a word, keeping a silent vigil through the grimy back window, which was fine because somewhere along the way, during that hour, Tyler had reached over and taken hold of my hand. It hadn't stopped him from focusing on driving though, as he alternated his attention between the road we were flying down and the rearview mirror.

I thought for sure he'd have to let go of my hand eventually whenever we'd hit a particularly treacherous pothole or when he had to make a perilously sharp turn, especially since my dad's ancient truck clearly didn't have power steering. But he never once did.

And every now and then, his thumb would stroke my palm, or his fingers would tighten, just enough to let me know he still knew I was there, and even though we were running for our lives, I'd momentarily forget to be terrified.

"I think we lost them." My dad shot one last look over

his shoulder, a just-to-be-sure look, before settling forward in his seat. If he noticed that Tyler didn't have both hands on the wheel, he didn't mention it.

"Who?" I asked, my own gaze dropping to Nancy beside him. She hadn't stopped making those warning sounds from the back of her throat . . . not growls exactly, but low mistrustful whines. "And why is she doing that?"

My dad rubbed Nancy's head and she quieted down a bit. "Your eyes. Pretty sure it's your eyes. Spooked her." He leaned over my shoulder and pointed to the glove box. "In there. Sunglasses. See if those don't help some."

My eyes? I mean, weird since she'd seen them before, over the past few nights, but I supposed it was possible; we were all a little spooked right now.

My hand felt cold when I let go of Tyler's to dig through the cluttered contents of my dad's glove box. I moved aside stacks of worn receipts and crumpled paperwork—an old tire warranty, several outdated registrations, fast-food receipts, and some maps. Beneath them my fingers brushed something more substantial and at first I thought it must be the sunglasses. But when I lifted the mound of mostly garbage out of the way, a hard jolt shook me from the inside out.

A gun.

My dad had never been that guy: a gun guy. He'd always been opposed to guns. Opposed to violence of any kind, and now he was what? Packing heat?

My gaze slid sideways to Tyler, to see if he'd noticed what I had. He raised his eyebrows, letting me know he hadn't missed it.

I flinched again as my dad's hand closed over my shoulder. Yet his touch was familiar, comforting, and my tension eased somewhat. "You okay, kiddo?"

"Dad, what's the gun for?"

"Things have changed, Kyr."

If I'd have been standing at that moment my knees would've buckled because of the way he said my name. It was the way he used to say it, like I was still the old me. But that wasn't what this was about, and I couldn't let my emotions sway the fact that my dad had let this . . . *this whole situation* change him. "Yeah . . . but a gun? Is that really necessary?" I was sure I was being unreasonable. Weren't Agent Truman and his guys armed? Didn't it make sense for us to have weapons too?

But wasn't that just it? What was it my dad always taught me? Two wrongs don't make a right.

Did that even apply when we were talking life and death?

He squeezed my shoulder again, so much like before, the way he used to do just before a big game or whenever I needed cheering up. "I gotta make sure I can protect you. Keep you kids safe."

I crossed my arms, not feeling cheered at all by his response. I didn't feel safer knowing my dad had altered his entire belief system . . . all because of me.

"So what do we do now? We lost pretty much everything

back there." My gaze slid to the glove box, and the gun inside. "Where do we go from here?"

My dad tapped Tyler enthusiastically on the shoulder. "Pull off up ahead there," he directed. "First thing we need to do is regroup."

We'd crossed into Wyoming now, which wasn't so strange. For days we'd been zigzagging across state lines as my dad tried to steer clear of the Daylighters, and considering my current obsession, it shouldn't have surprised me that the next exit was exit 17. We were on a highway that could barely be called a highway and there was a roadside diner with a flashing neon sign that had a pig wearing a cowboy hat. The pig promised the World's Best Pie.

I had no idea what one had to do with the other.

Unlike the narrow road we'd been on, the parking lot was wide and vast, and way more congested than the time of night warranted. When we pulled in, I had to ask, "You sure this is a good idea? There're a lot of people here. What if the Daylighters catch up with us?" Just to make my point, I turned to scan the road behind us, but no one was there.

My dad scowled at the mention of the Daylighters, but he was already buttoning the flannel shirt he'd been clutching when he'd come sprinting out from between the trees, which was probably a good thing because there were still sweat marks beneath the underarms of his T-shirt. "It'll be fine," he said. "Trust me, they won't find us here."

Sliding me a sideways glance, Tyler pulled into the crowded lot without saying a word. He managed to wedge the battered pickup between two enormous semis, making my dad's truck look miniature-sized, like some sort of windup toy.

I still wanted to talk to Tyler, but not here. Not with my dad listening.

"Wait here," my dad told Nancy as he ruffled her head, but she refused to be appeased by a little affection. "Don't be like that," he promised. "I'll bring you some leftovers." As if that was the reason she growled when I reached for my door.

Whatever had really spooked her, she'd definitely transferred her fears onto me. In her mind, I'd become the boogeyman.

Transference—I'd learned the term in psychology, but now the word itself held so many more meanings to me.

Transference could literally mean moving something from one place to another, like the way I'd been taken, literally plucked from the road that night on Chuckanut Drive. Or the way my memories had been moved from my old body to this new one.

My dad reached back in the truck and came out with the pair of sunglasses I hadn't been able to find. He offered them to me. "It's still dark. We don't need anyone noticing us."

"Me," I corrected, hardly able to hide my annoyance at being singled out, even though no one else's eyes were glowing. "You don't want anyone noticing me, you mean."

"Kyra . . ." My dad sighed.

"Whatever." I took the sunglasses and slipped them on. "It's fine. I get it."

I hoped the tint actually disguised my eyes rather than just making me look like some dork who thought it was cool to wear sunglasses at night.

Coffee. That's why we'd risked pulling over. My dad needed coffee.

The World's Best Pie was just a bonus.

"So how long do you think we have? Until they find us again?" Despite my strange choice in eyewear, I hadn't drawn a single glance. Maybe because I wasn't the only one with questionable fashion sense. I'd spotted at least half a dozen oil stains, several pairs of suspenders that were definitely *not* of the hipster variety, and more than a few (not-even-trying-to-hide-them) butt cracks. There was even one guy sporting a "Free Mustache Rides" T-shirt and an idiot's grin. As if he really believed he had a shot at someone taking him up on his offer.

My dad ignored me and signaled to one of the waitresses wearing a cotton candy-colored uniform before she rushed past us with her coffeepot.

"Can I get a refill here?" He wore his own version of a cheesy grin as he waved his cup in her direction. She paused just long enough to top him off, and didn't even acknowledge Tyler or me before rushing away again, eager to escape into the kitchen, probably hoping to steal a quick smoke break before having to go another round with Free Mustache Rides.

My dad settled the lip of his mug just beneath his nose,

lingering before actually taking a sip. I could smell the strong brew from the other side of the booth and tried to decide if that was a good thing or not. But from the blissed-out expression on my dad's face I guess I had my answer. After finally downing several long slugs, my dad dug into the pie and that blissed-out expression shifted to shameless ecstasy.

"You have *got* to try this," he said through a mouthful of the crumbling apple confection. He held out his fork, offering me a bite.

At any other time, and maybe for Old Kyra, the offer would have been tempting. But now, and to New Kyra, who had different, and less than impressive taste buds, the suggestion wasn't all that appealing.

I shrugged. "Maybe next time," I refused, like we were regulars and I wasn't passing up my one and only opportunity for the World's Best Pie.

"Ben, seriously," Tyler interrupted. "Who the hell was that back there? Did you get a good look at them? Did they see you?" Tyler was leaning forward, his face screwed up in determination.

My dad scowled, the fork halfway to his mouth, and then he glared, first at me and then at Tyler, before setting it back down again. After a second he shook his head. "No, I didn't get a good look."

"Then how do you know it was them?" Tyler pushed, and I wondered if maybe it was never Agent Truman at all. If maybe my dad had seen—or heard rather—the same people Tyler had.

The Returned must die.

The hairs at the nape of my neck prickled.

My dad cleared his throat and then gazed at me intently. Despite the fact that my dad was sitting right there, Tyler threw his arm over my shoulder and yanked me closer to him reassuringly.

I wasn't sure which of us was more surprised, me, my dad, or Tyler, but I smiled just a tiny bit.

Tyler wasn't thinking the way I was. He still thought the Daylight Division had tracked us down. "How do you think they figured out where we were? Where did we go wrong?" he asked.

Ignoring Tyler, my dad reached across the table, his hand closing over mine. "I don't think they did, kiddo. I don't think it was that Truman guy or his jackbooted thugs." He was hedging. For whatever reason, he didn't want to come out and say what he thought.

I nodded. "So? What are we doing here?" I gestured to the diner around us. "If it wasn't the Daylighters, then who were you and Nancy running from?"

He sighed again, a giving-up kind of sigh, then looked around, making sure no one was listening. And then he glanced up. Like *up-up*, toward the sky. "Them."

My stomach dropped, and I wondered why I felt this way. Why I had that same sick feeling I'd had in his trailer, back when I'd first been returned. Back when he'd told me he thought I'd been abducted by aliens.

Back then the aliens had all been in his head. Make

believe. Fiction. The stuff of fairy tales.

Now . . .

Now I knew better. Now he was only confirming what had already been bugging me. What I'd already been telling myself couldn't be . . . because no way was it them. Not here. Not again.

I tried to swallow but my throat felt like it was one long inflexible steel pipe, and my breath rattled along the hollow tubing. I kept my voice low . . . super, *super* low so no one could hear the kind of crazy talk coming out of our mouths. "What . . . makes you say that? Why do you think it was"—I leaned closer, our heads almost touching over the top of the table—"*them*?"

"I think they're trying to send a message, Kyr. I think they're after you."

I stayed inside the bathroom stall for way too long, surrounded by metal walls that were plastered with so much graffiti they looked like they belonged in a high school locker room rather than an all-night diner. One particularly eye-catching piece—a Sharpie collage of a nude woman riding an elephant—was not only bizarre, but so detailed I had to wonder how much time the poor woman drawing it had been trapped in here. I hoped for my dad's sake it hadn't been The World's Best Pie that had done her in.

On the flipside, there were several penis sketches and one *For A Good Time Call* listing . . .

Seriously, you'd think grown-ups would be more mature.

I looked down to where my dad's watch was strapped firmly to my wrist. He'd given it to me so I could always track the time, knowing the way it anchored me. Made me feel safe.

But right now, there was no solace in the steady meter of the second hand as it wound its way around the dial. My dad's words . . . the things he'd said back there at the table haunted me.

Whoever Tyler had overheard, my dad had heard them too . . . only he hadn't heard them the same way Tyler had. He agreed that they were talking, or at least he thought that's what they were trying to do.

Communicate . . . but not in words.

It was Nancy who'd woken him, he'd explained. "She was growling, which put me on alert, being the middle of the night and all. So I got up to see what had her all riled." He shrugged, his face sagging as he rubbed at the memory. "That's when I saw them . . . two gals dressed like hikers. At first I didn't think anything of it, except it was dark out and I didn't know where you kids had gotten off to." His saucer eyes fixed on me, and I couldn't tell if it was a concerned look or that unsettling are-you-still-you? look I'd been getting from him for days. "Then one of 'em opened her mouth and this"—he winced—"this sound came out of her, like a hiss. And when she was finished, her friend opened up her mouth and did the same. They went back and forth like that, having this weird *electrical* conversation."

It was Tyler who questioned my dad. Tyler who had

admitted to hearing something similar by the pond—voices mixed with static. "So what makes you think they were aliens?"

My dad rubbed his temple. "I didn't say *they* were aliens. I said I think the aliens are trying to send a message to you, trying to . . ." He shrugged and wrapped his hands around his coffee mug.

"So who were they then, those two ladies? If you don't think they were aliens?"

"I can't say who or what they were—maybe *they* . . ." He'd nodded toward the sky again. "Figured out how to hijack regular people, like those lady hikers. Maybe *they*—"

"Dad, I got it. I know who you mean," I interrupted, letting him know the histrionics were unnecessary. "And I'm pretty sure people stopped saying things like 'lady hikers' with women's lib, if anyone ever said it at all."

A half smile tugged at his lips. "You're probably right. All I'm saying is maybe that's how they're trying to reach you. All I know for sure is something's out there, and I don't think it's just that Agent Truman dude we gotta watch out for anymore."

Something was out there.

Something, not someone.

If there was *something* out there—something that spoke like static—then what . . . who was it? What did they want with us?

I sighed as I stepped out of the stall, feeling a little punch-drunk from everything thrown my way. I'd asked my dad if he had any idea where we'd go next, after we left this little slice of heaven—pun totally intended.

But the truth was, I had an idea, something we needed to consider: it was time to get ahold of Simon.

Something was happening out here that Simon and the others needed to know about. Something that involved weird languages and people talking in strange static-y voices. Something that maybe wanted Simon and the other Returned dead.

Still, I felt better having a plan in place. Knowing we wouldn't be alone much longer.

Slipping off my sunglasses, I examined myself in the mirror. Beneath the light of the bulbs my eyes hardly glowed at all. They just looked plain old Kyra-colored. Brighter maybe than before I'd been taken, but ordinary enough. Passable.

I tried to imagine when that had become the gold standard. When *getting by* had become *good enough.*

I jumped when the door to the restroom swung open, and quickly dropped the shades back in place as I pretended to be engrossed in simply washing my hands. The blond girl who stepped inside glanced at me, her brow lifting slightly when she noticed my sunglasses.

From behind the safety of the tinted lenses, I watched her. She reminded me a little of Cat, just a few years older than me—the way Cat was now—and there was something bold in the way she'd gone to the sink right next to mine rather than one of the open ones down the counter. I tried to be sneaky about my glances, but when I felt her eyes slide my way I put all my effort into the soap dispenser instead.

Even though it was only from the corner of my eye it would have been impossible *not* to be aware of her laser-intense scrutiny. As if she were trying to peel back the outer layers of me, picking a scab she couldn't leave alone.

Before I could stop myself, I glanced up, accidentally meeting her stare. This time, she didn't blink, or even attempt to look away, which made me think even more of Cat—no shame.

After a second of blatant inspection, she narrowed her blue eyes and bit her lip. "Do I know you from somewhere? You look . . . *so* familiar." She chewed more thoughtfully, scouring her mental archives to sort it out.

But I was already shaking my head and backing away. "Sorry. Not me." I wiped my hands on my jeans, not bothering with the electric hand dryer mounted on the wall. "I'm not from around here."

I was suddenly desperate to escape the confines of the restroom and those unwavering blue eyes of hers and questions about who I was and where I was from. I turned and bolted for the door, suffocated by my own panic. It was bad enough we'd been sitting in a diner full of people who'd seen our faces. Now I'd stumbled across someone who thought she recognized me.

But I hit the door too hard and grossly miscalculated how easily it would swing open, so when I shoved against it, I fell through, tumbling out the other side.

Thankfully, Tyler was there to stop me from falling

face-first . . . and causing more of a scene than I already had (you know, with the sunglasses and all).

"Hey there! I got you," he gasped as I slammed into him, sending the both of us crashing into the opposite wall. My cheek smashed against the hard muscles of his chest and his arms closed around me.

For several seconds I stayed there, inside that space. I remembered a time, not so long ago, when that was the absolute safest place in the world. When Tyler's touch could fix everything.

But things were different now.

I drew away, grimacing as I gave him a sheepish look. My sunglasses had slipped down my nose. "Sorry," I offered, my cheeks practically sizzling.

And then, when Tyler's arms didn't move, when his grip actually tightened, my cheeks got even warmer. "Don't be." His voice was lower when he said it, gravelly in a way that made my heart stutter. "Kyra, I've been meaning to . . . I've wanted to ask you . . ." Now he was the one who was stuttering. He frowned, an adorable kind of frown that almost couldn't be called a frown. I wanted to tell him not to say anything, to just stand there and keep looking at me like that.

Except now I was curious too.

His grip loosened, and for a moment my stomach clenched because I didn't want him to let me go. He drew me farther away from the clatter of dishes and voices that came from the diner, and into a dark hallway where there was an exit, where we couldn't be overheard by anyone headed to the restrooms. "I . . . ," he started again. "I have so many questions, and I think you might be the only one who can answer them." His hands moved back to my hips as he pulled me close to him. It was so familiar I thought my heart would explode because maybe-finally-*at last* he might remember how he felt about me.

"Yes." The word came out like a whisper. A breath.

His forehead puckered as he tried to piece his thoughts together. "I had a dream. And I think you were in it."

I waited, my mouth going unexpectedly dry. "A dream?"

"Yeah," he answered, and then his hands slipped up and down, like he was wiping them on my hips. Like he was nervous. "More than one I think. And in them I have this strong sense that you're with me, even when I can't see you."

This is it, I thought. *This is what I've been waiting for.* I leaned closer, all my attention focused on him. On his lips, on the sound of each breath he took. On waiting for him to say the words out loud.

At last he tried to see through my sunglasses when he said, "But we always have to be somewhere, and I know how to get us there because I have these maps—"

I jolted, stopping him midsentence. For a moment, I'd let myself believe we were on the verge of something—a breakthrough. That Tyler might be remembering how we'd been . . . before. Now I realized I'd misread the situation. His dreams weren't lost memories, they were just that . . . dreams.

I wanted to hug my dad for insisting on the sunglasses because at least Tyler couldn't see the tears crowding my eyes. "Maps?" I managed. "What kind of maps?"

Unaware I was on the brink of a total meltdown, Tyler gave one of his signature shrugs. "Maps. I don't know. Thing is, they don't even make sense, really. They're just these"—he made a face—"weird squiggly lines and symbols. But to me, at least in the dream, they make perfect sense."

Even as he tried to laugh it off as a nothing kind of thing, my skin began to tingle, and suddenly I wasn't thinking of the old us. His laugh wasn't convincing because he definitely thought there was something to it . . . and so did I.

His hands had been running anxiously back and forth along my sides, and I reached for them, gripping them. My stomach felt heavy and tight, and my nerves were zinging with electricity. "Tyler, it wasn't a dream," I insisted. It was time to tell him about the night in the desert. Maybe more.

Maybe all of it.

I'd seen what he was talking about, those squiggles, the symbols—the ones he'd been drawing.

His *map.*

I looked up and whispered, "*Ochmeel abayal dai.*"

I might have said it wrong. The words felt strange on my tongue, but it didn't seem to matter. The moment they crossed my lips, Tyler's eyes went huge as he stared back at me.

He knew.

He clung to me, his fingers working their way through

mine until they were interlaced. Until he was holding me like I was the only thing tethering him to this world. Then he translated the words for me, in the same strange cadence he had before: "The Returned must die." His eyes searched mine. "That's right, isn't it? What do you think it means?"

"I don't know. But tonight, at the hot spring, it wasn't the first time you said that to me. I found you a few nights ago, right after we'd left Blackwater—I thought you were sleep-walking in the desert because you were totally out of it—but you were drawing on the rocks. Strange lines and swirls, just like you described." I let out a hard breath, cringing. "Maps, I think. And you said those weird words—*Ochmeel abayal dai.*"

"The Returned must die."

I hated the way he could say it so easily. "I think we need to tell my dad so he can get in touch with Simon and the others. We need their help to figure this out. . . ."

Tyler nodded, letting go of my hand and touching my jaw. "Whatever you want," he said. "I'll go along with what-ever you think we should do." And that was it; I couldn't stop the tear from slipping down my cheek. Tyler had always been that guy, supporting me no matter what . . . even if he didn't remember. He deserved the truth.

"Don't," he whispered. "Whatever you do, don't cry. I swear I'll do everything I can to protect you."

My forehead crumpled. "It's not that. I'm not afraid about what you said or what you or my dad heard tonight."

His palm cupped my chin, his thumb stroking my cheek like he was drying it, but it was already dry. "What is it then?"

I couldn't claim temporary amnesia the way he could. This . . . *what we'd been to each other* . . . hadn't just slipped my mind. I had to hope-pray-*cross my fingers* I could find some way to make him understand why I hadn't told him before.

I lifted my chin, searching the green eyes I'd fallen for and telling myself I could do this. "There's something I need to tell you, Tyler."

His gaze clouded over at my serious tone.

I swallowed. "When we ran into each other, back at Blackwater . . ." My voice was hoarse so I swallowed again. "That wasn't the first time I saw you after I'd come back."

His tone was uncertain. "What are you talking about? Are you saying you saw me around camp before then? Why didn't you say something?"

I pressed my lips together. I needed to be clearer. Braver. "No. What I mean is, I saw you *before* you were taken. Right after I'd been returned, when we were both back in Burlington. At home."

Tyler's hand dropped. He looked more confused than ever. "What are you saying?"

I started to reach for him, but stopped myself. It would be too weird to touch him, to hold his hand, at a time like this. "I'm saying those gaps in your memory, the part you can't quite remember . . . I'm in those. You and me, we were together then."

He shook his head. "I don't . . . No . . ." He took a step away from me and ran his hand through his hair. I knew the gesture so well I almost could have predicted it. I waited for him to absorb what I'd just told him. After a second he asked, "Wait, so all the stuff I told you, about Austin and Cat . . . you already knew that?"

I nodded.

"And we . . ." He raised his eyebrows. "We were friends then? Before I was taken?"

I started to nod, then fell off to a shrug. "Sort of."

An almost smile found his lips. "We were sort of friends?"

Cringing, I bit my lip, feeling a thousand knives plunge through my heart. "Sort of *more than friends*."

"More than friends . . . ?" His eyes scoured mine. "How much more?"

I blinked several times, trying to speak but coming up blank. This was humiliating. It would have been one thing to confess my feelings to someone who felt the same way I did, where everything was new for both of us. But it felt like I was opening an artery, explaining to Tyler we'd already fallen in love before . . . he just didn't remember it.

"A lot more," I finally managed, my hollow voice ringing in my ears. "Tyler," I started, thinking this was the dumbest idea ever, and wondering why I'd thought it had to be done. Why I hadn't just let him go on living in blissful ignorance, the absolute best kind according to the cliché. But I was past the point of no return . . . "I love you," I blurted. My voice sounded hesitant but not half as unsteady as I felt. "What I mean is, I'm . . . *in love* with you. I know you don't remember this, and maybe you won't believe it, but before you were taken . . . before your memory was so messed up, you felt the same way about me." I ended in a rush, relieved, so damned relieved, to have it over with at last.

The silence that followed was something you could feel and taste and probably touch if you'd tried. It was smothering me. And on his face, he had that look again, that taking-it-all-in look. Like he was absorbing the bomb I'd just dropped on him.

I wanted to crawl out of my skin.

When I couldn't stand another second, I whispered, "Say something."

He blinked, remembering he wasn't totally alone in the hallway. "Why didn't you tell me? Why not say something when you first saw me at Blackwater . . . with Griffin?"

I struggled for a good answer . . . for *any* answer. I wished there were one. If I were in his shoes I'd be pissed to discover that *he'd* known things about *me*, and that he'd kept them from me all this time. I shook my head, and settled for the truth. "I guess I was worried you'd hate me."

"Hate you? Why would I hate you?"

Closing my eyes, I went for it. The rest of it—the truth. "Because it was my fault you were taken in the first place. I was the one who infected you. It was a mistake . . . I didn't know . . . about my blood being dangerous . . . and I bled in front of you." I inhaled, squeezing my eyes even tighter, too afraid, too chicken to even peek at him. "You got sick. So, so, *so* sick. And the only way to save you was to let them take you." *God, saying it out loud sounded a million times worse than in my head.* "And then you were gone, for so much longer than you should've been. We couldn't find you, and I was so worried I'd never see you again." Opening my eyes, I looked at him. "When you were there . . . at Blackwater, I thought, *This is it. Our second chance. I can finally tell you how sorry I am.* But then . . ." Then. "Then you didn't remember any of it. Not about us, or the time we'd been together. And there was Griffin . . ." I glanced at my feet and swallowed again, and felt the knives in my heart stabbing and stabbing and stabbing. "And I thought"—I shrugged—"you and her . . ." My eyes lifted. "I'm sorry." I waited. There was so much quiet, so much time . . .

"Kyra," he exhaled. "I'm not sure what you want me to say." It wasn't an answer or a vindication or anything really. His brow crumpled as he shook his head. "I don't know what to think, how to process all of . . . this. I . . . think . . . I just need some time alone."

It wasn't what I thought he'd say. Yelling would have been better. Getting it out of his system.

Time alone . . . I had no idea what to make of that.

He left me there, in the hallway. I turned and the exit sign blurred while I blinked hard. I wished I could take it all back. Not just my confession but everything—infecting him, letting him be taken, loving him in the first place.

I was about to go after him, to tell him, one more time, how sorry I was. How honestly-utterly-*truly* sorry I was, when the ground shook and the power flickered.

It wasn't like when we'd broken into the Daylight Division headquarters in Tacoma, but I recognized it as an explosion all the same. It had the same forceful eruption, the boom that lasted just a split second, like the sound of a huge cannon being fired.

Tiny fragments of dust and maybe some plaster filtered over me, and from the diner I heard what could have been screams or sharp gasps. I turned toward the restaurant, toward where Tyler had just disappeared and to where my dad was, but before I'd even rotated all the way around, she was there.

The girl from the bathroom.

She reached for me and slung her arm hard around my throat before I could stop her. She dropped me to the floor, pinning me.

I saw a flash of blond . . . right before I felt the sting of a needle slide into my neck.

SIMON

"HEY! *HEY!*" I SHOUTED AGAIN. "IS ANYONE EVEN listening?" Some poor kid walking by stopped, looking far too twitchy for his own good. "Yeah, you. What the hell? How much longer 'til we have some decent hot water around here? What are we, animals?"

He glanced around, and I could see him wondering how he'd ended up in this position in the first place when this clearly had nothing to do with him. "I . . . uh . . ."

Griffin saved his sorry ass when she appeared outside the makeshift shower stall, doing that thing again where she showed up at the least opportune moments—like when I was naked. "Stop your bitching," she half ordered and half sighed, pulling no punches. "At least you have running water." The kid seized his chance and scurried away like his shoes were on fire.

I took my frustration out on the spigot, twisting it harder than necessary, and the hose dangling above my head stopped spitting its glacial runoff all over me. "Easy for you to say, they're not your nuts being turned to ice cubes." I pulled aside the sheet being used as a shower curtain and shook off.

Griffin threw a towel at me. "Cover up. No one wants to see your blue balls."

"That's not what I said—" I sputtered.

But Griffin cut me off. "Relax. After all these years running a camp, it's nothing I haven't seen before. Besides, that's not what I came to talk about."

Water still dripped from my head and chest as I cinched the towel around my waist. "What, then? Something happen?" Suddenly the cold-ass water wasn't my number one concern. "You hear something, from Kyra . . . or Thom?"

I didn't want Griffin to know how badly I wanted her to say yes. Or how much more I wanted it to be about Kyra than Thom. It had been days since the Blackwater attack, since I'd had to leave Kyra with her dad and Tyler, but I hadn't stopped regretting that decision, not once.

At least when she was with me, I'd known she was safe. I'd seen to that myself.

Now they were out there, on their own, and I had no way of knowing where they were or what might be happening to them.

That shit was eating me alive.

All because of Thom. Thom, who I might not have liked, but at least I'd trusted. Thom who'd turned us in to the Daylighters before running off to save his own ass. Now we were stuck here in hiding. I had people out there, some of them still at Silent Creek, Thom's old camp. What if Thom went back there? What if he decided to turn on them too?

Prick!

My fingers curled into fists as I imagined wrapping them around Thom's throat, something I wanted to do almost as badly as I wanted to wrap my arms around Kyra, just one more time.

Now who was the prick? I thought. I shouldn't be thinking about Kyra, not in that way. She'd made her feelings more than clear—she had a guy . . . and it wasn't me.

I stomped after Griffin who was already halfway down the hill. "Tell me. What do you know?"

"Nothing yet. But there was an incident at a diner in Wyoming, not far from a town called Sheridan," Griffin explained as she trudged ahead of me.

We'd blown out of Blackwater after the attack, knowing the No-Suchers would never just leave it at that. They'd come after us. And when they did, they'd bring an army and enough weapons to annihilate us.

The mess at Blackwater had been bad enough, a massacre—the body count on both sides was inconceivable. As prepared as Griffin had been, it hadn't been enough. Agent Truman's Daylight squadron had come suited up in combat grade hazmat gear and bore an arsenal that far outmatched our own.

In Returned alone, we'd lost over two hundred. Good people

destroyed beyond their ability to repair. So many victims . . . so many sacrifices.

Griffin still hadn't forgiven herself for letting Agent Truman—who'd turned out to be her long-lost father—slip through her fingers after Willow had knocked him unconscious. She'd only left him unattended for a minute . . . maybe two, while her camp was being overrun. But by the time she'd come back he'd vanished, either lugged away by his own men . . . or healed enough to walk away on his own, since he was a Returned as well.

Eventually, Griffin had finally realized her soldiers couldn't win the battle against the NSA's Daylighters and she'd given the signal . . . a signal Agent Truman's troops had been unaware of, and the Blackwater survivors had disbanded. Griffin's strategy had been simple: scatter far and wide into the Utah desert and wait a full forty-eight hours—an inside joke for the Returned, since that was the amount of time aliens had kept us—before meeting at the designated rendezvous points.

It had been almost unbearable to just scatter the way we had. To up and leave the bodies of our fallen soldiers. But the promise of a second wave of attacks by the Daylighters left us no alternative. We couldn't even stay and give our people the burials they'd deserved.

But that's the way it always was with the Returned—we didn't get the lives we should; why should our deaths be any different?

Still, some of those soldiers had been mine. Some I'd even called friends.

When all was said and done, only twenty-three surviving

Returned had showed up at the rendezvous sites.

Twenty-three out of two hundred forty-nine. That was the official count we'd come up with between the two of us.

That's one in eleven, according to Jett who was one of the twenty-three to make it out. As had Nyla.

Willow . . .

Christ, I could hardly stand to think it, but Willow was still unaccounted for. Griffin chalked her up to the over two hundred dead, but because there was no body, until we could go back to search for remains, her death could neither be confirmed nor denied, which left me in this strange sort of limbo where I couldn't quite let myself accept it. Acceptance was too damned final.

I also couldn't stand the idea that some douche bag Daylighter had gotten his hands on her.

So I let myself hope she was out there, working her way back to us. Same way a man gives himself just enough rope to hang himself. Eventually I'd probably end up on the wrong end of that noose.

It had been the right thing, sending Kyra away. She would have been a distraction if she'd been around during the massacre. Then maybe I wouldn't be here either.

"What kind of incident? Did you get word about them or not?" I pushed away memories of the battlefield, of the dead Returned, as Griffin came to a stop in front of her new command tent, which was really just an ordinary canvas tent where she'd set up shop.

Griffin tossed a shirt at me. Not clean exactly, but clean-ish.

Cleaner at least than the one I'd been wearing before I'd hosed off, which was four days past rank according to pretty much everyone I'd come in contact with.

Combat wasn't the only thing Griffin had prepared for. She'd planned for potential evacuation too, and as much as I might have despised her—and I had despised her—I'd come to credit her for this much: when push came to shove, she knew how to handle herself.

In other words, she'd saved our asses.

"An explosion," she explained. "A big one."

"Fuel line?" I asked as I shimmied into a pair of cargo pants she'd also thrown my way.

She shook her head. "Not according to reports. No gas lines involved, and not an engine fire either. In fact, not a single vehicle was dented. Only damage was to a Dumpster out back. Blew the hell up. Detonations like that don't happen spontaneously."

"So?" I waited for the punch line. "What does that have to do with us?"

"This." Griffin held up a grainy image queued up on a prepaid cell that Jett had assured us was safe enough to activate. "Someone posted this on their FotoStream account."

I leaned closer. The image wasn't just grainy; it had been taken at night and the lighting was total crap. "Yeah. Okay . . . ?"

"Who does that look like?"

I reached over and used my thumb and forefinger to zoom in on the picture. I assumed the parking lot was from the diner she'd mentioned. After a second, though, I saw *who* she meant.

I snagged the phone out of her hand and held it right up to my face.

She was there. A girl who looked a whole helluva lot like Kyra—*my Kyra*—being toted away by two people toward what looked like a black van. The side door of the van was wide open, like it was waiting for them. Kyra didn't look like she was in any condition to fight her abductors.

I gripped the phone in my palm, trying not to lose my shit. "No, goddammit," I cursed. I was losing the struggle to keep cool. "Where the hell were Tyler and her dad when all this was happening?"

Griffin peeled the phone out of my fist. "You can ask 'em yourself. Call came in about an hour ago—they're on their way here now."

CHAPTER THREE

Day Unknown

VOICES. FROM ABOVE OR BEHIND, OR FROM somewhere inside my own head . . . I had no idea. But there were definitely voices.

"*. . . fought . . .*"

"*. . . Returned . . .*"

"*. . . escape . . .*"

I heard other things too, or I thought I did. It was hard to tell. Everything was muddled, like words in a blender set on high speed.

I wanted to say something back. To tell them I was here, in case they didn't know.

I opened my mouth . . . or thought I did. My lips were hot and thick. I tried to make them move.

"M-m . . ." *My name is Kyra.*

There was a sudden shuffle . . . a skirmish of sounds, blurry like all the rest.

Had I said it? Had they heard me?

And then: "*How* . . . ? She should be out for hours."

Another voice: "Doesn't matter. Hit her again."

Me? Were they talking about me?

I didn't get the chance to ask—or even attempt to—because something pinched me in the side of my neck . . . and then everything went hopelessly, endlessly black.

SIMON

I DAMN NEAR TORE THE TRUCK'S DOOR OFF ITS HINGES before the rusted-out piece of shit had come to a complete stop. Eight hours. That's how much time had passed since we'd gotten the call, and I'd worn a path right through the grass with all my pacing while we waited for them to get their asses here.

Had they gotten lost?

Changed their minds?

Been captured the way Kyra had?

The whole time I'd cursed them for not doing a better job watching her. Protecting her. If I'd been there, no one would've touched her. She'd be safe . . . not lugged away like a lifeless sack of wheat to be tossed in the back of some murder van.

Where the hell was she, goddammit? Where the hell had they taken her?

The dog, the one Kyra had been so excited to see when I'd dropped her off to meet her dad, wiggled through the opening first, and hit the ground running. She tore around in circles, whipping between my legs like we were long-lost pals. I gave her a halfhearted pat on the mangy fur of her head . . . whatever it took to calm the beast down.

I'd never been much of a dog person.

Griffin stayed behind me, exuding a nervous energy that was atypical for her. She and I had different goals in this. She wasn't worried about Kyra the way I was. But she was worried about appearances, so she put on her leader face and did her best to keep her shit together.

Maybe she was fooling the others, but I had her pegged. She had a thing for that Tyler kid.

I should be glad Griff wanted the boy.

Except, I wasn't. For reasons I couldn't even explain, not even to myself, it irked the shit out of me that he might like Griffin back. That Kyra would end up getting hurt because of her.

Stupid, I chided. Especially since *I* wanted Kyra for myself. Wouldn't it be better if the two of them hooked up? Gave me the opening I'd been waiting for?

Well, I'd never been accused of being a genius.

Unlike the dog, Tyler waited to jump down until Ben Agnew had legitimately parked the truck. He glanced at me, which felt more like he was looking right through me, until his eyes landed on Griffin. "Where is everyone?"

I wanted to punch him. The first words out of his mouth should've been about her. About Kyra. This shouldn't be about Blackwater or the other Returned.

I stepped into his line of sight and *made* him see me this time. "Tell me what happened."

There was a slam, and Kyra's dad came around the front of the truck. "We're not sure exactly," he said. "We stopped at this restaurant, off the interstate—"

I thought about the rules we'd had in place, the carefully drawn guidelines I'd laid out. "Why'd you stop? You weren't supposed to be in public. No one should've seen you."

Tyler answered this time. "We had to leave our campsite. Someone . . . I don't know, some*thing,* maybe"—he shot a glance at Kyra's dad before finishing—"found us."

Griffin slipped in next to me. "What do you mean by *thing*?"

Tyler shook his head. "I wish I knew. Ben said they were trying to send a message to us . . . to Kyra."

"The No-Suchers?" The idea of Agent Truman and his men getting their hands on Kyra made it hard to swallow for a second. I wanted to rip these guys' throats out for letting her down this way.

But Tyler shook his head again.

"Who, then?" Griffin was so much calmer than I could manage. She almost sounded . . . gentle. "Did you get a good look at them? Do you know who took her?"

Ben answered. "I was trying to tell her what I heard at the

campground—hikers maybe, with strange voices like static. I said I thought the aliens might be coming for her, but she didn't want to hear it." His eyes were watery as he rubbed his beard. "She needed a few minutes so she went to the bathroom. That's when we heard the explosion out back. That's when Kyra disappeared."

"Jesus-H," I exhaled. "So you thought *something* might be after her and you left her alone?"

"Just for a second," Tyler explained. His expression was bruised, dark and heavy like storm clouds before a tornado sets down. "Only for a second. We looked everywhere for her, but she was gone." His face crumpled.

Goddammit, I cursed in my head as I realized that whatever happened, he didn't do it on purpose. *The kid genuinely likes her.*

Maybe I should step aside and let Griffin work her magic, get her hooks in the kid once and for all. Get him out of the way for me.

Then I wouldn't have to feel guilty about his damn feelings. I could just swoop in and take his place with Kyra.

Or maybe I was a head case.

I shot a look at Griffin. Why hadn't she told them what she knew, about the picture Jett had come across? I turned to Kyra's dad. "What do you think happened to her?"

He looked lost. He reached down and scratched his dog's head, seeking comfort in the one place he could still find it. "No idea. That's when we called you. We were hoping you could help."

Griffin stepped closer. Closer, namely, to Tyler. "Start at the beginning, at the campsite. Tell us everything you know."

I bit my tongue through most of Ben's explanation. Even after everything we knew . . . even knowing what we were . . . hearing him talking about those hikers and their strange voices, I had to admit he sounded like a nut job. I could see why Kyra needed to take a breather.

But that wasn't what bugged me. I was sure I'd been called a nut job before, worse probably. Back in the day, as a recruiter for Blackwater, my role had been to explain what had happened to us—the abductions and the genetics modifications—to the newly Returned. Being called crazy was par for the course.

No, there was something else wrong with Ben's account. Something in the way he told the story, but I couldn't quite put my finger on it. My gut said Ben Agnew was lying . . .

No. Not lying . . . withholding.

I kept my eye on him, evaluating every action. Every mannerism—the way his eyes kept sliding back to us, watching us just as warily. The way he described their narrow escape, and then the diner explosion. How he talked about Kyra. I couldn't figure it out. Couldn't figure *him* out. He loved his daughter, I didn't doubt that, but did he know something more?

As far as I was concerned withholding at this point was just as bad as an outright lie. I didn't tag him on it . . . not yet anyway. I let him talk. He got to the part where he hadn't stopped Kyra from going to the restroom all by herself, and it was all I could do to keep myself from choking the guy. The both of them.

What had they been thinking? Especially if they seriously believed they'd been sniffed out by something trying to communicate in some sort of white noise?

Goddamn it!

"So what now?" I asked Griffin, bypassing the two jackasses who'd already managed to lose Kyra once.

She pursed her lips, and I wondered if her head was even in the game, or if her brain was scrambled from being so near Tyler again.

Jesus, what the hell was wrong with everyone? Was I the only rational one left around here?

When no one answered, my impatience reached the boiling point. "Nothing?" I prodded. "Then let me break it down for you. I think one of you knows more than you're letting on." With supreme discipline, I managed to keep from stabbing Kyra's dad with my critical gaze. "But this isn't the time to hold anything back. Kyra's in trouble and if we don't figure this thing out, who knows what they're gonna do to her."

"They . . . ? But how can we get her back if they've taken her again?" Tyler started, and I couldn't help thinking he was a few bricks shy of a load.

"Jesus, Griff!" I exploded, pissed we were talking about alien abductions when we knew damned well this was foul play of the human variety. "Show them the freaking picture."

Griffin's eyes turned to accusatory slits, and I wondered when she'd planned to share. Without explanation, she pulled out her phone and passed them the image of Kyra's limp body being hauled through the parking lot. "Do any of these guys look familiar?" she asked.

I knew the moment Ben recognized his daughter in the crappy photo, because his shoulders stiffened. "Kyr," he breathed, and the way he said it redeemed him for the moment. That kind of anguish can't be faked. But he shook his head. "I don't know these guys."

"Me neither," Tyler added, his voice hollow. Then he leaned closer. "Wait a sec." He squinted, his finger lifting to the phone and tapping it. He pointed to a fuzzy image of a girl with pale blond hair who was off to the side. "Her. She was there. She went in the bathroom right after Kyra did."

Hope swelled inside me. A lead. Flimsy, but a lead all the same. "Jett's gotten nowhere trying to ID the two guys. Maybe he'll have more luck with the girl. It's worth a shot." I hoped to God Jett could work his magic.

"Look, right before she . . . well, whatever happened to her." Tyler hesitated, took a deep breath, then continued. "Kyra and I were talking. I was telling her about something . . . a dream I'd had about her."

I scowled at him. This wasn't the time and I really didn't want to hear about them . . . not about them talking and especially not about dreams he'd had about her. Frankly, if Kyra wasn't in trouble, I wouldn't be sitting here listening to him at all. Ever.

When I glanced Griffin's way, I saw the same thing in her expression. While I had a knot in my stomach, hers was smack in the middle of her forehead, in the pinched crease between her eyebrows.

Oblivious, because he was Tyler and "oblivious" should have been his middle name if you asked me, the kid kept going. "I told her I think there's someplace we're supposed to be . . . maybe go. I keep dreaming about these . . . maps." He made a face, like this was supposed to be tough on him too—a stupid dream. "But the thing was, she already knew about it."

Griffin leaned forward, more interested than I could pretend to be. "Maps?" she asked, her eyebrows screwed up in a different way now—less worried and more curious. "What kinds of maps?"

"That's what was weird about it. Not ordinary maps, of roads or anything. Just a bunch of"—he shrugged—"I don't know . . . scribbles mostly."

Scribbles? Kyra was out there, and he was blathering on about scribbles?

"Can you show them to us?" Griffin asked.

Tyler looked uncertainly from me to Ben and then to Griffin. "I can try."

He reached down in front of him and used his hand to clear a spot in the ground, brushing the dirt so it was smooth and flat. Then he picked up a stick and began to scratch out shapes. There were lines, both straight and curved. Loops that intersected other loops. Complete spheres, partial crescents, and sharp points with acute and obtuse angles.

Scribbles. The whole thing looked like complete garbage. A total waste of time.

I stood up, tired of doing nothing. I'd find Jett and together we'd figure out a way to get a lead on the blond girl in the image. We'd find Kyra with or without these useless lumps.

I was about to say as much when I glanced one more time at the second-rate sand sketches Tyler had drawn.

"Holy . . . ," I started. "That's no map. I mean it is, but it isn't, not really."

"What is it then?" Tyler asked.

Griffin figured it out too, as she got to her feet and stood beside me. She turned her head to the side, giving me a look that asked what it meant, and then looked back at the ground, a smile tugging at her lips. "He's right. It's a star chart."

Tyler's shoulders fell as his voice became distant. "A star chart? No. That doesn't make sense. How can that help us find Kyra? What does it mean?"

Ben chimed in for the first time in what seemed like too long considering this was his daughter we were talking about. "I'm not sure what it means, but I think I've seen something like this before. It's not just a star chart, it's a *reverse* star chart."

Griffin snapped a picture of the map using the disposable phone.

"There's something else," Tyler added, meeting my eyes, and I braced myself. "Kyra told me she heard me say something. In my sleep."

"What was that?"

Tyler swallowed, his expression guilty. "The Returned must die."

CHAPTER FOUR

ALERTNESS HIT ME LIKE A DOUBLE WHAMMY.

An intense, white-hot pain—a pickax trying to gore my insides apart.

Followed by the sudden-searing-*terrifying* awareness I had absolutely no clue where I was or how I'd gotten here.

I wasn't sure which was worse, but at that moment my stomach convulsed in a way that forced me to swallow back a scream ripping at my throat. With stark clarity, it hit me:

Daybreak.

Somewhere, even though I couldn't see it, even though I couldn't see anything, the sun was rising.

Abruptly, my body curled up at the cramps that wracked me, trying to wrap around itself. But even before I'd moved an inch . . . a centimeter . . . the restraints stopped me. They were at my wrists and my ankles, even my neck and chest.

My pulse skyrocketed as a layer of cold sweat chilled my skin and the trembling set in, and somewhere inside my head the number fifteen repeated like some kind of misfire.

Fifteen, fifteen . . . *fifteen* . . .

I was desperate to open my eyes, but each eyelid weighed a million pounds, making the task monumental. Willing myself to focus on one thing at a time, I concentrated on my breathing, exhaling slowly, evenly, through my nose, until eventually the tremors began to subside. My thoughts were a sticky jumble. Disjointed and disconnected, clumping together and making them hard to sort.

Voices . . .

I remembered that much at least. Hearing voices somewhere . . . sometime before this. And now, here, I was sure I heard voices again.

No, wait . . . not voices. Voices *and* sound . . .

Familiar yet somehow not at the same time . . . like . . . what was that?

It was fuzzy and faraway.

I swallowed hard, thinking, concentrating. *Concentrating.*

My throat was raw, my tongue thick and dry.

The word seeped into my awareness like molasses, slow and gummy: *music.* The sound with the voices was music . . .

It was significant, that victory, as if I'd crossed some sort of invisible line that divided the imaginary from the real. Dreams from consciousness.

You are now entering life. Population: everyone but you.

It was like being reborn.

I focused on the music, something you'd hear in an elevator or a doctor's office—a crooner from some bygone era. From even before my dad's time, which was practically prehistoric.

There was a smell too. Definitely-certainly-*absolutely* nothing I'd ever smelled before. It went beyond musty and past decayed. I tried to put a name to it, but it wasn't any one thing. It made me think of corroding metal and decomposing leather and rotting documents or papers all at once. Whatever it was, it was definitely old, ancient, and it singed my nose hairs all the way to my brain.

"She's awake," someone said. A girl.

An image flashed through my head, fleeting and incomplete, but it was her—the blonde from the diner bathroom. "*Do I know you?*" she'd asked. And now I wondered if she had, even though I most surely hadn't known her.

"Watch." The girl's voice again, and I wondered what they were watching because I wasn't giving them anything to look at. My eyes were sealed tight, and at this point, I was barely even breathing.

Then came a guy's voice. "There it is! Go get Ed. Tell him the girl's heart rate's spiking. Ask if he wants us to shut her down again."

Monitors. They must have me hooked up to some sort of monitors.

I wished I had control over my heart rate the way I did my breathing. *Stupid heart!*

Guess there was no point playing dead. Might as well get a look around.

This time when I tried to open my eyes, they felt less heavy, but still gooey, like someone had glued them shut. The effort was crazy, and it took me several tries before light clashed against my retinas, stinging them all the way to the core.

"Hey there," the girl said, only this time I was sure she wasn't talking to someone else.

She swam into focus and then I could see her and it was most definitely the blond girl, standing directly in front of me, her blue eyes migrating over me. "You were dead to the world for a while there. Took a helluva lot to knock you out though."

Knock me out. I turned her words over.

My last truly conscious memory was the flash of her pale-colored hair, followed by a sharp burn in the side of my neck.

That must have been it, the burn. No wonder I'd been so hazy. She'd jabbed me with something, a needle probably—drugged me.

Right after I'd been returned my parents had taken me to the hospital. One of the lab techs had stuck a needle in my arm to draw blood and my skin had healed so rapidly the needle had gotten stuck. I wondered if that had happened this time too.

It made me wonder about the blond girl and whoever she'd been talking to, because when the lab tech had exposed himself to my blood—something the NSA called a Code Red—he'd gotten sick, the same way Tyler had. Only that guy had died.

I studied the girl. Had she been exposed too? Would she die? That's what I'd call karma.

I tried to lift my hand, to check my neck for a needle or punctures or injuries, but it jerked to a stop. Some sort of cuff, brittle leather, kept me bound in place.

Right, the restraints.

My eyes scanned downward.

I was bound to some sort of chair. It reminded me of a dentist's chair, except it was really, *really* old. I could feel the metal at my back, and not of the spotless stainless steel variety. I could only see part of it at my sides, but where I could it was like a grimy, rusted-out stretcher. Cold and unforgiving.

Above me there was an enormous box light attached to an equally rusted pole. The bulb wasn't on, but the way the lamp was directed, aimed right at me, made it clear it had been positioned there for me.

Beyond the light and all around me—around *us*—were crumbling and decayed brick, and the smells suddenly made sense.

The building was in shambles. Everything . . . other than

the monitors and machines connected to me, the electrodes and wires that slipped beneath the blue-green gown I was wearing, was rotting.

There were two faces watching me—the blonde and some guy. I continued to ignore them. I wanted to get a feel for my surroundings before deciding the best way to handle them, whoever they were.

"Fifteen?" the girl asked, licking her lips intently. "What does it mean?"

Her question caught me off guard, but I managed to swallow my surprise. I gave her an I-have-no-idea-what-you-mean stare, even though I knew exactly what she meant. I must have been mumbling in my sleep, before I'd come to.

A boy came racing into the room then. "Ed says keep her awake. He'll be here soon."

I started a mental file, compiling a list of the things I knew:

This Ed guy the boy mentioned must be in charge.

They'd drugged me at least once, and for whatever reason, it hadn't been easy.

It was morning—something I knew because of the sharp stabs that had awakened me earlier. (Which day, I had no clue.)

And finally (and this was the biggie in my book), there were no fewer than four of them—one girl and three guys.

My guess: they were Returned, because none of them were sick from whatever needle they'd shoved in my neck—the whole drugging thing. If I was more heartless, more of a soldier like Griffin or Willow, I'd test that theory by biting my own tongue and exposing them to a Code Red. But I wasn't a soldier, and even if Blondie and the others were holding me hostage, I couldn't stomach the idea of watching someone else get sick the way Tyler had.

Not without knowing why they were holding me in the first place.

"Where am I?" I prodded, hoping to add to my list of facts. My voice came out a croak.

The girl tilted her head and her blond hair draped over one eye as she deliberated. "An old asylum," she answered decisively. "No one'll ever come looking for you here." She smirked then, the corner of her mouth ticking up slightly. "The exact 'where' doesn't matter."

An old asylum. Made sense considering the condition of the place. It also explained the creepy hospital vibe it had going for it. Wherever it was, it must've been deserted years ago.

A guy appeared then. Marched in, was more like it. His presence filled the corroded space and made even the grubby air we breathed seem somehow antiseptic . . . sterile.

Blondie snapped away from me like a tightly strung rubber band. She threw her shoulders back and her chin shot toward the ceiling.

It wasn't hard to deduce this was Ed I was laying eyes on, even through my drug-addled fog.

Acting as if I didn't exist at all, their conversation went like this:

Ed: "How long's she been conscious?"

Blondie: "Not long, sir. We sent word soon as we realized." She almost, but stopped herself short of, saluting him. Yeah, this was definitely the guy in charge.

Ed (Looking me over): "She say anything?"

Blondie: "Nothing important. Just wanted to know where we were."

Buzz. Wrong answer!

Ed jerked his head to glare at the girl.

Short temper, duly noted. No wonder she'd gotten so tense the second he arrived.

Then he snapped, "I'll decide what's important." To which she nodded, a silent but obedient, *Yes, sir.*

His I-could-break-you-like-a-twig stance relaxed, but only by a hair. "You answer her?" he asked, turning back to me.

The way he assessed me gave me the creeps. He didn't touch me or get too close, only eyeballed me, turning his head from side to side. His eyebrows lowered from time to time. It reminded me of the way people walked through the reptile exhibit at the zoo, crouching and squinting as they tried to glimpse the most venomous predators where they coiled beneath logs or in dark crevices behind the thick sheets of glass. They were fascinated and horrified all at the same time.

Ed was both fascinated and horrified by me.

He ran his hand over the side of his jaw. "Might as well get started. Hand me Lucy, will ya?"

Blondie passed him something I couldn't quite see, a

stick or wand of some sort and I tried to figure out what, exactly, we were "starting."

He leaned closer, and even his breath was sterile, almost to the point of being caustic. "Let's start with something easy," he said, this time most definitely talking to me. "Where are they? How much longer do we have?"

I frowned, searching the room to see if anyone else knew what the hell this guy was talking about. "Where are who . . . ? How much longer to what?" I gave an uncertain shake of my head, wishing he'd get out of my face. "I have no idea what you mean."

He lifted the thing in his hand, showing it to me. "Know what this is? This is ten thousand volts of truth serum. Answer me, or you'll know the true meaning of hotshot." He spoke slowly this time, enunciating each syllable. "Now, tell me what you know."

I shook my head, still clueless. But he had that short temper thing I'd already noted, and before I could even open my mouth to ask, he jammed the end of whatever that thing was against my bare thigh.

My entire body jolted, wracked by a sudden surge of electrical current. The straps made it impossible to escape, but my wrists and ankles and chest all strained against them nonetheless as my muscles seized involuntarily. The skin where the thing jammed into me burned.

After a few excruciating seconds, he pulled it away and grinned like the sick bastard I was starting to realize he was. "We call her Lucifer. Lucy for short. Best damn cattle prod on the market. Better'n a stun gun 'cause you stay alert." He was proud of himself, and he smacked a now inert Lucy against the open palm of his other hand. "Your tongue feelin' a little looser yet?"

If I had better control over it, this would be the perfect time to use that telekinesis ability of mine. And I tried, the way Simon and I had practiced . . . to get mad . . . really, *really* pissed off, because I was. I was genuinely pissed that Ed had just jolted me with an effing cattle prod. One that he'd named no less.

But nothing happened. Maybe I was still numbed by the drugs, or maybe the electricity had short-circuited my brain. Either way, I couldn't manage to throw one of those bricks that were lying all around us at Ed's head.

Damn!

"Fine," he stated, clearly taking my silence as a challenge. "We can definitely do this the hard way." And I wondered when, in all this craziness, we'd been doing things the easy way. He lifted the pronged end of Lucy up so I could see it, and I swore I could smell my own flesh burning on it. "Tell me why you're so damned important? Why is it we got someone so eager to get their hands on you? What makes you so special?"

I blinked, but this time didn't hesitate. I didn't want Lucy to find her way into my skin again.

"Me?" I rasped. Could I tell them I'd been abducted? And even if they were Returned, was it safe to admit I was a Replaced? Was that even what he was getting at? "I have no idea . . ."

"Don't play dumb with me!" He was yelling now, getting right in my face.

He didn't elaborate, just shoved the prod against my shoulder. Crashing against the metal chair behind me, my body went crazy stiff as pain jolted through me. Without meaning to, my teeth clamped on to my own tongue, even as I screamed at myself to release it.

By the time it was over, blood filled my mouth, and I could feel where my upper teeth met my lower ones. I'd bitten completely through my own tongue and suddenly the whole exposing them to a Code Red thing wasn't something I had any control over. Blood was dribbling out of my mouth. I'd heal. Already the wound was sealing closed, repairing itself. If they got sick they'd only have themselves to blame.

But I wasn't sure how much more I could take.

Ed was relentless. And ruthless. "Tell me, and it ends. When will they be here?"

"Please"—I choked on the blood—"I don't . . . know . . ."

Wrong answer.

He hit me with Lucy again. Only this time he didn't just zap me once, he waited until I'd finished convulsing the first time, and then added one more for good measure. Two jolts for the price of one.

I got the sick feeling he was just getting warmed up.

I was already panting, my skin damp with a layer of sweat when the second bolt of electricity released me. I lay back, my eyes rolling skyward as I prayed they'd just knock me out again. *Please God, just stick another needle in my neck.*

"Answer me!" he grunted, only this time he wasn't waiting for an answer. I saw the prod coming at me already, making its way toward me, and all I could think was *Is he really going to shove that thing into my face?*

But then I heard her voice, and he did too because his hand froze right where it was, just inches from my cheek.

It wasn't Blondie who'd interrupted him. There was another girl here with us, and I swear, even in my state of utter pain and confusion, I knew who it was. If anyone was watching the monitor it had to be going crazy, because my heart was beating a thousand times a minute.

But when she stepped closer, away from the shadows and into my line of sight, it tripled.

"Eddie Ray, stop," she said, right before her perfect hazel eyes fell on me.

Right before she gave the signal, and Blondie plunged something into a line I hadn't noticed before, one that must lead to somewhere beneath my skin, because suddenly my vision tunneled and everything faded away.

Natty.

Natty was here at the asylum. With me.

I wanted to add that to my mental file but it was almost too weird to believe. If I hadn't seen it with my own eyes . . . if I hadn't heard her voice . . .

But I had. She was here, all right.

So did that mean Thom was here too?

Last I'd heard of him, we'd all been at Blackwater. Just

after Thom had betrayed us by sending word to the Daylight Division so they could attack us.

He'd turned traitor.

Or maybe he'd always been a traitor. I had no way of knowing since he and Natty had vanished right afterward. We'd never had the chance to interrogate him. To find out if Natty had gone willingly, or if he'd kidnapped her.

I'd known about the two of them—their relationship, the one they'd worked so hard to keep under wraps, so it made sense that if Natty was here, Thom might be too.

But there was that other thing, this strange niggling thing somewhere in the back of my mind. The name Natty had mentioned just now: Eddie Ray. That's what she'd called Ed—Eddie Ray.

I'd heard that name somewhere before, I was sure of it.

That drugged sensation made everything fuzzy, impossible to process. But the information was there, waiting for me to dredge it up. I just had to be patient . . . to wait for it.

"I know you're awake." It was Natty's voice that intruded on my thoughts. I found it more than a little unsettling, the way they could do that, monitor my body's reactions without either my awareness or permission.

I didn't bother pretending the machine was mistaken, that there was some bug in their technology. I opened my eyes. "What are you doing here, Natty?" My voice sounded as if it was months out of practice, as rusty as the abandoned equipment surrounding us. "What do they want with me? Why are they holding me like this?" I glanced down at my cinched wrists to emphasize my point.

Natty's shoes crunched across the gritty floor until she was looming above me. Her hair was still the same jet-black it had been after we'd dyed it in a gas station restroom, back when we'd gone on the run from the Daylighters. It was just as striking today against her perfect porcelain complexion as it had been then. But her hazel eyes seemed somehow colder, more intense.

"We have our reasons," she stated flatly, like that was a real answer. A complete explanation.

We. Not they. And with that admission I added her to the list of accomplices to my kidnapping. To whatever they were up to here.

Blondie, the two as-yet-unnamed guys, Ed (aka Eddie Ray), and Natty. Five of them that I knew of, and possibly Thom.

At least one of them—Natty—was a Returned. But considering their youthful appearances, and the fact that none of them were taking any precautions to avoid my blood, they all must be.

More things to add to my mental notes.

"Why me? What did I ever do to you?" I didn't mean for it to sound so pathetic but that's the way it came out.

Natty had been my friend. Ever since Simon had dragged us to Thom's camp at Silent Creek, where I'd met her. She'd been the one person to look after me, to take care of me. She'd stuck to me like glue, making sure I ate and that I was never lonely.

But what if I'd been wrong about her? What if it had never been about making sure I wasn't lonely?

What if it had been about making sure I was never *alone*?

My stomach churned at the idea. She'd been my friend, my confidante. Natty's lips parted and suddenly I wondered how I'd ever mistaken her for sweet. Quiet. Unassuming. She looked predatory, sharklike.

"Because you exist," she answered.

I was glad no one was watching the monitor, because my heart rate had reached an all-time high. I had no idea who she was, this Natty. She was a stranger. A virtual-absolute-*unmitigated* stranger. I realized I'd never known her at all, and alone with her was the straight-up last place I wanted to be.

Nervously, I glanced her way.

She closed the remaining gap between us. "If you know anything, now's the time to say it."

"About what . . . ? Natty, I don't know what you mean."

She curled her lip. "The others. Like you."

"The Returned?"

She circled me, sizing me up . . . and I could tell by the way she narrowed her eyes I'd guessed wrong. "You have no idea how special you are, do you?"

Natty wasn't there when I'd discovered just how different I was from the others—a Replaced rather than one of the Returned. But since Thom *had* been there I assumed he'd told her. Surely he'd told her.

"No," I answered. I'm not sure I'd ever chosen my words

more carefully. "I know." I winced, watching her reaction closely. "I'm a Replaced. My body is made from one hundred percent alien DNA. My memories . . . my thoughts are all that's left of the old me."

"Not that, you idiot," she shot back venomously. "Of course you're a Replaced. Everyone knows that. But do you even know what that means? *Why* they made you?"

I'd asked myself that same question so many times, but figured there was no answer. I was just some experiment—an alien lab rat who'd landed in the wrong petri dish at the wrong time.

Even as I shook my head, a noose tightened around my throat. I hated how badly I wanted the answer . . . how desperate I was to know. "Tell me," I gasped.

"Do you feel them?" she asked.

Fifteen, my brain suddenly screamed.

She opened her mouth, and I held my breath, waiting. Eager.

"Leave!" Ed's voice boomed, echoing obnoxiously against the hollowed-out bricks that crumbled overhead.

Natty closed her mouth, but it wasn't like with Blondie, who jumped to obey Ed the second he gave an order. Natty was less responsive, not as comfortable in the submissive role. Strange, since that was the only role I'd ever known her in. The Natty I'd known had always been a dutiful follower.

She eased away from me, her lips tightening. She might not be happy taking orders, but she also wouldn't blatantly disobey him either. She had no intention of telling me anything. At least not with Eddie-what's-his-name hovering over her shoulder.

He'd ruined my chance of discovering anything Natty knew about me.

TYLER

FLINCHING HARD, I SAT UP STRAIGHT. IT ONLY TOOK A second to realize what was happening and where I was.

The dream by itself didn't make any sense, mostly because I shouldn't be dreaming at all. Maybe that's why I couldn't just blow it off. Ignore it.

Ben had taken us from location to location, campsite to campsite, choosing stopping points with no apparent rhyme or reason. But no matter where we'd gone—first driving west to Nevada, then backtracking to Arizona before heading north again—I always knew where we were. Not because he'd told us, he never did. But because in those rare instances when I slept, I somehow dreamed our locations.

And I was never wrong. That last campsite, where I'd overheard those creepy hikers by the hot spring, was somewhere in northern Colorado.

Now though . . . now I dreamed of Kyra.

Even with the fog lifting, I was left with an overwhelming awareness of her. Of the drive to find her, and the coordinates that were now ringing . . . echoing inside my head.

As much of a dick as Simon was, he was right about one thing: I should never have left Kyra alone. I should've acted like a man and stayed to face what she'd told me, even though it felt like she'd caught me unaware with her admissions about our history. If I had, Kyra might be here right now.

It was my fault she'd been kidnapped.

But it was her fault I was a Replaced. She'd told me as much. It was her fault I'd lost everything—my friends, my family, and not just my parents but my brother too. My entire life, all of it, gone.

So what that she'd done it by accident. So what if she hadn't realized her blood was poisonous, like she said. Did that really make everything okay? Make it all right that she offered me up to aliens to mess with my DNA and snatch away my humanness?

And what about that other part, where we . . . she and I . . . had been . . . what? A couple? What did that even mean?

She loved me, she'd said. *She'd actually said that.*

Was *that* supposed to fix things between us? How could it?

But her getting kidnapped didn't make us even either, it

just made me feel shittier about this whole effed-up situation. And now I was here, with Griffin and the others, and I had to face the fact that so many from my former camp were gone. Unaccounted for. Dead.

Being here among the survivors made me even more restless. Or maybe that was about Kyra again.

Even though I was mad at her, I needed to find her, and until I did, I doubted I'd be able to breathe.

All I could think about was her . . . somewhere out there . . .

And instead I was stuck here with Simon, who didn't even bother to hide his feelings for Kyra or his suspicions toward me.

If we hadn't wanted the same thing, I would've told him what an asshole he was. But this wasn't the time or place. He made it more than clear he was willing to risk his life to save her, so I kept my mouth shut.

Griffin, on the other hand, had her own reasons for helping me. Not so much for Kyra's sake, but because of the message—the Returned must die.

What if there was something to it? What if the aliens really were trying to communicate with Kyra, and we needed her to figure it all out?

Otherwise, Griffin might never help Kyra at all. Sure she put on a good face, but I got the feeling if Griffin had her way things would go back to how they were before, to a time when she was the only girl in my life. Like we'd been a couple or something.

I always knew that was what she wanted. But even before Kyra had shown up there'd been . . . *something* stopping me.

Something unfinished I couldn't quite put my finger on.

I guess I knew what that was now—Kyra. Maybe a part of me had known all along, about Kyra and me. Maybe that's why Griffin had never quite managed to wear me down.

Almost, though.

Griffin had *almost* gotten through to me, and I'd almost made a move on her. It sounded bad, like I was some prisoner she'd been subjecting to torture—withholding food, waterboarding, putting on the rack, that sort of thing. It wasn't like that. I liked Griffin well enough. She was tough and practical and loyal.

Like I said, I liked her. Just not the way she wanted me to.

Then Kyra had arrived and everything had changed. That thing, whatever it had been, had clicked into place. It was like Kyra's presence—just Kyra being Kyra—had been enough, even without knowing our history. Not in the whole "you complete me" way . . . except, yeah, kinda like that.

Being near Kyra had made me feel . . . *like me again.*

God, I sounded like a Hallmark card. Even now. Even while I was pissed at her.

It hadn't made sense at the time; as far as I'd known she'd never been mine in the first place.

So, why then, when I'd seen her there, standing in camp, couldn't I remember a life where I hadn't wanted her? Where she hadn't occupied my every thought, even after she'd vanished? Even once Austin and Cat had grown up and moved away? I couldn't recall a time I didn't wonder: *What happened to Kyra? Where did she go? Will I ever see her again?*

So getting a second chance with her the way I had . . . there was no way I could . . . I wouldn't let it slip through my fingers. Besides, it's not like I hadn't felt guilty for pushing Griffin away, because *didn't I owe Griffin*?

But that wasn't how feelings worked. I couldn't be Griffin's just because *she* wanted *me*, or out of some misplaced sense of loyalty. I decided I needed to find out if Kyra could ever . . . if there might somehow be *something* between us.

And I guess I got my answer. We could and there had been.

Yet here I was again, with Griffin and without Kyra. How had that happened? How could Kyra be gone all over again?

I closed my eyes against the dull pulse ticking away inside my skull. This guilt was different from the one over cutting Griffin loose. This was a punishing, unbending, grotesque sort of thing that lashed at me. Burning me, scoring me, using me up.

Like Simon, who said it over and over and over again, I wouldn't rest until we found her. I just didn't have to say it out loud, to everyone within earshot every freaking five seconds.

Jett's trace of the van's license plate had led to a dead end and every hour that passed was another hour wasted. I felt like I might lose my shit once and for all.

But now . . . I had this new dream.

Maybe it was nothing. *Probably* it was nothing, because it was just a goddamned dream after all. But I was running by the time I reached the others all the same. Breathless and sweating when I gripped Ben's shoulder.

"I might know where she is," I gasped. "I think . . ." I had Simon's attention. Jett stood up from his laptop. "Wyoming," I said, moving over to where Simon had a map we'd been using to mark where we'd been and to track any possible leads. I concentrated on the lines—longitude and latitude—on the geographical landmarks and the names of the cities. I worked it out in my head, trying to interpret what I'd sensed in my sleep.

In the same way I'd seen the map I'd drawn in the sand, I'd seen Kyra. Sensed her in my dream. Only she was brighter, like a pulse of light I was being drawn to. Compelling me to find her.

"Here," I dropped my finger to a location in the upper northeast corner of the state.

"Why there?"

There was no point lying about it so I braced myself. "A dream."

Simon's eyebrow lifted, and his skepticism was of the loud-and-clear variety. For once I couldn't blame him. "A dream? You seriously expect us to make a decision based on a dream?"

"Look, no matter what you think, you guys haven't exactly hit it out of the park here. It's not like we have a lot of other options at this point."

Simon came at me. "Don't go pointing fingers. This is all your fault," he was shouting. "If you'd done your job in the first place, she wouldn't be out there, and we wouldn't have to 'hit it out of the park.'"

Griffin shoved her way in between us. "All right, you two. Cut it out." She pushed Simon away. "This isn't helping anything."

"No!" I shouted back. "I'm tired of his dictator bullshit." I looked past her to Simon. "You know what? I don't give a shit what you think. You're right, I shouldn't have left her alone, but right now my dream's the best chance we have of finding her, and if you don't wanna come, then stay here. But I plan to find out if she's there because for some reason, that's where I'm being drawn. There's something—some part of me—that says that's where we'll find her." I was breathing hard, daring him to argue, daring the others as I glanced around at them to say I was full of crap or tell me they wouldn't come either. If that was the case, I'd go alone.

I'd find my own way to get there.

After several tense moments, Simon seemed to calm down. His voice was edged with reluctance, but reluctance wasn't refusal. "How can you be sure that's the place?"

"I can't." I smiled. I shouldn't have, this was serious and I was hoping like crazy this dream of mine was a real lead. A solid one. A *not* dead-end one. But I was sick and tired of Simon acting like he was in charge of everything and everyone and I couldn't stop myself. "How could I, man? It was just a dream."

CHAPTER FIVE

I WOKE ON A GASP, BUT IT WASN'T THE PAIN OF sunrise. This was more like I'd been jolted awake by Lucy, that ten-thousand-volt bitch of a cattle prod. My entire body convulsed and my eyes rolled back in my head, and all I could do was wait for whatever was happening to pass.

When it did, my head collapsed against the metal stretcher behind me with a solid *thunk*.

A new number rattled through my brain—*fourteen*—and I realized I'd somehow missed the new dawn.

Gasping, I looked around, surprised to discover I was alone. There was no one who could have electrocuted me, at least not with Eddie Ray's cattle prod.

The room, me and everything in it, was a landscape painted in darkness, which meant not only had I missed the morning, but most of the day as well. Of course they'd drugged me again, they must have. It was the only explanation for the way my brain felt like mush, and my skin buzzed like Lucy had just been jammed into the side of my neck.

For several seconds . . . minutes . . . maybe hours, I waited for someone to call out the alert that I'd regained consciousness. But no one seemed to be manning the equipment monitoring me.

I glanced down to my bound wrists and wondered how much time I had left. I thought about Natty, and tried to imagine how I'd misjudged her so badly. I thought about Blondie and her "Do I know you?" routine back at the diner, and Eddie Ray with his stupid cattle prod. I squeezed my fists.

Still, no one called out the warning when I knew for damned sure my pulse spiked.

I focused my thoughts the way Simon had taught me, concentrating on more things that upset me . . . things that would make my blood pressure rise . . .

The attack at Blackwater . . . the way Agent Truman had shot Griffin—his own daughter—just to prove a point . . .

I flexed my wrists, but they held tight.

Simon and Jett and Willow, and all the others we'd left behind. Who might be dead for all I knew.

My skin tingled and burned.

Tyler. Oh god, Tyler . . . there were so many things I needed to make up to him. So much I owed him.

The glow from my eyes intensified, and I heard . . . no, *felt* the buckles at my wrists vibrate. I glanced down at my right hand and realized the buckle was loose, not fastened at all. The tiny silver pin had never been secured into the leather strap. It only took a little jiggling for me to liberate my one hand.

And then use that one to release the other.

Without waiting for an alarm, or for someone to cry for help, I groped for the restraint at my neck. It was another buckle, easily undone. My feet were just as simple.

Like that, I was free.

The fog in my brain cleared in an instant as I yanked off every wire and probe and electrode attached to me.

The game had just changed.

Despite the darkness, I could see with perfect clarity and I made my way to the doorway. The sign outside the door read room #14—giving me that same strange sense of déjà vu.

Fourteen.

The hallway beyond my room was long and wide with crumbling brick slabs and broken-out windows high overhead. There were mounds of discarded furnishings, broken chairs and splintered tables.

There was no one around. Not a single person in sight—not Blondie or Natty or Ed. If I hadn't known better, I would have sworn the entire building was deserted.

Spasms continued to rack me, and my legs were all rubbery like I'd just finished sprinting several miles. I had a hard time staying upright, but I didn't have time to be unsteady, so I heaved myself toward one of the walls, using it to support myself.

I still wore the flimsy blue-green hospital gown, which only added to the surreal sensation I had that I was some sort of escaped mental patient. This whole situation was just that, insane. Being kidnapped from the diner, held hostage in this crumbling building . . . being shackled and tortured.

Finding Natty . . . here.

It was more than crazy.

My feet were bare, so I walked as carefully as I could, but it was impossible not to step on shards of broken glass and jagged chunks of cracked concrete and brick. There were even split tiles with edges sharper than any knife. It was like navigating a razor blade obstacle course.

After just a few steps I had deep gashes in the soles of my feet and ankles that made me wince. It didn't matter that they healed almost as fast as they occurred. That didn't stop them from hurting like a mother.

I refused to give up, though. I couldn't afford to coddle myself, no matter how incredibly-horribly-*brutally* painful it was.

This might be my one and only chance to escape.

My pulse thrashed, propelling me forward, and I was hyperalert as I searched for signs that someone had noticed I'd awakened and was trying to get away.

So far though, it was still just me.

If someone came around the corner or anywhere in my line of sight, they'd surely see me—the glow from my eyes would be a dead giveaway.

All I could do was run . . . across the carpet of glass and broken tiles beneath my exposed feet.

I passed several open doorways, each one another glimpse into the asylum's past. There was so much old junk—trashed hospital beds and gurneys, old-fashioned wheelchairs, outdated medical equipment and instruments discarded in piles and heaped in corners. Graffiti streaked the walls, which meant this place wasn't entirely out of reach, the way Blondie had led me to believe. But I had no way of knowing how long ago anyone aside from my captors had stepped foot in here.

I saw no way out, though. There were no exterior doors, and the windows I did see—even the smashed-out ones—were barred.

Claustrophobia crept in on me, a sensation I was far too familiar with, as I realized I might never get out. Each breath become harder and harder to find, and the walls began to narrow just as the ceiling suddenly seemed like it was pressing right on top of me.

I told myself it was all in my head—the hallway hadn't changed—but I ducked all the same.

I had to get outside.

I had to feel air . . . real air . . . fresh, nondusty air . . .

My feet continued to tear and heal . . . rip and repair . . . split and mend in an endless rhythm. I tried to concentrate on that rather than the part where I was suffocating.

I reached a corner near the end of a seemingly endless corridor, and stopped as something caught my eye.

Ward 14 was painted high on the wall in faded blue paint. I'd probably passed other wards and never even noticed the numbers.

My heart bucked when I heard something. A voice.

I waited, to hear it again. For someone to shout for me to stop, or to call for reinforcements.

Instead, when it finally came again, it was ragged and weak and not at all a cry for backup. It was one tired simple word: *help.* Just that, "help" coming from behind a doorway I'd just passed.

I froze, trying to convince myself in a million different ways to keep going, to . . . *ignore it.* It wasn't my problem. I couldn't save anyone if I didn't save myself. Someone else would come . . . someone else would *help.*

Not. My. Problem.

But who was I kidding? What kind of person would I be if I sneaked away and pretended I hadn't just heard that? What kind of *monster* . . . ?

I dropped my chin to my chest and took a step back. My feet bled as the cracked tiles beneath me sliced them again, and I had to hope whoever was in there wasn't human, or else I'd already sentenced them to death—maybe not this second, but within a day or two. And knowing the way Tyler had suffered, they'd be begging for the end to come.

But it wasn't a human I found, at least not a full human.

And I couldn't decide whether I was glad I'd come back when I realized who was trapped in the room.

The idea of leaving, taking off the way he had when Blackwater was attacked, became real again. Make him someone else's problem.

Except he didn't look like the Judas I'd thought he was. I'd been sure Thom had been the one to send out the message, letting the Daylighters know I existed, sending them our coordinates.

But here he was . . . tied to the same kind of ancient table I'd been strapped to, so I had to wonder . . . had we been wrong? Was Thom a victim too?

"Thom," I whispered, keeping my distance.

"Kyra?" His voice sounded like a dried-up riverbed. No way that could be faked. This wasn't a trap. He'd been tortured too.

"It's me." I went to him, but my fingers shook as I unfastened his neck and his hands. If you'd have asked me five minutes ago, I would have called Thom a backstabber. Now . . . now, I was setting him free. His skin was cold and I wondered if that was a bad sign. He didn't have electrodes or machines hooked to him. No IV. But he seemed weak. "Are they drugging you?"

"They were," he said as I worked to get him upright. His shaky grip clutched my shoulder. "Do you have water?" Even his whisper was feeble. "They haven't given me water in"—his black eyes searched the room helplessly—"I . . . I don't know how long."

The Returned might not need as much food, but that didn't mean they—that *we*—could survive without it. Same went for water. If Thom had been here since the raid of Blackwater, which, if I'd counted right, had been at least five days ago, maybe more if they'd kept me comatose through any other sunrises, then no wonder he was so weak. He wasn't hooked up to an IV the way I had been.

"Come on. Let's get you outta here." I hauled him up, and he leaned heavily against me. It wasn't ideal; I wasn't superstrong, at least not the kind where I could carry a grown man, but he wasn't able to carry himself.

I was sweating within seconds, my arms and legs trembling beneath his weight. Neither of us had on shoes, but my wounds healed at speeds his never would. He barely winced though, and I couldn't help wondering if he was even aware of all the cuts and gashes, or if he was too far gone from dehydration or starvation or whatever else they'd put him through.

"Just a few more steps," I told him. I kept repeating that like a mantra, to urge him on whenever he slowed. The truth was, I had no idea how much farther we had.

When I saw the exit, I nearly buckled from sheer-elating-*thrilling* joy.

An *honest to goodness* exit.

The door was clearly marked, with a sign and everything. But just like the rest of this place it was blocked by debris—a discarded mattress with stuffing and springs erupting from it, a lopsided heap of worn and broken strips of timber, garbage . . . so much garbage.

No big deal; they'd be easy enough to clear.

"Stay here." I propped Thom against a wall, as if he had any say in the matter. It's not like he could take off or anything.

I climbed over the garbage mound, and began shoving it out of my way. After several minutes, I'd already made a serious dent when I felt rather than heard the presence of someone creeping up behind me.

Even without looking, I knew it wasn't Thom. I don't know how I managed *not* to puke.

This couldn't be happening. Not now, not when we were so close.

"Eddie Ray . . ." It was the defeat threaded through Thom's voice that somehow reminded me where I'd heard the name before.

I turned to face him.

Eddie Ray. How had I not recognized it sooner? The name wasn't common.

Eddie Ray—the guy Simon had told me about when he'd been explaining his long and complicated history with Griffin—his back-in-the-day story. As in, Simon had known Eddie Ray back in the day, when the two of them, along with Thom and Griffin, had all been recruiters at Blackwater Ranch . . . years earlier.

I tried to remember the things Simon had said about Eddie Ray, in case there was anything useful. But he hadn't said much. Just that Eddie Ray had gone missing around the same time the camp's former leader, a guy named Franco, had vanished. Simon had made it sound suspicious, like Eddie Ray might've had something to do with their leader's disappearance, mostly because he'd also said something about Eddie Ray being some kind of power monger.

In my brief experience with Eddie Ray, Simon hadn't been wrong.

Standing over me now, Eddie Ray gave me a look that made my skin pucker. "You didn't think we were really letting you just walk outta here, did ya?"

I glanced back toward the exit, evaluating my chances for escape. I might be able to make it, but not if I had to carry Thom. I'd have to leave him . . . send help for him later.

But if I gave up now, neither of us stood a chance.

At the back of my neck, the prickling in my skin had begun to stretch. It expanded until it spread across my shoulders and down my arms.

I was trapped, I told myself, feeding on the growing panic. Letting it fuel the weapon inside me.

It consumed me, buzzing all the way to my fingertips.

I focused on Eddie Ray. Eddie Ray . . . and the garbage around me.

I didn't stop myself with worry over whether I might actually hurt him. He'd hurt me. I concentrated, instead, on getting out of here, reminding myself he was standing between me and freedom. Between getting help for Thom.

It happened then, like a whirlwind . . . the first pieces

of debris shooting up and hitting Eddie Ray from behind. Pelting him in the back of his skull.

He tried to shield himself, the way anyone would. He raised his arms to defend himself. But even I saw the pieces he couldn't guard against, tearing his cheek and chin. A jagged-edged brick cut into his forehead, slicing wickedly down and across his face. If he hadn't been Returned, he'd have been left with a gruesome scar.

Blinking through the screen of blood, he tried to wipe his eyes. But the debris kept coming at him.

It was more than I'd meant to summon, but I had no idea how to curb it. Maybe I didn't want to.

Thom took some hits too, smaller stuff mostly, and I felt bad for that, but it couldn't be helped. I didn't have enough experience. I couldn't control where it struck.

I didn't stay to watch. Instead I bolted, leaving Eddie Ray curled in a fetal position, crippled by the rubble that viciously pelted him. I'd come back for Thom, but one of us had to get out.

Climbing the rubble I hadn't yet cleared, I hit the release lever to the exit. Relief coursed through me as the crisp nighttime air rushed in and I lifted my face to meet it.

This was it. I was going to make it. Just a few more steps and I would be free from these lunatics forever.

My feet sank in the unmowed lawn. It was soggy and damp, and its moss-laden patches were soothing to my bare feet as I ran.

When the alarm shrieked, it wasn't a result of the door

I'd opened . . . not even a delayed response would have been *that* delayed. But the sound was more intense than anything I'd ever heard, causing me to stumble.

Reaching up to cover my ears, I scanned for its source, concentrating on each step I took . . . one and then another. The noise filled my head, bouncing off the walls of my skull and making my teeth rattle. My steps felt sluggish.

When I staggered again, I glanced up. Planted around the perimeter, high on tall steel posts, were loudspeakers. Ones I hadn't noticed before.

I noticed now, though.

The pain in my head was a thousand times worse than the cuts and tears that had shredded my feet, and I wondered if this was the kind of damage that could ever be repaired.

Like Eddie Ray behind me, I finally gave in to the assault and dropped all the way down, even while I told myself . . . screamed at myself to run, run . . . *run*!

Except . . . I couldn't manage it. And in a single instant I knew: there'd be no escaping. Not today.

There was only this . . . folding in on myself, tucking my knees to my chest as I covered my ears against this horrible, incessant blaring that rattled and echoed and made my brain vibrate.

When the hands closed in on me I knew . . .

It was over. They'd beaten me.

And then somewhere, in the jumble of noise and ache in my head, I felt it again, the stab . . . the sting . . .

TYLER

"HOW MUCH FARTHER?" IT WAS THE ONLY QUESTION that mattered, and Jett answered without skipping a beat: "Less than two hours."

He'd already done the math; that was two hours taking into account our breakneck speed.

One hundred twenty minutes.

A lifetime.

I liked Jett, maybe more than I liked anyone else in the vehicle we were in—one of the two we'd taken. Ours was the SUV. Ben took his truck, along with two of Griffin's guys, and Nancy.

I liked that Jett thought in terms of numbers. Statistics. Percentages.

I'd never been a numbers whiz, I was always more into books and music and art. But Jett didn't make me want to shove my fist down his throat the way Simon did. Jett was ordered, logical. Simon was rude. The kind of guy my dad always called an SOB.

Even more though, I liked that Jett was almost as anxious to find Kyra as the rest of us, but without all the ulterior motives Simon and I had. Jett didn't have something to prove. He wasn't thinking about her lips or how he could convince her to choose him.

Or at least if he was, he was hiding it like a champ.

"What have you found out about the place?" I asked.

"It's an asylum," Jett announced. "Look." He turned the beat-up laptop he carried everywhere and showed us some sort of official site with titles or deeds or something.

I leaned forward to get a better look even though I had no idea what I was looking at. "I didn't even know those things existed anymore."

"They don't. Or this one doesn't. It was shut down in the early seventies. According to the public records, it's been bought and sold a couple times, but never actually converted into anything useful. Empty mostly. The bank foreclosed on the last owner over five years ago." He tapped the screen again.

Simon, who just had to know something about everything, added, "Makes it the perfect hideout."

Jett nodded, as usual agreeing with everything his fearless

leader had to say. The hero worship was nauseating and a strike against Jett as far as I was concerned. Beside me, Griffin stayed silent, which from her was as good as agreement. An asylum it was, I supposed, and prayed Jett was half as smart as these people thought he was.

I leaned back and looked out the window, thinking of what I would say when we finally found Kyra.

I wasn't sure I'd know until I saw her face. I wished I could be like her and remember everything she did—the things she'd told me about. I know she said some of them were bad, but some of them . . .

My breath had fogged the glass and I absently traced a pattern with my finger.

Some of them must've been good too. Kyra had said so.

She'd told me she loved me.

Two more hours. Two more hours until hopefully, with an arsenal to outfit a small army and some luck, we'd get Kyra back and maybe we could talk again. Maybe she'd help me sort it out . . .

I could tell her all the things I've been thinking . . . feeling. About her.

I looked up at the words I'd written in the steam:

I'll remember you always . . .

CHAPTER SIX

"HEY, SLEEPYHEAD." THE SINGSONG VOICE sounded like it was echoing down a tunnel. "Someone slept the whole day away. Glad you decided to join the land of the living."

Living. Is that what this was? If my head hadn't been pounding and my ears ringing, I might have laughed. As it was, all I could manage was to open my eyes. Not bad, all things considered.

When I turned, Blondie was at the monitor, observing my heart rate.

Ever since being returned, I'd been envious of normal

humans—people who needed a solid eight hours sleep. Now, if I never lost consciousness again it would be too soon.

Although I wasn't sure you could really compare the comatose state these freaks had been keeping me in with *actual sleep.*

"Go to hell," I rasped.

She chuckled. "Aw, don't be like that. Did you think we *accidentally* left you all by your lonesome?" She made a *tsk*-ing sound while she came around to check me out. "Come on, Kyra. You're not stupid. Natty told us what you could do . . . that little trick—moving things with your mind. Eddie Ray just wanted to see it in action. Have a little fun with you." Her mouth twitched slightly. "Guess he didn't realize how much damage you'd do."

But I was too focused on the other thing she'd told me, about my escape not being an accident. My chest felt heavy. "So . . . you . . . were just messing with me?" Why hadn't I considered that sooner?

Shrugging indifferently, she tapped an IV line that I assumed was how they kept me in various states of consciousness. "Just separating truth from fiction, so to speak. Eddie Ray likes to test the merchandise—calls it quality control. Plus, we needed to find out whether that little trick of yours was something we could defend against." Smugly, she kept talking as she moved around, checking machines and connections. "Those sirens . . . those were my idea. You dropped like a rock. They should give us a good second line of defense against you since the meds haven't been as . . .

effective as we'd hoped. Not bad, huh?"

I blinked, my eyelids still heavy from the sedation. "They seem pretty effective to me," I told her, thinking about the way I'd missed entire days . . . entire sunrises.

"That's because you're on a dose high enough to kill an elephant, and even that has to be on a continuous drip or your body just"—she chewed her lip—"metabolizes it."

"What's to defend against? What did I ever do to you?" My voice wobbled. I tried to turn away, but the collar around my neck prevented me.

Blondie grinned. "Might as well get comfortable. We can't transport you until we can guarantee it's secure." My face screwed up as I tried to figure out which part to focus on first. She must have thought she could pinpoint my confusion. "Oh, the transfer. Yeah, we're not keeping you here forever. We're just the . . . how do I say this? We're what you could call brokers."

"Brokers?" I managed to squeak out.

"That's right, middlemen." She cocked her head to look down at me. She was definitely enjoying this. "We're not the ones you should be afraid of. The folks who bought you paid a lot to get their hands on someone like you."

"Who is it, the Daylighters?" But of course it was Agent Truman or one of his lackeys. He was probably already here somewhere, waiting for his chance to take me into custody. To strap me to some other table in some other lab and start experimenting—slicing and dicing. "Are they taking Thom too?"

She made a face. "No. I mean, yes, we're selling Thom to the Daylighters, but not you. You should be so lucky. Once your buyers get their hands on you, they're never gonna let you go." She said it as if Agent Truman would have, and I think we both knew that wasn't true.

I wasn't sure who I was more sorry for: me, heading off to the unknown, or Thom, who'd be passed off to the dreaded Daylight Division. But all I could focus on was the one word she'd used: *never.*

She and Eddie Ray and Natty were planning to hand me over to someone who had no intention of letting me leave. Ever.

I practically choked myself trying to turn away again. I didn't want her to see the tears building behind my eyes. I hated crying, but I was far too groggy to stop it. Even though I'd healed and my body was 100 percent, I was finally realizing that she and Natty and Eddie Ray had beaten me. I was thoroughly-completely-*utterly* defeated.

Even though I didn't respond, my elevated heart rate probably said it all.

I'd never see my mom or my dad again. Never get the chance to see my little brother, Logan, or Cat or Austin.

I'd never get the chance to tell Simon how grateful I was that he'd saved my life. How much I appreciated everything he'd done for me, to keep me safe, to reunite me with my dad and Tyler.

But even I knew I was a liar, because my feelings for Simon weren't all about gratitude. If whoever they were planned to kill me, or let me die, then why shouldn't I at least be honest with myself?

Simon mattered. More than I meant for him to.

And if I was really playing the truth game, so had that kiss . . . the one he'd given me when he'd said good-bye.

That sweet, demanding, puzzling kiss that reminded me so much . . . too much of Simon himself. Demanding and complicated. And sometimes, when he really wanted to be, sweet even.

I squeezed my eyes shut and my vision blurred. Hot streams poured down my cheeks.

Then there was Tyler. I'd never see Tyler again.

"Don't you want to ask again? I heard you asked Natty *why you*. Don't you want to know the truth?" Blondie tugged the tube that disappeared beneath the sleeve of the hospital gown I was wearing. She didn't try to be gentle since she must know by now that my skin had definitely healed around it, locking it firmly in place.

"No."

"Aw, c'mon. It was more fun when you were playing along," she coaxed.

Any other time I would've added a little something to my inflection, but I had nothing left to give. "Screw you," I said flatly.

She laughed, because that's what I was, a big, fat joke.

Kneeling down so she was right in front of my face, she whispered, "But here's the thing—I wanna tell you. No harm in it, I suppose. It's not like you can tell anyone, right?"

She reached out, her cold, spiderlike fingers stroking my cheek, and even though I felt dead inside, I couldn't stop from inwardly cringing. "You're not like us," she said, like this was some major revelation.

It didn't matter what she said. If she was right, if they were planning to pass me off to someone else—someone who'd apparently paid a lot of money for me—then I didn't give a crap what their reasons were. My fate had already been decided.

It didn't stop her from pretending we were having a conversation. "What?" she chided. "You think I mean that you can do things we can't?" She spoke quietly, a whispery sort of venom to her tone. "Did someone forget to tell you the part where those things up there might not be as peace-loving as we've been led to believe? And . . . *whatever you are* . . . whatever they made you into . . ." Her fingernails sank sharply into the flesh of my cheek. "Don't even kid yourself we're the same because I know what I am. *I'm* still part human."

She may as well have jammed Lucy right into my heart. I could no longer ignore her, even though part of me was convinced she was insane—the way she touched and prodded me, her low, boastful voice.

What was she saying—that it really was us versus them? That I was the enemy?

"You're wrong," I started, and then changed my tactic. Pissing her off seemed like a seriously bad idea. "You're confused. I want the same thing you do. We're on the same side."

She leaned closer, and the notion she might be crazy amplified. "This is bigger than us. Way, way bigger. You know they're up there. I know you know it. You feel them, don't you?" She did that thing my dad had, where she nodded skyward as if to say, *Them, the aliens.*

This conversation was getting weirder and weirder. "What do you mean?" I asked, wondering where she was going with this.

"I mean," she insisted, her nostrils flaring angrily, "tell me you don't you feel them. You don't sense them getting closer?"

Feel them . . . ?

I blinked, not sure how I was supposed to respond to that. Not sure what she was even saying. How would I know if they were getting closer?

Then I thought about my dad saying he thought they were trying to send me a message—through those hikers.

"We've seen you, each time it gets close to sunrise, the way your pulse and your blood pressure skyrocket. How long has that been happening? Days? Weeks?" She grinned, standing upright. "It's getting stronger, isn't it? Those people who want to buy you say it's only a matter of time now. They think it's not much longer 'til they get here. Is that what it meant, the number I heard you saying?"

Sweat broke out on my upper lip as I thought about the knife-twist that came with each sunrise, and the way it had gotten stronger, more intense each dawn.

With each passing day.

Even for a girl who'd lost five years of her life, whose memories were now thriving inside an entirely different body—*an alien body*—this was almost too much. What if she was right? What if I could somehow, some way, sense their approach? "So why me? If you're right, why do *I* feel them?"

She shrugged. "Because you're one of them? Because they want something from you?"

"Want what?"

"How'm I supposed to know? My job is to make sure you're delivered in one piece."

She continued to watch me, and I wanted to tell her to look away, even as the thought struck me: my obsession with time. My preoccupation with the passage of days, hours, minutes, and seconds . . . ever since I'd returned.

Was it possible . . . could that have been why all along? Had my body been somehow programmed to sense their arrival?

"So what . . . I'm some sort of . . . *clock*? Like a countdown—"

Blood sprayed across my face, almost before the sound of the gunshot split the air.

I blinked blood out of my eyes, and tasted it between my teeth. It had splattered all over my arms and on the blue-green of the gown I was wearing. No wonder it took me so long to register what had happened.

Blondie never had that luxury—that moment of clarity—before her eyes, which had been clear blue and laser-focused on me just a second earlier, had gone suddenly and absolutely blank.

Then every muscle in her body wilted as she'd collapsed to the floor. On her way down, her forehead banged solidly against the side of the metal gurney I was strapped to. It was the only sound I'd heard, other than the bullet that disappeared inside her brain.

I was still gaping. Trying to comprehend what . . . and . . . why, when I saw Eddie Ray standing in the doorway, holding a gun.

"Oh my god . . ." I gasped at him. "What . . . ? *Why did you do that?*" Chunks of bone and flesh clung to my skin. *Blondie's* bone and skin.

"She's a talker."

I shuddered at his icy explanation, the realization that the head shot wasn't the kind of wound Blondie could heal from finally sinking in.

"About . . . *me*? Y-you . . . you didn't have to . . . kill her." I'd never stuttered before, not the old me, but my teeth were chattering and my words tripped over my tongue. "Sh-she . . ." My throat stung. "Said it d-didn't matter if I knew. She s-said I w-was never getting away."

"Not her place to decide." Eddie Ray set the gun down next to one of the monitors. I had no idea how he could be so cavalier, so *whatever* about what he'd just done.

This time, drugs had nothing to do with the spinning of the room. I needed to get a grip. To be as collected as Eddie Ray was. "Was she right? About what she said? *Am* I some sort of countdown clock?"

Eddie Ray reached for a stool, one that didn't look as

ancient as everything else in this place—this asylum. He avoided Blondie's body, parking it instead on the other side of the table. Straddling the seat, he cocked his head to look at me.

Then he reached down and brushed at something near the corner of my eye, and I felt it . . . like he'd picked a wound that hadn't quite scabbed over all the way. I knew what it was: a piece of Blondie.

I was wearing a dead girl all over me.

He chuckled. *Chuckled.* Like this was somehow funny. Like there was even the remotest humor to be found in any of this. He leaned close and the urge to flee kicked in.

I'd heard of animals that had literally chewed off their own limbs just to escape the jaws of a bear trap, and that's how I felt. Like I would be willing to chew off one of my own arms or legs if it meant getting away from Eddie Ray.

"According to our buyers, those alien fuckers are already on their way . . ." God, why did everyone have to do that eye tic thing? I knew who he meant. "It's just a matter of when. Could be days."

Days.

I concentrated on that rather than the stomach acid eating my throat. Days could mean anything. Days could add up to weeks or months, or even years.

I thought of all the mornings I'd been gripped by pain . . . was that what I'd been sensing? Their approach? Their nearness?

How many days had there been already?

I thought of the way I'd been tracking time, the strange numbers I'd heard in my head and wondered why I hadn't thought of it before.

I concentrated, trying to remember what today's number was. Which number was repeating itself in my head right now, at this very moment?

Thirteen. That was the number.

Was that the countdown to their arrival?

They were coming. But why?

"So?" he asked. "Are they right? Can you feel those little mothers?" Eddie Ray angled his face so our mouths were almost touching and I wished I couldn't taste the rancidness of his breath.

I refused to answer him. No way would I ever, not in a million years, tell him anything.

He didn't seem to need my answer. "Are you afraid?" he asked, grinning down at me.

I curled my lip at him. "Aren't you?"

But Eddie Ray scoffed at the idea. "I won't be anywhere near you by then. But don't worry, don't take it personal. In the end, this is really just about business."

"Business? You mean all of this just comes down to making a couple of bucks? That girl . . . she was . . . you just shot her, for what? Money? If you really believe they're coming, then you're talking about an alien race heading to Earth, and you don't even know what they want." My voice rose. "How is this just *business*?"

I thought of the message—what Tyler had said, what my

dad had overheard: *The Returned must die.* Maybe I shouldn't even care about any of that when this was the end for me—they'd already beaten me . . . beaten us.

But I did.

"It just is," he spat, his patience with me reaching its end. His cheeks and neck and forehead went red and splotchy. "And it's more than just a couple of bucks. It's enough to buy our freedom if I play my cards right. Freedom from all this. From the No-Suchers. From pretty much everything. We'll never have to worry again. All we have to do is deliver you in one piece." He jumped up, knocking the stool out from behind him. "The thing is, though, it'd be even better if we could've gotten our hands on the other one too—that Tyler kid. We could make a helluva lot more for two of you. That was the plan, you know? She was supposed to grab both of you. Her mistake." He moved to where the blond girl was lying and stared down at her. I couldn't see her body, but I watched as Eddie Ray nudged the dead girl with his foot. His eyes were glittering when he looked up again. "Like I said, it's just business."

Tyler. They wanted Tyler too.

There was no way. That could not—would not—happen.

He came back over to me. "Just tell me where the kid is . . ." His voice dropped all conspiratorial-like. As if we were somehow partners. Pals. "In fact, if you tell me, I'll put in a good word for you. Let your buyers know how *cooperative* you've been. Never know, maybe you'll get lucky and they'll take it easy on you." He winked, and bile blistered the back of my tongue.

I shook my head, emotions pounding through me.

The buddy-buddy expression vanished from Eddie Ray's face. He gave me a strange look then, one I couldn't quite decipher but probably it was better that way. I didn't want to know what was going on inside that head of his.

"I don't need your help," he finally said. "I'll find him myself. I'll sell you and then I'll track him down on my own."

"Please . . . no . . ." But I wasn't sure who I was trying to convince, him or me when I said it.

Because it was too late. He'd doomed himself the moment Tyler's name had rolled off his lips.

This wasn't like before, where the sensations began mildly—the slow build of prickling, itching, tingling.

This was wild. Uncontrollable. A storm unleashed.

Like *I* had been unleashed.

And I had been, in more ways than one. Energy tore through my body, blistering from the base of my neck and shooting all the way to my fingertips and toes.

This need to save Tyler made me strong. Stronger than I'd ever been. And before I could think the word "control"—before Eddie Ray realized anything was happening at all—my right hand had yanked free.

But that wasn't Eddie Ray's undoing; it was the part where I managed to move the gun. *His* gun.

It was like that night up at Devil's Hole when I'd mentally stripped Agent Truman of his weapon . . . only this time I wasn't trying to disarm anyone.

This time the gun flew directly *into* my other hand. And just like the time with Agent Truman, it occurred so fast, whipping through the air, it was barely a blur.

And because of Natty's training, I knew how to use the thing. *Eddie Ray had her to thank for that.*

Before he'd even recognized the weapon in my hand—the still-bound one—or the fact that the other one was free, I'd reached across and released the slide.

Then I switched hands and raised the gun right at him.

Quickly. In one arcing motion so he didn't have time to run, or even duck out of the way.

I didn't ask if he'd change his mind. I didn't clarify how he planned to track Tyler down, or ask him to explain how he planned to sell him or to whom.

I pulled the trigger.

The gun's kick threw me back against the steel table. My neck was still bound, so it's not like I had all that far to go, but the impact was solid, making my vision blur.

Eddie Ray had only been standing a few feet away and I hadn't missed. It had been like watching the blond girl go down, only in reverse.

The bullet struck him just above his left eye, in his forehead, which hadn't exactly been where I'd been aiming . . . but it did the trick all the same.

By the time seven minutes had passed, it was down to just me and Natty, and I needed to find her before she found me.

After I'd shot Eddie Ray, I'd scrambled to get off that damned table—I couldn't do it fast enough, but the entire time all I could think was, *I shot someone . . . I shot someone . . . I shot someone . . .*

It made no difference that he meant to capture Tyler, or that he would've killed me if I'd hesitated. What I'd done was inconceivable, and I was still trembling. Still, none of that stopped me from snagging Blondie's boots so I wouldn't have to navigate the hallways barefoot again.

I hadn't made it far when the two guys whose names I'd never even learned found me.

When they came ricocheting around the corner, I was almost as surprised to see them as they were to see me. Almost, but not quite.

My hands were shaking but I got off two rounds, one into each of their heads, and then, as if I were as coldblooded as Eddie Ray, I stepped over them on my way out.

Next it was Natty's turn.

I wish the thought disturbed me more.

The last time I'd seen Natty I'd learned she'd never been my friend. That she was responsible for the Daylighters' siege of Blackwater. Responsible for me losing my dad and Tyler all over again. Now I had a chance to get my revenge against her for everything she'd done.

A satisfied smile curled my lips.

My borrowed boots crunched across the littered floors. Natty was here—I could feel her. Practically smell her.

If only.

I kept the gun in front of me as I moved from room to room. My only knowledge of searches came from movies and TV, so I was sure I looked like one of those jacked-up cop-actors Austin and Tyler's dad, who was a real cop, always made fun of.

But so what? All that mattered was that *I* found her before she found me.

My heart was beating against the over-tight muscles of my chest like a mallet. Beat-BEAT, beat-BEAT, *beat-BEAT.* NO way Natty didn't hear *that* from a mile away.

I stopped when I heard something, but the noise was all wrong.

It came from overhead, not in front or behind me, and I squinted to get a glimpse of whatever was up there, trying my best to see past the rotting rafters. I had to find it—that scuffling, scraping sound. And still, my heart beat-BEAT against my ribs, pulverizing them.

Something came at me then, faster than a shadow.

Flinching, I nearly dropped the gun as I used my hand to shield my face. When I crouched, a nail along the baseboard raked across my knee.

It's okay. I'm okay, I told myself, biting back a hysterical bubble of laughter when I realized it had been a bird. Trapped the way I was inside the asylum. It flew down the hall one way, and then came back the other, its wings frantically stirring the dust-filled air as it searched for a way out.

"Jesus . . . ," I muttered, getting to my feet again.

"Jesus can't help you." Natty's voice was like liquid ice.

Had she been standing there, watching the entire time? Waiting for me to mess up?

When I turned, it was slow and deliberate . . . and not complete. I came to a stop when I saw her. When I saw the gun in her hand, not a handgun like mine, but one so large she had to grip it with both hands.

One that was aimed directly at me.

"I know they're dead," she told me coldly. "I know you killed them."

"I'll kill you too," I stated matter-of-factly.

She shrugged, not at all concerned. Not at all believing I would do it. "You know, it was dumb luck that we tracked you down. Your dad made it tough. He was better than I gave him credit for. We had eyes on several state DOT traffic cams for days before we finally picked up that damn truck of his outside Fort Collins. Good thing for us his piece of junk is hard to miss, because he was smart enough to switch the plates." She took a step closer, and my heart picked up a notch.

"Don't," I warned her, but she just kept talking, ignoring the gun I was holding.

"We almost lost you again after you tore outta that campground. If you hadn't stopped at that diner, things might've ended differently. Worked out in the end though . . . at least for us." She took another step. "Tyler won't be as hard. He's a sweet kid. Trusting." Her voice changed then, and I heard her, the old Natty. The meek girl who'd been my friend. "He'll believe me when I say I just want to help him find you." She squeezed her brows together, a tortured sort of look. "We're in this together, Tyler. Kyra's my friend too." Her voice broke, and if I didn't know the real Natty, I would have believed she was going to break down and cry.

My shoulders fell because she was right. She was so totally-completely-utterly convincing. Tyler would buy this act of hers hook, line, and sinker. If Natty got to him, there was no way he would ever suspect her of what she really had planned for him.

I couldn't let her get away with it. I used both hands to raise my gun to point at her head.

When she laughed, it was an insulting sound. "Let's just get this over with." She wasn't afraid of me. She didn't believe I could do it.

And maybe she was right. Already my hands were shaking again, and the beating in my chest had resumed.

Beat-BEAT . . .

. . . Beat-BEAT . . .

Don't let her get to you. It was a silent prayer.

Natty . . . Natty who I'd once believed was my friend. My eyes traveled down to her gun at the same time I concentrated on the one in my own hands. I saw her nod toward me . . . at me.

I recognized the nod. I'd seen that nod on the field a million times. Athletes gave it whenever they were feeling overly cocky. Too confident for their own good. It was a *Fuck you* nod. She didn't have to say it out loud.

I focused, telling myself Natty was wrong. She was full

of crap. She was the reason I was here in the first place. She was the reason Blondie was dead and I'd been forced to kill Eddie Ray and the others. She was the reason Blackwater had fallen. But she wouldn't take Tyler.

I slowed my breathing . . . and my heartbeat. I counted to three.

One, two, three.

Beat-BEAT!

Then, like lining up a pitch, I fired.

SIMON

I HALF EXPECTED FREDDY KRUEGER TO JUMP OUT AT us with his knife-fingers at any second. Vines snaked in and over every surface of the crumbling building, choking it out. The lawn needed a serious dose of weed killer, and the driveway, which had one of those massive iron gates at its mouth, was now a disintegrating mess of broken asphalt, and was lined with creepy, spindly limbed trees.

I wondered what it must have been like, back in the day. Jett had mentioned that people used to drop off their relatives at places like these . . . dump them when no one could, or wanted to, care for them.

What was that like, to live behind these massive brick walls, cut off from the rest of the world?

Nothing like now, I guessed. Now this was a place time forgot. Just like us, I couldn't help thinking. Now it was an empty shithole crumbling to the ground. I wondered who we were about to come up against in there. And for the millionth time, I hoped to God Tyler was right, that Kyra was inside. That he hadn't just led us on a wild-goose chase.

"Cut the lights," Griffin whispered, but I was one step ahead of her, already switching them off. Then, she added, "We should go the rest the way on foot."

No one said much, not even Jett, who usually rattled off numbers whenever things got tense. This time, he kept his mouth shut. No data about our odds or the probability we could be walking into a trap.

We'd figured that one out all on our own.

Kyra's dad took his cue from us, and the lights from that piece of shit pickup behind us shut off too. The world—the run-down grounds around us—went black. When we parked, he cut his overloud engine too. If anything had given us away so far, it was that goddamn truck of his.

Getting out of the SUV, my adrenaline kicked into overdrive, pumping so hard I could taste it. I signaled for Griffin to bring her AK-47, and Jett, and to stick with Tyler and me. We'd be going directly through the front entrance. Ben Agnew's party would take the rear, searching for an alternate way in.

I lifted three fingers—our channel on the two-way—the only way we'd be communicating from here on out. But until there was something to report, everyone knew to stay off the comm. No point giving those sons of bitches any other clues we were on to them.

I joined my fingertip to the tip of my thumb: *okay?*

When there were nods all around, we broke apart. The other group took off ahead of us and disappeared into the night, just as planned. Griffin, Jett, Tyler, and I waited a beat or two longer, giving the other team, Ben Agnew and two of Griffin's best Blackwater soldiers, a ten-second head start. Then we took off too, slipping silently through grass that reached my knees and overgrown bushes that tangled menacingly along what had once been a driveway.

In operations like these, darkness could be your ally, the shadows swallowing you whole and giving you the element of surprise. But it could just as easily work against you, creating unseen obstacles and making it next to impossible to discern friend from enemy.

I'd been on those missions. Seen allies fall simply because we were shooting blind.

I never wanted to live through that kind of clusterfuck again. If I shot someone, I wanted it to be intentional. I wanted to see their faces when they died.

For every action there is an equal and opposite reaction, I'd heard that somewhere, maybe in school back when things like school mattered.

With each step, I waited for a reaction, equal or otherwise. A warning shout, an alarm, a bullet chiseling through the night. But nothing happened as we got closer to the building. Silence and darkness seemed to seep out from it equally, and I started to believe Tyler had screwed us. Wasted our time.

No one was here. No one had been here in a very, very, *very* long time.

Griffin and I took opposite sides of the massive entrance doors. They were solid, making them impossible to see beyond, but we stayed to the sides anyway—no point taking a face full of bullet spray if it wasn't necessary, right?

Griffin and I eased forward, while Jett and Tyler stayed back. Time slowed and I was aware of everything—the stars overhead; the still, almost oppressive heaviness of the air; the sound of every breath I took. I balanced on the balls of my feet, settling my weight as I crossed my left hand over my body to reach for the door's handle while my right shoulder slid over the heavy wooden door. The assault rifle stayed at the ready in my right hand.

I wasn't the least bit surprised to find the door locked.

I nodded once at Griffin. We'd been here before, in situations like this, back when we'd both been recruiters under Franco. The job had landed us in some sticky situations. More than once we'd had to bust into private residences, medical clinics, even a police station or two to rescue a newly Returned. Like me, Griffin knew the drill.

Silently, we watched each other, counting in unison. Neither Jett nor Tyler was even aware. It was so ingrained; we didn't do it out loud.

When I reached three, I stepped out of the way and Griffin smashed her boot near the handle, heel first. The frame splintered as the door gave, and I rammed my shoulder against it, shoving my way through first.

Griffin and I cleared the entry within seconds, with Tyler and Jett coming in right behind us. We were all armed, although the rifles Griffin and I carried made the others look like water pistols.

"Stay close!" Griffin whispered.

The inside of this place was an even bigger mess than the outside. The guts of the asylum were everywhere; long-dead electrical wires dangling from walls and ceilings, wreckage spewing out of doorways, and a rotted stench that combined everything from human waste to musty decay to something . . . fresher . . .

"Gunpowder," I mouthed to Griffin. It was a scent I'd have recognized anywhere, even mingled in this shithole of sensory overload. But Griffin had already noticed it, and now she was leading the way, making quick work of picking her way through the rubble.

The first body we came across was facedown. Relief that it was a boy wasn't a strong enough word. The fact it wasn't Kyra almost renewed my faith in God. Almost.

The kid was wearing khakis and a T-shirt—normal crap. I wasn't sure what I'd expected, old-fashioned hospital scrubs? Maybe a killer clown or two? Somehow his ordinary street clothes were even creepier in this place.

If he was Returned his body never had the chance to heal. The point-blank bullet through his forehead had sealed his fate the second it had shredded his brain.

Dropping his face back into the debris, Griffin gave the *Let's go* signal.

Body #2 was another boy, just a few feet from the first. This kid had a gun, but apparently it had done him little good. Same precise bullet hole, same destroyed brain.

From behind me, I heard the two-way crackle to life.

I turned to Jett, who held it to his ear, listening with intense focus.

"They got a body," he whispered. "Near the rear exit."

I closed my eyes, wishing I could ask if it was her—Kyra—but knowing we needed to stay off the channel as much as possible. We had no idea who might be listening.

I nodded. We'd get there. At least I hoped we'd get there.

Before we did though, we reached a strange inner chamber. That's where we discovered another body—a blond girl who matched the image Griffin had found online. It looked like Tyler's dream had been right after all.

In the center of this room with its over-high ceilings, there was an old-fashioned gurney of some sort . . . an ancient metal table with leather straps. I could only imagine this was where they'd done electroshock or lobotomized the hospital's residents in days gone by.

There was fresh blood smeared across it, splattered in thick viscous puddles. And all around the table were machines. But not old-school ones. These things were high tech. Monitors, IV stands, machines that had no business in a place like this.

I signaled for Tyler to come around. "That her?"

When Tyler nodded, my breath loosened. Not all the way,

but enough. Someone had been here before us, someone armed. Someone gunning for the bad guys, same way we were.

Still, just because they weren't on the kidnappers' side, didn't mean they'd be on ours. And there might be more of them.

It also didn't mean we wouldn't find Kyra among the rubble, a bullet between her eyes too.

All it meant was there were fewer kidnappers to contend with.

"Over here." Griffin's voice was less quiet. Less cautious. When I moved around to the other side of the table, I saw it too—body #5, if we were counting the one Ben Agnew's team had come across.

Strange thing was, Griffin and I recognized this corpse—a guy we'd known years ago, a sneaky little prick named Eddie Ray. I wasn't sure what to make of that, finding Eddie Ray here, dead at the asylum where Tyler said we'd find Kyra. How the hell did Eddie Ray fit into all this . . . after all this time?

Making our way toward the rear exit, we were intercepted by one of Griffin's soldiers. He led us to the body they'd stumbled upon, a girl who was lying facedown in the dark.

"Who is it?" Griffin asked from behind me, and I hated her for the almost hopeful edge I swore I heard in her voice. Couldn't she at least pretend she didn't want it to be Kyra?

Beside me, Tyler froze, and for the first time we exchanged a look. I hated him because I understood him—the pain in his face.

Ben was kneeling beside the girl, and when he glanced up

and saw us, he simply said, "It's not her."

Then I saw how small the girl was, and how short and dark her hair was. Of course it wasn't Kyra, how could I have been so stupid?

Tyler hunched over her, his brow furrowed as he reached for her. When he rolled her over, I rocked backward.

Just like with Eddie Ray, we knew this girl . . . it was a face we recognized all too well.

Natty.

Things weren't adding up. What was Natty doing here with Eddie Ray? Natty, who was armed, and had an almost identical bullet hole through her forehead as Eddie Ray and the other two guys. Did it mean anything that the blond girl had been shot through the back of her head and not the front like the others? Had Natty been abducted the way Kyra had? Or was this something more sinister? Did she somehow belong with them?

This time it was Griffin and I who exchanged glances, both of us wondering the same things: Had Natty been involved in the destruction of Blackwater? Had she gotten all those Returned killed? Had she been the one who'd kidnapped Kyra?

If that was the case, I wished I'd been the one to pull the trigger.

TYLER

AFTER FINDING NATTY, WHO KYRA HAD TOLD ME WAS her closest friend since being returned, I made the decision not to trust anyone, and that included Griffin and Jett. I even had a hard time with Ben, despite the fact he'd just lost his daughter again.

As for Simon, well, he'd never been on the list.

It didn't take long to figure out Kyra was gone, although we had proof she'd definitely been held here—the clothes I'd last seen her in—the jeans and T-shirt she'd pulled on after we'd gone for a dip in the hot spring—were bagged in a corner of one of the rooms.

It made me wonder what she was wearing now, which was stupid, because who cared? All that mattered was finding Kyra alive.

God, I hoped she was alive.

It had taken us almost an hour to clear the place, to make sure whoever had done this—whoever had killed Kyra's kidnappers—were no longer here. The asylum was a maze of winding hallways and dead-end chambers and there was all this crap in the way, like some sort of hoarder's paradise. Almost an hour gone and we still had nothing to show for it, just a lot of useless equipment and enough drugs to supply a zoo.

But we still hadn't dredged up another body. Most importantly, not Kyra's. Whoever was responsible for this massacre hadn't shot her and left her for dead.

"If someone else did get to her first, how are we supposed to find her now? Any clue where she is?" Simon turned on me, like it was my fault we hadn't gotten there in time, rather than thanking me that we'd found the place at all.

"It's not like I can turn this thing on at the drop of a hat," I tried to explain, but Simon spun away.

Griffin wasn't much better. "Well, standing around here isn't going to help! We've wasted enough time in this shithole." Her voice echoed off the rafters as she walked in nervous circles. "We need to get moving."

Griffin was right. If whoever had done this had a head start, it couldn't be by much. Hours. Maybe less. If they had Kyra with them, was it possible she'd seen our headlights as we passed on the road?

Ignoring Simon, I turned to Jett. "What about the reverse star chart thing, the one I drew? I might not sense Kyra now, but maybe we can figure out where that thing was pointing. When I dreamed it, I had the feeling I was supposed to be there, maybe that means something. Maybe there's a clue to finding Kyra there."

Jett stopped what he was doing, a mission he'd been on to liberate some of the hard drives and cables from the kidnappers' equipment. "Maybe," he said, intrigued by the challenge. "It might take me some time to sort it out. But yeah, I could probably do it." He handed an armload of crap to Ben who'd been helping him. "Shouldn't take too long."

Just as Jett logged into his laptop, we heard it: a crashing sound.

It came from beneath us. From the basement.

I glanced to Griffin, who looked at Simon, who took a quick inventory. We all were present and accounted for.

Someone else was down there . . .

What if that someone was Kyra?

CHAPTER SEVEN
Days Remaining: Twelve

"YOU SURE YOU DON'T WANT SOME?" FROM THE driver's seat, Chuck wiggled the bright yellow bag of generic potato chips my way, making the cellophane-y wrapper crinkle.

It was the third time he'd offered, and for the third time I declined with a simple, "I'm good. Thanks anyway."

The cab of his eighteen-wheeler was big, but that didn't stop it from feeling cramped. Claustrophobic. I shrank into the leather bucket seat, trying to disappear.

"She always this quiet?" he asked on a chuckle, like it was just a girl thing, or maybe a teen thing. Like he had a confidant in Thom, who'd been even quieter than I had since the early hours, when Chuck had stopped to pick us up. If Thom hadn't been balancing on the edge of the mattress of the sleeper cab, just behind the seat, Chuck probably would've elbowed him in the guy-talk way that men sometimes do.

Thom didn't really answer, just bobbed his head, a pseudo-agreement.

Chuck nodded back. "Help yourself to another water if you want."

Thom reached into the mini fridge under his feet and untwisted the cap on his fifth water bottle. He downed the whole thing in less than ten seconds.

Chuck watched, but didn't comment. He turned his attention back to me. "West is a long ways away. Skinny gal like you might waste away before we get there."

West. That was as much as I'd told Chuck when he'd asked where Thom and I were headed. He'd done his best to pin us down. To get one of us to be more specific—a city, a state, even a precise region—but he didn't need to know our plan, so I remained adamant, and Thom . . . well, Thom was thirsty, so we'd simply left it at "west."

"Suit yourself," Chuck said, thrusting his hand into the chip bag once more. When he pulled it out again, his fist was overflowing. His grip reminded me of one of those crane machines, the kind they had at pizza parlors or in front of supermarkets. You almost never won at those things, but if you did, and *the claw* actually dislodged a toy from the rest, its grasp always seemed tenuous, like the slightest hiccup or breeze would knock your prize loose on its way to the chute.

Chips and crumbs spilled from between Chuck's fingers on their way to his mouth. Just like The Claw.

"You're lucky I came along when I did," he announced through his half-chewed food. "That road doesn't get a lot of traffic."

He was right. I'd *felt* lucky when he'd stopped.

My parents had always made a big deal about *not* hitchhiking—just like I'm sure all parents did. They'd try to scare me with warnings about Stranger Danger and murder vans by showing me news stories about girls who'd hitched rides only to never be heard from again.

If you're ever stranded, stay where you are, my dad had counseled me. *We* will *find you.*

Great advice for a sixteen-year-old who believed that the worst that could happen was missing curfew and losing her cell phone privileges.

That was before I'd been swept away in a flash of light and lost five long years of my life. Before I'd come back and found out I was no longer the same person.

And before I'd been kidnapped and tortured and forced to kill a girl I'd believed was my friend.

Maybe I was braver because I wasn't alone, but to be honest, after everything I'd been through, in the grand scheme of things hitchhiking kinda seemed like no big deal.

Plus, other than his poor nutritional choices, Chuck seemed like a decent enough guy. Nothing about him screamed ax murderer, so he had that going for him.

Thom and I had stayed hidden as long as we could, waiting to make sure my head count at the asylum hadn't been off. That there wasn't anyone left to come after us. Even as weak as he was, Thom had put up with my questions, managing to answer mostly in single syllables and groans.

During that time, I'd pieced together why Natty and the others had been torturing him, even while they planned to sell him to the Daylight Division.

Without Thom, Silent Creek had no leader. And after the massacre at Blackwater, the Silent Creekers were probably still trying to sort through their contingency plans.

Which meant they were weak.

And locked inside Thom's head was a code word that would win the camp's confidence.

If Natty could wiggle her way back inside now, she and Eddie Ray could hit them while their defenses were down. Hadn't Eddie Ray said that's what this was all about, *business*?

Through it all, Thom had held out, never giving them that code word despite their liberal use of Lucy on him. He was loyal to his Returned, and I was more sorry than ever that I'd doubted him.

I'd asked him about the watch too.

He'd looked at me, his eyes moving from mine to my wrist as if he'd only just noticed I wasn't still wearing the cheap plastic wristwatch he'd given me as a gift—the one I thought he'd used against me.

I winced. "You weren't the one who put the tracking device in it, were you?"

He reached over and squeezed my hand, giving a faint shake of his head. *No*, he told me silently. *Somehow, Natty had done that too.*

Probably to make sure she could find me.

The sun had only been up a couple of hours when Chuck had found us, wandering lost and alone on the side of the small road. He hadn't questioned why I was propping Thom up, or why Thom had been so dehydrated when we'd finally gotten him into the cab of the truck. He also hadn't commented on the way Thom had gone from looking like roadkill to your regular, healthy, normal-looking teen (at least if you didn't know any better) so quickly.

Just add water!

At first glance, I didn't have much to say about old Chuck either. There didn't seem to be anything special about him. He was just your average-ordinary-nothing-special kind of truck driver.

But then he'd turned toward me, and I'd seen it . . . the way the left side of his face dimpled. The way it creased and sagged so much more than the right. He didn't say why, but it wasn't hard to guess it was sun damage, caused from years, maybe even decades of being on the road. From one side of his face being more exposed than the other.

It was like Chuck had been time-lapsed—a Before and After of him that had been cut in two and reattached down the middle.

But considering I'd just seen someone's entire face blown off, my attitude was somewhere along the lines of it-could-have-been-worse. I barely blinked at ol' Chuck.

My attention drifted toward the fields that ran along the freeway, punctuated with low mountains covered in soft grass. They were nothing like the harsh red deserts of Utah or the brown barren ones of eastern Washington.

"Where are we?" I asked Chuck absently.

Appraising the stretch of highway, Chuck nodded. "My guess is somewhere outside'a Channing."

"Channing," I echoed, trying to decide if the name rang any bells.

I glanced back to Thom who looked so much more like his old self again. He shrugged.

Turning back to Chuck, I tried again. "So that's the name of the city . . . ," I drawled, and then, because I knew this was going to sound weird, I bit my lip. "Which *state*?"

Chuck eyeballed me. "You kids pullin' my leg or something?" And when he realized it was no joke, he did a full-on double take. I wouldn't mind playing cards with Chuck sometime—he had the world's worst poker face.

There was no point pretending. "We're just a little lost is all." I sighed. "And if you could help us out, that'd be great." I smiled, hoping I looked sincere, and not like some crackpot who'd literally just shot her way out of an asylum.

My life got stranger and stranger.

It must've been pretty good because Chuck nodded a sort of, *Sure, I guess so* kind of nod, and answered. "Wyoming. 'Bout an hour south'a Gillette."

Gillette—I had no idea where that was either, but

Wyoming gave me a better sense. Geography might not have been my strongest subject, but I knew I was nowhere near Blackwater Ranch, back in Utah, and even farther from home . . . if I even had a home anymore.

"Can I ask you something else, Chuck?" I mean, why not, right? Might as well go for broke.

"Shoot."

I winced at his choice of phrasing. The gun was still pressed against the small of my back, stuffed inside the waistband of a pair of jeans I'd found in a duffel bag. They could have belonged to anyone—the Levi's 501s—but the fit was close enough so I'd taken them, along with a spare shirt. It was better than trying to catch a ride in a blood-splattered hospital gown.

I spit out my next question. "What . . . What *day* is it?"

Chuck just shook his head. Not in a sad way, or even a shocked way, but more in an I'd-stumped-him way. "When you kids say you're lost . . ." He slid a sympathetic gaze my way and then up at his mirror to look back at Thom. "Man-oh-man, girl. Thursday," he said. "It's Thursday." When I frowned, mentally, trying to get my bearings he took pity on me and added, "The first."

My breath came out in a whoosh. "The *what*?"

"July first." He sat a little straighter than before, his eyes darting to where my hands were gripping the sides of my seats. My knuckles had gone bone white. "You okay?" He sounded nervous, and maybe he was right to be. The chill in my bones had spread to my skin and I was swallowing back my own stomach acids. I hadn't puked after shooting four people, or even when pieces of Blondie sprayed all over me when Eddie Ray killed her. But the possibility was real now.

"You don't look so good. Should I pull over?"

I leaned forward, taking slow and shallow breaths. After a second I released my death grip and held up my hand.

"Kyra?" Thom asked from behind me.

"It's okay. I'll . . . I'll be okay." They were the same words I'd whispered to myself over and over after I'd rescued him at the asylum. After I'd shot Natty.

Five days, I repeated in my head.

How was it possible that I'd been kidnapped almost a week ago? How had I not noticed the passing of an entire week? Felt the knifing pain that came each and every daybreak?

But I knew how . . . the IV drip. The drugs.

"One of you got family out west?" Chuck asked, still trying to pry information from us.

The word "family" brought a whole new kind of pain. A week was a long time to lose track of my dad. I had no idea where he'd gone after I'd been taken from that diner.

Hopefully he and Tyler had gotten in touch with Simon and they were all together now, someplace safe.

Where? I had no clue. Blackwater was out of the question—Agent Truman and his Daylight Division had seen to that. And since they didn't know that Thom had never been the traitor we'd all believed he was, there was no way they'd go back to Silent Creek.

That left me with no idea where to start looking.

But Thom and I needed a place we could lay low until we sorted things out, and because our options were limited, we planned to take advantage of the code word—the one Natty hadn't been able to pry from him. Silent Creek might be reeling, and it might even be compromised, but it was the only place Thom felt safe.

He trusted his people and their ability to hide us until we could figure out our next steps. We had to hope the NSA hadn't found them, and that we could get there without being captured.

"Something like that," I told Chuck, not an outright lie. My family was in Washington State. They just weren't who we were planning to see.

Swinging his face to me, he grinned. "Can't blame a guy for tryin'." He turned back to the road. "Better get comfortable. Even if we drove straight through, it'd be 'bout another sixteen or so hours 'til we reach Portland, and that's as far west as I go."

I settled back, smiling to myself when I said, "That's close enough, Chuck."

SIMON

GRIFFIN'S SOLDIERS HAD ALREADY CLEARED THE basement, but five minutes after hearing the sound, Griffin and I were back down there. It was worse in the basement than even upstairs—darker and moldier. Scarier than fuck, basically.

I wasn't above admitting it wouldn't take much for me to crap my pants at that very moment.

But if there was even a chance Kyra was down here, it would all be worthwhile.

Even if Jett hadn't been working to decipher his map—check that, *reverse star chart*—the delay meant he and Ben had more time to pilfer whatever they could of the high-tech components the group had been using—radio equipment, computer hard drives—anything they could grab and stuff into a duffel.

I couldn't fault him. When we'd fled Blackwater, we'd had to leave behind the entire array of computer and communications equipment Griffin had amassed over the years. All that remained was the laptop Jett rarely let out of his sight.

I tried to stay focused on the job at hand, finding whatever had made that noise, but my mind kept drifting back to Eddie Ray.

Talk about a ghost from the past. I hadn't given Eddie Ray a second thought in years, not since before Willow and I had snuck out of Blackwater in the middle of the night to save her ass from Franco's wrath.

How the hell had Eddie Ray ended up in a place like this? What were he and Natty doing together?

None of it made any sense. This whole thing was one shitstorm after another. "Shh!" I lifted my finger to my lips, signaling Griffin to stop. I cocked my head just so, not bothering to ask the question out loud. Griffin knew what I meant: *Did you hear that?*

She listened too, and then frowned an *It's nothing* frown back at me.

She was wrong. It definitely wasn't nothing. I hauled ass toward the not-a-noise, warning myself not to get my hopes up.

"Simon . . ." There was a waver in Griffin's voice, something I'd rarely ever heard. It was dark as hell, but Griffin wasn't the scaredy-cat type. Even spooked, I knew she'd never stand for being left behind.

I heard her boots crunching along the passageway and the flashlight she held swept across the trash all around us. I barely noticed; my concentration was zeroing in on something else.

A mewling . . . a low, almost imperceptible yowl.

Whatever it was—a cat . . . a dog maybe—it didn't sound at all like Kyra. Had some animal gone and gotten itself trapped below these ruins?

It sure as hell wasn't Ben's dog, that much I knew. He'd left Nancy back in his truck. He hadn't wanted to, but no way was I letting that spastic mutt anywhere near this place; she would have given us away in a second, with all her jumping and running around. We might as well have let her come though; her constant howling had been a dead giveaway, even from behind the truck's closed windows.

That's what this sound reminded me of, a muffled howl.

Not willing to take the chance of running into some feral animal, I held my gun at the ready. I wouldn't be proud of myself if I was forced to shoot an innocent creature, but if it came down to it or me, I chose me.

"There," I whispered insistently to Griffin. "That! Did you hear it that time?"

When I looked over my shoulder at Griffin, her face was cast in an eerie veil of shadows. She held her position, straining to decide if she had heard it or not. *Maybe,* her expression told me. *I don't know . . .*

Keep moving, I answered with a head nod and this time she

followed because she wanted to know too.

Then she grabbed my arm.

We were close. The whimpering sound was on us all at once, louder, and clear enough to leave no question. Griffin shifted the beam of light so it scaled the walls. She used it to search for a doorway, a window, some means of access. Then she let it hover over piles of garbage while I kicked at them, looking for an animal caught in the wreckage of this place.

Whatever was making the sounds was nearby. So nearby it should be right here, where we were standing. Yet . . .

There was nothing. Just Griffin and me and rubble for as far as we could see.

I kept moving, thinking we'd misheard, miscalculated. It was farther down. But after several steps the sound faded, got more muted, and I realized we'd passed it.

Even before I said anything, Griffin had already turned to go back.

"Here," she said, stopping at the same spot we'd been in before. She secured the flashlight under her arm as she used her fingertips to explore the wall. "We must've missed it."

While she probed, I pounded, thinking I might dislodge a hidden door or something.

The sound came again. We were in the right place, and the thing, whatever it was, wanted to be found. It grew louder, more insistent.

"No, Griff. Christ. It's right here."

That's when we realized there was a hatch of some sort cut into the floor itself. A trapdoor. The handle was flush with the ground, making it almost unnoticeable in the dark. If it hadn't been for the sounds coming from below us, we'd have missed the damn thing entirely.

"You sure about this?" Griffin asked, when a long keening moan reached up to us.

"Of course not. But we've come this far, haven't we?"

The hatch screeched when I lifted it—the kind of nails-on-a-chalkboard sound that made your skin prickle.

Griffin aimed the light from the flashlight into the hole. It was darker down there, infinitely more sinister. The stairs going down looked as if they'd been hand carved into the dank earth itself—hard-packed and uneven, a death trap waiting for one misstep.

"Ladies first," I proposed breathily.

But Griffin was Griffin and no way would she back down from a challenge, joke or not. When she started toward the steps I grabbed her arm.

"Stop. I'll do it. You stay here and . . ." I tried to think of a good excuse that didn't sound like I cared what happened to her one way or the other. Finally, I ended with, "Just stay here."

But Griffin . . . Christ, she was stubborn, and she was right at my back the entire way down the steps.

"Watch it!" I grumbled, when she almost shoved me over.

She didn't apologize or back off, and although I wouldn't tell her so, I was glad I didn't have to face what was down there alone.

Her flashlight slashed through the darkness, landing just about everywhere in spastic fits, combing the carved ground. Until it landed on the thing responsible for bringing us down there to begin with—the demanding mewls that had turned to full-blown wails, still muffled but unrelenting.

"Willow!"

A wave of emotions slammed into me, leaving me speechless and stunned and horrified.

Willow was here. Willow was alive. Willow had a rag stuffed in her mouth, and her hands and feet were bound.

But Willow was . . . *here of all places.* Buried in the hollow depths of this abandoned pile of rubble. And if we hadn't heard her, if we hadn't come to investigate . . . I shuddered. I didn't want to think about it.

She didn't look too bad, all things considered. She didn't have a bullet hole in the center of her forehead, and right now, that was a major triumph.

In fact, she looked completely uninjured, the way any Returned should. That didn't mean she hadn't been hurt, it just meant enough time had passed that she'd already healed, and that was good enough for me.

Good enough because we'd found her. Somehow we'd found her.

"Jesus. *Willow* . . . ," I repeated, yanking the gag out of her mouth. "What happened? Who did this to you? How long have you been down here?"

In the surreal light from Griffin's flashlight, Willow grinned. She freaking grinned! "Good to see you too."

I'd have hugged her—really, I considered it—but I liked my face the way it was, and Willow wasn't what anyone would call the hugging type.

"Griffin," Willow said, nodding toward the one person she'd always believed was responsible for getting her kicked out of Blackwater all those years ago. "Thanks for coming." There wasn't a trace of sarcasm in her voice.

Griffin was even less comfortable with displays of affection than Willow. "A little light deprivation and some gentle torture, and you go all soft on us?"

Willow shot Griffin a tolerant look—huge for Willow. If I didn't know better, and if we weren't holed up in some grimy underground dungeon, I'd swear I smelled a friendship brewing.

"We gotta get outta here before she comes back," Willow insisted, when I finally managed to free her from the archaic straps that had held together long enough to restrain her.

"She . . . ?" I started, and then realized Willow was in the dark, literally. "Do you mean Natty and the others?"

Willow jumped to her feet and swayed slightly, looking like a drunken toddler. It took her legs a second to adjust as she flexed her wrists and her shoulders. "Natty *and* Eddie Ray," she told me with an intensity that made it clear she had no idea what had happened just one floor above her.

I shook my head and said flatly, "Dead. All of 'em."

"Is that what was happening up there?" She nodded at the ceiling. "I heard something. Did you at least question them first? Find out why she did this? What they wanted?"

"We were too late. They were like that when we got here," Griffin answered. "What do you know? Did they tell you anything? Maybe you overheard something."

Willow screwed up her face in concentration. "I didn't.

Nothing useful, at least that I know of. But Natty's dead too, you're sure?" Her eyes searched mine. When I nodded, she just shook her head. "Too bad. I would've liked a shot at her myself." She frowned. "After I bailed camp I lost track of everyone, but I wanted to be careful not to draw attention to myself so I laid low . . . didn't reach out to any other camps in case the No-Suchers were listening to chatter. I hitched rides, listened for word of anything interesting to see if I could pick up your trails, but nothing." She stretched. "Then I heard about a group staying up at this place in Wyoming—kids, the locals called 'em. Apparently they weren't too careful . . . stocked up on supplies in town. Made a lot of stupid mistakes. I waited, hoping to catch sight of one of them, and when I did I was shocked to lay eyes on Natty."

"What did you say to her? Did you ask her about Thom?" Griffin interjected.

"'Course I did," Willow said, making a face to let her know what a stupid question it was. "And she fed me this cock-and-bull story 'bout how Thom tricked her, and took her hostage as he left Blackwater, but how she'd escaped and found this new group of Returned and was up here, living with them." She shook her head, raking her hand through her hair. "I fucked up, Sim. I fell for her bullshit, all of it. When I got here, that bitch drugged me with something." She rubbed the side of her neck. "Next thing I knew I was down here, and that SOB Eddie Ray was breathing down my neck."

"What about Kyra?" I asked. "Did they tell you why they took her?"

Willow dropped her hand, her attention captured. "Kyra? What's she got to do with all this?"

"They were holding her hostage too," Griffin said.

"*Were* . . . ?" Willow stated as if this was news to her. "But not now?" Then her expression cleared and her face fell. "Aw, shit. Is she dead too?"

Griffin answered, "Not dead, but missing. We're hoping to find her before it's too late."

"Then what are we still doing down here?" This was an accusation. The old Willow was ready for action.

TYLER

WE HAD IT—A LOCATION.

Jett refused to give us all the details—plausible deniability, he maintained. But if I had to guess he'd somehow hacked into NASA or some other space agency, and had used the reverse star chart to come up with the coordinates of a location here on Earth. Even better, it was in California.

The guy was a freaking miracle worker.

Now we just had to get there.

It was too far, and way too cramped, to make the 1,200-mile trip packed into two vehicles with eight people and a hyperactive dog. Or maybe it just felt that way.

Whatever the case, we stopped by Griffin's temporary camp and dropped off Nancy and whoever else wanted to get out, which turned out to be Griffin's two soldiers, who weren't invested in finding Kyra the way the rest of us were. Ben made the poor guys promise to guard the dog with their lives and to feed her only the best rations. They agreed, but only after their eyes slid to Griffin for authorization.

Nancy howled and both men had to hold her back while our two vehicles rolled out of camp.

"She's a dog," Simon told me, the only thing he'd said to me in hours. "She licks her own butt. She'll forget all about him in two seconds."

Somehow, I doubted that. But I didn't want to debate the Nancy-Ben relationship with Simon, either, so I dropped it.

Less than a day and we'd be there. And with any luck at all we'd find something—some shred of information that would lead us to Kyra. Because right now it was killing me not to know where she was. That I couldn't pinpoint her location the way I had before—that beacon of light I'd sensed, leading me to her.

Simon didn't seem to notice the part where we had no real plan. He just charged ahead like it would all work out, because Simon was like that—like a bull, never thinking, never planning, just bulldozing his way through life. Willow sat up front in the SUV, seeming no worse for the wear, even after being imprisoned down in that asylum, while Griffin sat in back with me.

I stared at the back of Willow's head.

Everyone was so quick to accept her story, that of all the places in all the world, she just happened to cross paths with

Natty in the middle of Wyoming. That Natty just happened to pull a fast one on her.

I wasn't saying she was lying, I just wasn't entirely convinced.

Still, it wasn't like I had many options. Right now, finding out where this map led was our only hope. Which meant this had to work. That, or we might never see Kyra again.

It wasn't easy though. I couldn't wipe the images of the mess we'd left behind back there at the asylum—the bodies, the strange equipment. What had they done to Kyra?

I forced myself to focus on my primary objective—finding Kyra.

And the first thing I'd do was tell her I forgave her . . . for everything, because I did. How could I not? I'd had time to think about it, and if the roles had been reversed . . . if it had been Kyra dying and my only option had been to send her to them in hopes that they might save her . . . even if it meant she might come back *changed* . . .

Well, I'd have done it too.

Of course I would have.

Because I loved her.

I couldn't remember everything about us, but I remembered that . . . deep in my bones . . . in every cell of my being, I loved Kyra Agnew.

And I'd be damned if anything was going to stop me from finding her.

CHAPTER EIGHT

Days Remaining: Eleven

WITHOUT THE DRUGS IN MY SYSTEM TO SHIELD me from daybreak, those orange-tinged tips of the sun's arrival felt like white-hot fire pokers gutting me.

Eleven, I heard inside my head as I bolted up from the seat with so much force that my forehead nearly rammed into the dash. But Chuck's reflexes were lightning fast, and instead I crashed against an arm as solid as a tree trunk.

"Damn, girl. Nightmare?"

From behind, Thom's fingers cupped my shoulder more gently. "You okay?"

Working to get my breathing under control while still

being branded from the inside out, I clung to the lie Chuck had offered me. "Yep . . . nightmares."

Chuck hadn't noticed that for the last hour or so I'd been faking sleep just to avoid his endless barrage of conversation. He was seriously the nicest guy ever, but I couldn't help myself. I was just so *tired* of dodging his questions—about where we were going, where we'd been, who we were, and what our plans were.

Thom was better than I was at being evasive. At giving nonanswers.

For me, fake sleep had been a million times easier.

And now I was *real* wide-awake, and as the sun began to climb, the last of the pain evaporated.

"Where are we?" I asked. Even if my eyes hadn't been closed, I'd lost track of where we were over the last day. Chuck had a stop to make in Idaho, a quick drop and pick up that took him less than an hour start to finish. But unlike Thom and me, he couldn't go on indefinitely, and he also had to stop for food and to refuel, and once even to catch a quick nap. He'd only slept a few hours, and after being tied up for days on end I'd taken advantage of the time to walk around and stretch my legs.

"Just outside'a the Tri-Cities," Chuck answered, grinning back at me, like this time it wasn't so weird I was asking. "In Washington, nearabouts to the Oregon line."

Washington.

Maybe it wasn't just the sun that was painful. Maybe it was the memories.

Glancing around at the dry rolling hills, I realized we weren't so far from Devil's Hole—the place Simon and I had taken Tyler after I'd infected him.

I closed my eyes, sick at just being so close to the place where I'd doomed Tyler to a life on the run. A life without family and without ever growing old.

Saved was the absolute wrong word for what I'd done. Sure, he hadn't died that night, but he was no longer the same person he'd been before.

Now he was like me, a replica of his former self. Replaced.

And what had Blondie said, that at least she still had a human side worth fighting for? Not Tyler and me—we were something else.

And on top of that I was apparently some kind of countdown clock . . .

But to what? And was there any way I could stop it?

I inhaled, trying to tell myself to drop it—the whole thing was stupid.

But saying it was stupid didn't mean I could just pretend it didn't exist. I needed answers.

Silently I watched the scenery, and when we saw the sign, *Welcome to Oregon*, I felt something in my stomach unknot.

We were so close now. Just a few hours to Portland, and then another five-, maybe six-hour bus ride to Bend. We'd have to hope to hitch another ride from there to Silent Creek, but we'd figure it out.

For now, Chuck was decent company. It was nice to be with someone who didn't have an agenda. Someone *normal.*

Chuck had tuned into some evangelical station on the radio. The preacher had been going on about love and forgiveness in a voice that would rise to thunderous highs that demanded action, and then plunge to resonant lows begging for reflection. It was like being on an amusement park ride, trying to keep up with him. He quoted bible verses to hammer his sermon home to his listeners. And every now and again, Chuck's eyes would go all misty and thoughtful, as if something the evangelist said had struck a chord deep inside him.

I wondered if there was someone he should forgive, someplace he should be heading instead of Portland where he could make amends.

When the Columbia River came into sight, the radio went all static-y, and the preacher's voice got lost to the hum. I thought Chuck would try to tune the knob to find a better signal, or maybe turn it off altogether. But he did neither; he just kept driving, navigating the bridge that led us into Oregon.

I waited several minutes, and even several more, until we were back on solid ground on the other side. The truck moved evenly, steadily over the highway, and then my gaze slid to Chuck. His focus was as intent as ever, listening. Concentrating.

On what? I couldn't help wondering, my eyes shifting to the radio, which was still spitting out static and only static.

It hadn't gotten any clearer, only louder. Sharper. Harsher.

The grating sound grew until my ears began to hurt, and

I finally blurted out, "Chuck . . ."

When he didn't respond, I reached for the knob myself, meaning to switch it off and put us all out of our misery. But Chuck's hand shot out and caught mine.

His grip was cruel, not at all like the Chuck I'd come to know.

"Jeez, Chuck!" I tried to yank my hand away but he was merciless, and his fingers felt like they were going to crush my wrist.

"Hey! What the hell's the matter with you?" Thom leaned forward, reaching for us when the radio screeched.

Chuck's attention snapped toward it, and away from the road. It was so strange the way his head cocked, almost birdlike, that I nearly forgot that he'd stopped the flow of blood to my hand.

What was he hearing that I couldn't?

Then, in that same weird birdlike way, his focus swiveled back to me.

He was still Chuck, with his lopsided jowl and his hair peppered with dandruff flakes. But there was something in his eyes that made my stomach pitch. Eyes that were no longer his own.

Even in the morning light, I swear it looked like they glowed. The way mine did.

But that wasn't possible . . .

It couldn't be . . . I knew that.

Still . . .

I almost couldn't get the words past the giant lump in my

throat. "What's happening?" I wasn't sure which of them I was asking, but Chuck heard me.

He no longer pretended to watch the road, yet somehow we stayed on course. I'd heard of cruise control, but this was like full-on autopilot.

Real sci-fi crap.

Like glowing eyes.

Chuck's voice, when he answered me, was no longer his voice either. I'd heard that sound before . . . in the desert, the night I'd found Tyler. That freaky wheezing I realized now sounded almost electronic, as if someone had hijacked Chuck's voice box and was transmitting *through* it, just like the radio.

But . . . no . . . that wasn't . . . it couldn't . . .

Except wasn't that exactly what my dad had heard, the two hikers in the woods with their radio-static voices?

"Time," Chuck said. "Time . . . time . . . ," he repeated, and I tilted my head closer, trying to hear his message. He opened his mouth almost impossibly wide and spoke again: "Time . . . is . . . running out."

Time is running out?

And then Chuck blinked. "Eleven." Blink. Blink. Blink. "Eleven . . . eleven . . . eleven." Today's number—isn't that what I'd heard at daybreak?—eleven. And then, his voice still electrical, "The Returned must die."

How could Chuck possibly know that? How could he be speaking in static the way the hikers had?

I wondered if the hikers' eyes had glowed too. I thought

of the way Nancy had growled at me, and a thought hit me: Had Nancy seen them? Was that why my eyes had suddenly spooked her?

"What the hell . . . ?" It was Thom, dragging me back to this. To now. To Chuck.

Every cell in my body seemed to freeze and explode at the same time—microscopic nuclear reactions going off in every sector of my being. And even though only a second or two passed, a million things flashed through my mind at the same time, congesting my thoughts: What was happening to Chuck? What did they—*eyes to the sky*—want from me? Why was this happening, and what could it mean?

Chuck's grip started to loosen, and just as I thought he was finally coming around, that they were releasing whatever hold they'd had on him, the same way they'd eventually let Tyler go, he said, in a not-quite-normal voice, "What's happening? *What . . . did you do to me?*" He looked at me with his strange glowing eyes, like this was my fault, all of it.

And then I saw it—the mile marker—green marker number eleven on the side of the highway, and everything started to move in double time.

Taking his other hand off the wheel, Chuck reached for me. Before I could react or move out of his way, he had ahold of me and was shoving me—my head anyway. "Make it stop!" he shrieked, remnants of static still shadowing his voice as he slammed my face hard against the passenger's side window. I heard Thom shout, but that was only a split second before my cheekbone smashed against the glass, rattling my brain so hard I expected the window to explode.

The glass didn't, but the bone definitely did. Not explode exactly, but when the bone beneath the skin disintegrated, there was an eruption of light behind my eyes that blinded me.

"What the . . . ?" Through the flashes, I saw Chuck reaching for me again at the same time Thom was launching himself at him. I tried to shield myself, thinking, *This time for sure. The glass will definitely break this time.*

Thom got an arm around Chuck's neck from behind, but that didn't stop Chuck, and rather than shoving my head, he reached behind me. Before I realized what he was doing, he had his hand in the exact place where my gun was hidden.

There was no way he could have known about the gun . . . except somehow he did. Just like there was no way his truck could be driving itself—staying exactly on course without wavering the tiniest bit—since Chuck's hands weren't even touching the wheel. But it totally was.

"Chuck, no. Please . . . don't," I begged because all I could think was I didn't want to die, and I didn't want him to shoot Thom. Not like this. Not after everything we'd been through. Out in the middle of nowhere, with none of my questions answered. Without saying good-bye to my dad or Tyler or Simon.

Even if I'd wanted to use my telekinesis thing, it was too late because everything was happening too fast.

"Make it stop . . ." Chuck's voice scratched again as he raised the gun and pointed it at my temple, safety off.

I closed my eyes and whispered a silent apology to my friends for not being able to warn them about what I'd learned from Blondie.

The gunshot came and I jumped, waiting for it . . . the pain . . . the numbness. The *nothingness* of death.

"Kyra. Jesus. Kyra." It was Thom, and I snapped my eyes open.

What I saw made hot waves of shame uncoil inside me.

Chuck was slumped over his steering wheel, an obviously self-inflicted gunshot wound in the side of his head—his good side, the less droopy side. The driver's side window was splattered with pulpy fragments that were likely some combination of skull, flesh, blood, and brain matter. Thom had released Chuck's neck and had collapsed back so he was leaning on his heels. He had pieces of that same flesh and blood all over his face.

"What the . . ." But he was just looking down at his hands, like he'd been the one to pull the trigger.

I glanced back at Chuck. Whatever had been piloting the truck was no longer in control. The steering wheel shimmied as Chuck's bulk weighed heavily over it. At first the giant rig just vibrated beneath me, like the wheels were all out of sync. But then it pitched off course in wide sweeping arcs, first drifting lazily into the shoulder, and then coming all the way back and crossing out of our lane.

That was when I knew we were going to crash. We were headed toward the giant cement blocks that divided the highway.

"Hurry!" I shouted to Thom, already trying to unbuckle so we could shove Chuck aside, meaning to take the wheel. But it was far too late for that.

The impact was both brutal and disorienting.

The air rushed out of my lungs as the seat belt locked. My head—at least I thought it was my head—hit glass, or maybe it was the doorjamb. Everything got jumbled. I remembered sounds—rubber on pavement, metal screeching or tearing, glass splintering, maybe. And smells. They were bitter and caustic, like gasoline and oil and exhaust and burning rubber all thrown together in one toxic cloud.

From somewhere in all that, I tried to say Thom's name, to ask if he was okay . . . if he'd survived at all, but my voice was caught in the fumes.

I don't know how much time had passed, but I heard sirens. Someone must have seen the crash, or could see the smoke rising and called for help.

Inside of me, things were broken—bones most likely. Everything hurt, and already there was the familiar tingling and itching that meant the healing had started. But breathing was hard, each inhalation a painful knife stabbing up and around my left side . . . almost worse than daybreak. I gasped and gasped, again and again, testing the sensation, until I realized it wasn't like a stitch that could be worked out.

With my head still against the headrest, I took in the deepest breath I could and held it before fumbling for the seat belt. I had to find Thom, and if he was still alive, we had to move. To get away from here before the police came and found Chuck with a bullet through his brain and started asking questions.

Releasing the latch, I sat up.

"Thom," I rasped. I was woozy, but I could do this. I scanned the interior, which was filling with dark oily smoke. "*Thom!*" This time my voice took hold.

"Here. I'm . . . here . . ." His voice was weak, but I heard him. I scrambled out of my seat as quickly as I could, which wasn't all that fast.

He was crumpled in a position that didn't even look humanly feasible. But I guess that was the thing, he wasn't entirely human. I saw Chuck too, halfway lodged beneath the enormous steering wheel. It was grotesque the way his body had broken. Thom might be hurt—no, check that, he was definitely hurt. But he wasn't broken like Chuck, not beyond repair.

"Can you get up?" I winced when I saw the way he clutched his wrist to keep his arm from dangling; his elbow bent at an unnatural angle.

It was hard to distinguish where all the blood had come from, whether it was his or Chuck's. Likely both. But even if it were Thom's, the fact that his blood—*our blood*—was toxic to the non-Returned wouldn't make a difference to any rescue workers who arrived at the scene. It had to be fresh to do its damage. After sixty seconds it was no longer dangerous.

Thom was riddled with scrapes and bruises, but he managed to stagger to his feet, and staggering was enough.

While Thom lurched toward the passenger door, I slipped

over to Chuck. I had to work fast, and I did, rummaging through his back pockets for his wallet, not bothering to assess whether there was anything beneficial inside. I searched the floor, and beneath the seats. My hands were shaking and my heart was pounding.

I had to climb over Chuck, my fingers delving into the cavity between his seat and the driver's side door, but when my fingers closed around the gun's grip, I almost sighed out loud.

My relief was short-lived as the sirens came closer and closer.

Then, right before I was ready to follow Thom out the passenger's side door, I hesitated and turned back to Chuck, his mangled body. I told myself forget it, even as I climbed back over and stripped him of his watch.

I pocketed that, along with the wallet, and shoved the gun into the back of my jeans before hopping out of the cab as I half limped half ran into the thick brush that skirted the length of the freeway where Thom was already waiting for me.

Now, more than ever, we needed to get west . . . to safety.

If there was such a thing anymore.

PART TWO

Certainly, no fact in the long history of the world is so startling as the wide and repeated exterminations of its inhabitants.

—Charles Darwin

CHAPTER NINE

NOTHING SCREAMED LUXURY LIKE A THREADbare motel bedspread. But after being strapped to a rusting metal gurney for almost a week, I lay back and spread my fingers wide, running my hands over the green and yellow stripes, petting the polyester fibers like they were spun from gold. For the first time in days, my damp hair didn't contain bits of other people's brains, and even the scratchy motel robe was heavenly against my clean skin. I felt like I'd won the freaking lottery.

I was free. Not safe. Not yet . . . just *free*.

It was crazy how low my expectations had dropped.

At least I no longer hurt. The breaks in my right arm and wrist, and the cracked ribs—however many of them had been broken—had healed. I think my lung had been damaged too, punctured maybe by one of the ribs, but eventually even that had mended, and I could breathe just fine now.

The cuts and bruises were gone now as well, and I wondered when I'd ever get used to that, the remarkable healing abilities of this strange new body of mine. Also, when I'd get used to calling it "this strange new body of mine," since I still felt like just plain old me.

If only that were true.

As soon as Thom and I had run far enough from Chuck's "accident" to feel like we wouldn't draw too much attention to ourselves, we'd stopped at a small gas station where I'd planned on using the pay phone in the lot to call a cab. All we really knew was we were somewhere outside a town called Umatilla, a place so small I was pretty sure even the gas station would qualify as a recreational outing.

Turned out, though, that phone booths these days were really just props. The phone itself wasn't just dead; the handset was missing altogether.

So Thom and I had done our best to clean ourselves up in the dingy restrooms out back so we could go inside to see if there was a phone we could borrow. But there wasn't enough cheap hand soap in the world to make Thom presentable and he'd had to wait outside.

The kid behind the counter had been cool about it when

I'd asked to use his phone, not mentioning the smears of pink I'd made on my own shirt when I'd tried to blot away the blood. He'd passed me a grease-covered cordless phone that had a retractable metal antenna, circa 1990. But at least that phone had worked, and the cab had come for us within twenty minutes.

For an extra twenty bucks, the cabbie had even taken us as far as Pasco, Washington, which was back over the bridge Chuck had just brought us across, but it was also the closest place he said we could catch a Greyhound bus.

The bad news was that the next bus wasn't scheduled until eight the next morning.

The good news was that Chuck's wallet had been fat with cash; over three hundred bucks worth, which was partly why it had been like winning the lottery. If you could say "winning the lottery" after some guy blew his brains out while being hijacked by an interstellar transmission.

So, yeah, winning the lottery might not have been exactly right, but Chuck's money meant Thom and I could get a motel room for the night while we waited for the next bus to Portland, where we'd buy our connecting tickets.

It also meant I was able to take a nice hot shower. It was crazy how hard I'd had to scrub to get all the dried bits of brain matter off, both Blondie's and Chuck's.

While Thom took his turn in the shower, I switched on the news to search for reports of the crashed semi.

What I was really looking for was anything that said the cops had known Thom or I had been there. I had no idea how—fingerprints or witnesses—whatever it was they did to locate people.

"Anything?" Thom asked, when he came out of the bathroom. He was cleaner after showering, but he'd already put on the clothes he'd been wearing before, the ones we'd had to "borrow" for him back at the asylum. The sweatpants were loose on him, and not his usual neat, khaki style. Made worse now because they were torn and stained.

Chuck's cash would come in handy for more than just motels and bus tickets if we planned to go unnoticed.

I shook my head. "Not yet." I turned the volume all the way down, but left the newsfeed on, just in case. "You look better." And he did. The cuts on his face had healed, only a faint pucker remained to show anything had happened at all. With a little more time, those too would fade. Eventually there'd be no evidence at all.

He flexed his arm, nodding. "I feel better." Then his eyes met mine. "I'm sorry," he said.

I half shrugged and shook my head. "Don't." But then something heavy settled in my stomach. "Not about that anyway. Can I ask you something though?"

"About Natty?" He sat in one of the chairs at the small Formica table next to the bed I was on. He leaned forward on his elbows as if one had never been busted up in the first place.

"Yeah. About her." I sat up too, facing him. "What . . . *happened*? Did you have any clue . . . what she was up to?"

Thom looked offended. "God. No. I can't believe you'd

think that. I mean, of course you would, but . . . no." He rubbed his face, his dark, straight hair falling over his forehead. "I figured it out though. When we were at Blackwater. That last day . . ." He paused and cleared his throat before continuing. "I was actually stupid enough to think . . . well, I'm sure you know what I thought. I thought me and Natty, I thought we . . ." He gave me a chagrined smile.

"We all thought that," I told him, hoping it made him feel better to know he wasn't the only one who'd fallen for her innocent act. "She made it pretty clear she was into you."

"Yeah, well . . . she wasn't." He shrugged, and I knew he wanted to drop that part of it. "Anyway, Natty and I had gone for a walk that night, and she said she was going back to her tent. Said I didn't need to walk her back, but of course, I insisted. But she insisted just as hard. *Insisted.* I should've realized something was up—she was acting strangely. But I let her go." Watching Thom, I could see the truth filling in the gaps. He shoved his palms into his eye sockets. "The thing is, it bugged me, so I followed her anyway." He was still at the table, and he leaned his head back against the chair. "She didn't head for your tent after all. I guess I wasn't as careful as I should've been and she caught me when she came out of the communications tent. I thought she was in trouble—that's what I thought was going on when I followed her. I had no idea she was armed, or how far she'd go to stop me, or anyone else who tried to stop her." He looked up and watched me earnestly. "The worst part is, she knew my authorization codes. That's how she sent the message out. She led the No-Suchers right to us. Christ, Kyra, it was my fault. I even *told her* I was turning her in—like she could be reasoned with. But then she pulled her gun on me, and the next thing I know Eddie Ray and the others were there. The next thing I knew . . ." His voice cracked. "She wasn't the person I thought she was. I didn't know her at all. I never had."

He didn't have to say anything else, because I already knew the rest of the story. I'd lived it too. At the asylum, drugged and tortured, and who knew what else they'd have done if we hadn't escaped when we had.

If I hadn't killed them all.

"I'm so sorry," he mouthed.

"Like I said, no apologies."

The phone on the bedside table rang, and Thom's head jerked up. He gave a quick shake, but I was already reaching for it.

"Hello?" I said into the avocado-green receiver.

It was the clerk on the other end—the older woman who'd talked my ear off when I'd checked in. She hadn't balked at all at the fifty bucks I'd offered if she'd give us a heads-up if anyone came around asking questions about us. I got the feeling we weren't the first ones to check into this motel who wanted to be left alone. "You know how you told me to tell you if anyone asked about you? Well, a man just checked in, askin' about the boy you were with. Showed a picture and everything." Thom was standing right next to me now, his ear pressed to mine so he could hear every word she said. I would've asked her questions about the man, but I was waiting for her to take a breath, something she didn't seemed inclined to do. "I didn't tell him nothing, just like you asked. Said I'd never seen the boy before." The money thing had been risky. Truth was, someone else could easily have offered her more, but Thom and I needed to hold some of Chuck's money back for other things. "I don't think he bought it though. He's in the lot now if you wanna get a peek at him."

My pulse hammered hard in my throat. "Thanks, Mabel. I appreciate the tip."

"Anytime, doll. You kids take care—"

But I'd already hung up, and was racing to the window. I was careful with the curtains, not wanting to move them too far or fast. I didn't want to let whoever might be out there know we were here. That we were watching him.

"Goddamn it," Thom cursed from beside me, when he saw who I saw.

Even with an entire parking lot and a window to separate us, I felt my heart explode. It was my one true nemesis.

Agent Truman.

I glanced to Thom, a knot forming in my gut as I weighed everything he'd just told me . . . everything I knew about him. "How did he find us?" I asked. I reached for my clothes, piled on the edge of the bed. I yanked my pants on beneath the robe, my eyes never leaving Thom. He couldn't be the traitor after all this, could he?

"Kyra . . . ," Thom answered slowly. "I swear it wasn't me."

I wanted to believe him.

"How then?" I refused to turn my back, so I was forced to pull my shirt on in front of him. "How on earth did he know we were here?" I didn't expect an answer, but I searched Thom's eyes as I moved back toward the wall.

"You have to trust me. We're in this together. I have no idea how he found us, but you heard Mabel—it's me he's after, not you. For all we know, he doesn't even know you're here." He started to take a step toward me, but I held up my hand to stop him. "You can still get away. If you go out the back, I'll turn myself in. You can get a head start."

After a second or two, I dared another quick glance out the window.

He was still there.

Agent Truman hadn't always been part of the Daylight Division. Once upon a time he'd been the infamous Dr. Arlo Bennett. Aka, Griffin's dad. None of us had known the two were one and the same, not until he'd shown up with his army of Daylight Division goons to storm Blackwater Ranch.

That's when he and Griffin had come face-to-face for the first time in decades. The reunion hadn't exactly ended well.

I hadn't envied Griffin before then, when I thought her dad was a scientist who'd sacrificed her to the aliens just so he could experiment on her when she returned.

I envied her even less once I knew her dad had changed his identity and was working with the feds to round us up. And then he put the cherry on the worst-dad-ever award by shooting her right in front of me.

It made no difference that he was a Returned too.

The last time I'd seen Agent Truman had been at Blackwater, right after Willow had taken a baseball bat to his head.

He'd said that being older than the rest of us meant he healed slower than we did, but I had to say, considering less than two weeks had passed, he looked pretty good. It made me wonder what he'd told his cohorts . . . how he'd explained his miraculous—and exceptionally speedy—recovery, since after Willow had gotten done with him he'd looked like a crash test dummy on its way to the dump.

Now he glanced up, his eyes scanning the length of the building.

He saw us . . . he saw us . . . somehow, I'm sure he saw us . . .

Run. Thom wanted me to run. To get a head start. Did that prove it, that he wasn't a traitor? That he hadn't led Agent Truman right to us?

I let my eyes drop to Chuck's watch, dangling loosely on my wrist. The sight of it slowed my heart rate. Calmed me down.

Then I saw Agent Truman pull out what looked like a handheld radio or walkie-talkie, but with a screen. He entered something and held it out and up, toward the motel.

"Hey! *Jesus!*" Thom reached up and slapped his neck,

right below his right ear. "What the . . . *Did you hear that?*"

I slid my gaze sideways at him, and then back to Agent Truman, who was grinning now, and taking sure steps in our direction, his eyes moving upward, to the second floor where our room was located.

"Oh my god, Thom. It's you." I had to think fast. We had to act fast. "You *are* the reason Agent Truman's here. Somehow they . . . he or Natty and Eddie Ray . . . *someone* put some kind of tracker in you." I pointed to his neck, to where he was still rubbing the place beneath his ear.

I dropped the curtain, my mind spinning as I rubbed the back of my own neck. My blood was pumping hard. We only had seconds until Agent Truman would be here, and I doubted he'd give the courtesy of a friendly knock when he arrived.

"Okay," I said. "I got it. You have to stay here." I grabbed the gun I'd shoved under my pillow. "I'll be right here, ready to surprise him." I ran to the bathroom. "Hopefully he thinks you're alone."

I didn't give Thom time to argue—we didn't have time. I slipped on my boots—Blondie's boots—and disappeared into the still steam-filled bathroom. The near panic of waiting to be caught by Agent Truman was too much, and my chest constricted to the point I almost couldn't breathe.

I turned those emotions inward, focusing, trying to harness them into a storm I could use against Agent Truman in case the gun wasn't enough. In case it jammed. In case I ran out of bullets. In case Agent Truman disarmed me.

My ability—could I do that? Could I call on it at will?

I could try.

Suddenly this plan I'd come up with—granted, on the spur of the moment—this whole thing where I would ambush Agent Truman, I realized it was amateur hour. It was me trying to pass off a blob of unsculpted Play-Doh to a snooty art dealer.

I couldn't do this. It was pathetic. This was Agent Truman, a seasoned veteran. A man who carved up Returned just to see what made them tick.

What was I thinking?

Then I saw the window, the one above the tub, and I heard Thom's voice in my head: "Go out the back . . . you can get a head start."

I wasn't the one with an implant in my neck. Thom was right, I could escape unscathed.

I heard footsteps coming on the cement walkway outside the motel room door. Agent Truman wasn't even trying to be stealthy. He wasn't even remotely afraid of us.

For some reason, knowing how little he thought of us . . . of Thom and me . . . well, it pissed me off.

Suddenly the gun in my hand was vibrating. No, the gun wasn't vibrating, my fingertips were. I didn't think I'd be able to hold it steady enough to shoot. But then again, I had a better weapon now.

Outside the bathroom, on the other side of the flimsy hollow-core door I was hiding behind, I heard the doorknob to the motel room jiggle, and I could imagine Agent

Truman out there, testing the lock. I imagined Thom, too, waiting and feeling guilty because he was the reason Agent Truman was here. Blaming himself all over again.

A storm blew through me. A hot wind coiled, twisting and snarling when I heard the bright red metal door bang against the wall as Agent Truman let himself inside.

What a jerk!

This was what I needed, to be angry. Enraged.

It would give me the upper hand, and then the gun would be unnecessary. I held my breath, waiting for the right time.

I counted his steps.

Then, I heard his voice. "Hello again." He said it like he had everything under control, and something inside me unleashed.

The door to the bathroom flew wide—I didn't even touch it . . . it just . . . *happened.*

I was ready for it; Agent Truman never saw it coming.

He had his gun drawn on Thom—not at his head, which was a true kill shot, but at his chest. I wondered if a bullet through his heart would heal, or if that was as fatal.

Either way, Agent Truman never had the chance to shoot. I saw surprise register on his face at the moment I launched the bedside phone at him simply by looking at it.

The old rotary dial was heavy . . . clunky, but it was also still attached to the cord in the wall. The cord only seized for a second before detaching with a sharp snap, and then it hurtled at his head.

Agent Truman was forced to lift his arm—and the gun

in his hand—to shield himself from the phone. Thom used the split-second distraction to slam his shoulder into Agent Truman's midsection.

Agent Truman went down hard, with a gusty *Oomph!* His gun slid somewhere across the shag carpeting, maybe beneath one of the twin beds. But he wasn't giving up that easily, and from out of nowhere he had a pen, a cheap ballpoint. He jammed it into Thom's thigh.

"Son of a—" Thom howled.

Then Agent Truman rolled him over and was shoving his face down into the carpet.

I don't know why, but I became fixated on the blood. It was everywhere, Thom's blood. All over his pants, on the shag carpeting, and on Agent Truman.

Agent Truman punched Thom in the jaw then, and I tightened my grip around my gun. But before I could squeeze the trigger, I hesitated. What if I missed Agent Truman and hit Thom instead? What if I accidentally shot him in the head and there was no coming back from it?

The door to the outside was open, and maybe it shouldn't matter but I kept thinking, *What if someone walked past and saw what was happening in here? What if they were exposed to Thom's blood and died because of what we were doing?*

If I had better control over my abilities, I would have used them to close the door. But when I concentrated nothing happened, so I hurled myself at it instead. Agent Truman grabbed my ankle as I ran by, and I tripped just as the fingertips of my outstretched hand brushed the edge of it.

I kicked out, trying to dislodge his grip on me, and the heel of my boot connected with something solid. I hoped desperately I'd struck bone—jaw or nose or skull. Nothing in this world would make me happier.

Whatever I'd hit, the impact had been enough to loosen his grip on my ankle, and I was able to move those last few inches to reach the door. I shoved it closed with a solid, satisfying bang.

I rolled over, collapsing onto my back, at the same time Agent Truman, with blood streaming from his nose—blood that was also poisonous—swept his arm underneath the bed. When he came back up onto his knees, I saw the gun.

My heart bloated with fear. This time, he pointed it directly where it would do maximum damage: directly at Thom's head.

"Don't," I begged. I still had a gun in one hand and a supernatural ability I tried to call on, but it was useless. He had me right where he wanted me—I couldn't risk Thom's life. I was lying on the floor, on my back, and I raised *my* hands over my head to show I gave up.

Then, without giving him time to gloat over the fact that he'd managed to capture us, I whispered, "*Ochmeel abayal dai*," because those words were maybe our only hope at this point.

He was one of us, like it or not.

I'd tried to make them sound the way Tyler had, giving them the same inflection, but like before, they sounded strange coming out of my mouth—a foreigner testing the feel of a new and unfamiliar language.

Because it was *a new language*, I reminded myself. *These were not words I was ever meant to speak.*

Thom didn't flinch. My hands trembled as I forced myself to stay focused on him.

When Agent Truman finally reacted, it wasn't at all like I'd expected, although how *was* one supposed to behave when they heard an alien language?

Maybe *not* by reaching down and waving his hand back and forth in front of my face.

"*What* . . . are you doing?" I asked.

"Just making sure you're still in there." It wasn't a question, he was simply stating a fact, and I knew what he meant: that my body—*this* body—hadn't been hacked into the way Chuck's had.

"It's still me."

Bonelessly, like this was all suddenly way too much, he fell to his knees, his gun dropping to the floor with a dull thud. He ran his hands through his hair.

I stayed where I was, my eyes darting to Thom, while Agent Truman processed it all.

Finally, he asked, "What about *them*?" Only he, unlike everyone else I'd ever talked to, didn't look upward. "Are they here yet?"

I shook my head. "I don't think so, not yet anyway. But I think they're close."

He nodded, as if pulling himself together at last. "We better get a move on then."

Agent Truman locked the motel room's door, then slid the security chain in place, and wedged the back of one of the metal chairs beneath the knob, testing it twice before he was sure it would hold.

And I thought my dad was paranoid.

"We'll have to work fast," he said while he pointed at one of the twin beds. "You lay down there," he told Thom. "We need to get that GPS chip outta you, before they realize I'm not comin' back and decide to send someone else after the signal."

Thom reached up and rubbed the side of his neck, eyeing Agent Truman anxiously. "Why are you trusting him?" he asked me. And then to Agent Truman, "Why are you helping us?"

Agent Truman pulled out his keys and unhooked a small pocketknife from the ring. He inspected two of the blades, as if he were deciding between them, and then nodded, snapping one back in place. "I'm not. I assume you know what the message meant, that *Ochmeel abayal dai* garbage?"

I nodded. "The Returned must die."

Thom jolted. "That's what Chuck said. Right before . . ." He halted. "Right before the *accident*."

"Chuck?" Agent Truman didn't know about Chuck yet.

"We both know that was no accident," I said, then turned to fill Agent Truman in. "Nice trucker. Gave us a lift and then blew his brains out, right after he delivered that message. He also said: 'Time is running out.'" I pictured Chuck the way I'd last seen him alive, with his eyes glowing as he reached out and slammed my head against the window. That hadn't been him, not really.

"Trucker, huh?" Truman said to Thom. "We wondered what happened. When we couldn't get them on the horn, we thought they must've put you back on the auction block and sold you off to a higher bidder, so we activated your GPS to safeguard our investment. Had no idea we'd find you all the way out here." He almost cracked a smile. "How the hell'd you get away from them anyhow? They guaranteed us their facility was locked down tight as a tick."

I wasn't sure I wanted to answer him, but I couldn't think of a reason to lie. "They're dead."

If I expected a reaction from Agent Truman, I didn't get it. "I guess that explains the silence on their end."

I frowned. "If he has a GPS tracker, how come I don't?"

Agent Truman regarded me. "How do you know you don't?" He lifted his shoulders. "If you do, it's not one we were given access to."

A tracker. If whoever bought me knew where I was that would change everything. My stomach convulsed.

I hated asking, but I needed to know. "Can you tell if I . . . if they . . . put one in me too?"

Agent Truman rolled his eyes. "Relax. The one in him is ours. We supplied it to them. And unless the folks who paid for you have access to highly classified government technology, like the device we put in your friend here, then you're free and clear."

He didn't exactly set my mind at ease, but he had a point. What were the odds there were two government agencies bidding on hybrid alien teens?

I slipped closer to Thom, inspecting his neck. The skin was so smooth . . . as it would be, I supposed. He'd already healed around whatever they'd done to him. "So there's something in there? And they put it there, Eddie Ray and Natty?"

Agent Truman scoffed. "Natty? I heard that was what she was goin' by now. Cute." He used the knife's tip to point at the bed, indicating it was time to get started. Thom reluctantly settled down.

"You sure you know what you're doing?"

His eyes slid coolly, calmly, to the knife in his hand. "Haven't you heard, sport? I'm a doctor."

Thom closed his eyes as Agent Truman began probing his fingers over the surface of his neck, presumably searching for whatever had been planted inside. I shuddered—he may have been a doctor once, but he had a terrible bedside manner. To distract myself, I pushed for more information. "So you knew Natty?"

"I know . . . *knew of* her. She had an impressive reputation, that one. She and that partner of hers, Eddie Ray, worked the black market for years. Made a killing. No pun intended." He winked, making it clear the pun was totally intended. Also, making it clear he had a cold, dead heart. He glanced up at me. "I never really trusted her." His lips pursed. "Eddie Ray I got—his loyalty was all about the almighty dollar. Whoever had the deepest pockets, you know what I mean." He pressed his finger over something and Thom grimaced. He seemed to have found whatever it was he was searching for.

Then he got the knife ready.

I spoke up before there was no going back. "Aren't you at least gonna sterilize that or something?"

"He'll be fine. That's the beauty of healing at superspeed. It works to fight off bacteria too. Right, sport?"

Thom opened his eyes and gave me a he's-not-wrong shrug. I couldn't exactly argue. If Thom wasn't freaking out, how could I?

"About this black market you mentioned, what's that all about? How does that even work? What would anyone even do once they got us?"

Agent Truman gave me a quick but critical glance. "You're not that naive, are you? You can't tell me you'd be surprised to know how valuable you—*we*"—he corrected, because we all knew he was a Returned as well—"are on the open market. People pay big money for crazy shit. My division alone ponied up a crap ton for ol' Tommy Boy here, all in the name of science." He leaned over Thom and leered into his face, reminding me why I always thought of him as a shark.

"You're the worst."

"I doubt that. There are some sick SOBs out there,

people who like to . . ." He jammed the tip of his knife into Thom's throat, making Thom flinch. He didn't actually cut him open or anything, but it left a nasty mark. ". . . experiment," he finished.

"Like you?"

"You can't have progress without sacrifice." He shrugged as if it made no difference to him one way or the other, and I wondered if this indifferent attitude was all hot air—an act he put on to make me believe he didn't give a crap. Or if he was really as cold and as unfeeling as he made it seem.

"There are some who just like to 'collect' us, like freaks in a zoo. Create their own little museums." Another who-cares shrug. "And others who like to use our blood for sport. Stick some poor sap in a sealed container and expose them to it. Then they sit back and watch."

"Until what?" But I had the sinking feeling I already knew the answer.

Agent Truman didn't hesitate to fill in the blank. "The Code Red."

My stomach rolled as I thought of Tyler—the way he'd suffered before I'd decided to take him to Devil's Hole.

"What about me? If you were buying Thom, how come you didn't buy me too?"

"Your friend 'Natty' never told me she had you. I mean, I knew they had a Replaced, that was why we attacked Blackwater in the first place—we intercepted that message she sent out."

So the message Natty sent hadn't been to the NSA.

He glanced down at Thom. "As much as I like my experiments . . . and I do like my experiments, kids like you . . . well, you're chump change in the grand scheme of things." He grinned. "No offense." He offered it like it somehow absolved his vileness. Turning back to me, he explained, "Getting my hands on you would have changed everything."

I felt dirty. To my very core I felt sick and dirty and like I was the real traitor. *I* was the one who'd gotten Blackwater attacked, not Natty . . . not really. I turned to glare at Agent Truman. How had I ever thought he could be trusted? How had I thought this was a good idea, asking him to side with us? "And now? Is that what this is—your big chance to capture me?"

"Jesus, girl, if I'd have wanted to haul you in, I'd'a done so by now." There was an undercurrent of irritation in his voice, and I wondered if I'd struck a nerve. "If this is your way of thanking me for saving your friend here, then you're welcome."

"What about Alex Walker? When we were at Blackwater, you said you didn't need me, because you had him?" A thick cloud of guilt twisted and churned in my stomach, becoming something dark, something stormy.

"Kid from Delta?" Agent Truman clarified. "Yeah, I thought he was like you, but I was wrong. Turns out, he was just garden-variety Returned."

I let out a long, low breath. "What . . . *what* did you do to him?"

"I didn't say he wasn't *useful.* Just not as useful as you woulda been."

Dead air filled the room. A charged kind of silence that lasted weeks. Months. Years. Time we couldn't afford. I was powerless to change the past . . . I couldn't keep worrying about Agent Truman and the things he'd done or we might not have a future.

We had to move forward.

"You said the message Natty sent wasn't meant for you. Who then?" Thom asked from where he was on the bed.

"No, sir. The message was sent out for another buyer, the one your girl had waiting in the wings. When you went up for sale, we weren't even in the running. We were just lucky enough to be monitoring the signals, and picked it up." He looked at me. "Unfortunately, you got away." Truman took his frustration out on Thom as he dug the end of the knife into the thin tissue of Thom's neck. "Except I think she and Eddie Ray couldn't agree about it. I think the transaction woulda closed sooner if Eddie Ray didn't think he could get more money for you from someone else. He was right, you know? You . . . being what you are . . . you're worth big money." He gouged the tip of the blade deeper. Digging. Burrowing. He had all the finesse of a butcher with a rusty hacksaw. It gave me the creeps.

"Got it!" Agent Truman held up what looked like a miniature-sized SIM card covered in Thom's blood.

Thom sat up, wincing as he wiped his neck. "Did it really take that much work for something that small?" The gash in Thom's neck was at least four times the size of the tracker Agent Truman had extracted.

Agent Truman grinned as he snapped the device in half before tossing it in the wastebasket, where it barely made a plinking sound. Then he wiped the blade of his pocketknife on his pants. "I always did enjoy my work."

"You're a monster."

"We're all monsters. You most of all."

It stung, hearing him say it like that . . . the same way Griffin had.

What was her word? Chimera.

Didn't matter that she called it something else, though, it still meant the same thing: monster.

Thom lifted the edge of his shirt to his wound, to try to stanch the flow of blood, even though it was probably already slowing on its own. "Maybe this is a mistake, working with him. He's a Daylighter, after all." His voice lowered, until it was barely a whisper. "Even if he's Returned, what makes you think he'll help us?" Thom asked, and Agent Truman gave me a look that said he wanted to know the answer as well—an *Enquiring Minds Want To Know* kind of look.

"Because I have a trustworthy face?" he goaded.

"Because that message said 'The Returned must die,' and you'll do what you always do—save your own ass."

"And what about you. You're not one of us. You're not Returned, you're Replaced. Why should you get involved?"

I thought about the things Blondie—the dead girl—had said about me not being human. But she was wrong.

If what she'd said was true and these *beings* were coming, then where did that leave us—and I didn't mean *us* the way Natty said it, as in *us*, the alien race. Or even *us* as in the Returned. I meant *us* . . . people. Because that's who I was. That's who I would always be.

A human being. A person. A part of this world.

No matter what my DNA said.

"I wouldn't expect you to understand. I might be different now, but that doesn't mean I don't remember who I was. I can't just throw that part of me away. Simon, Willow, Griffin . . ." I ticked off their names, again waiting for some flicker of acknowledgment. Something that told me he'd heard his daughter's name. But he remained blank. Dead-faced. So I said the words he'd never be capable of, "They're my friends."

Agent Truman settled back now and somehow made it look even less comfortable than before, like he was balancing on razor blades rather than on a bed. "They're not mine though." He smirked, and frustration swelled within me.

"But if these aliens really are coming for us—for the Returned—we need to stop it from happening. Don't you feel a sense of loyalty to your old life? To protect any friends you *do* have? You're still half human. You can't want this to happen."

He frowned. "Look, you're not getting it. These things . . . these *beings* are far more advanced than we are. If they wanted to destroy us, trust me, they would. You think that Chuck guy *wanted* to blow his brains out? Poor guy had no idea what was going on inside his own brain." He inhaled, thinking it over. "No, there's got to be something more to it. They want something."

"You knew them. You made deals with them way back when. What do you think they want? And why would they want the Returned dead?"

Agent Truman's expression hardened and his jaw flexed. "We had no idea what they were up to in the beginning. We really thought we were getting the deal of the century—trading a few people for technology beyond our dreams."

"And you believed them?"

"We had no reason not to. They'd been studying us for years. They understood us better than we understood ourselves. They knew our weaknesses," Agent Truman explained.

"So what happened?" I asked, leaning forward now.

"We realized they were getting more out of the deal than we were. They were supposed to warn us before taking anyone, and then again when they sent them back so we could . . ." He pursed his lips, and I knew this was the part I wouldn't like. "So we could *intercept* them."

"So you could experiment on them, you mean? See what makes the Returned tick?" I criticized.

He shrugged, not bothering to deny it. "Then we realized they were taking people without consent . . . sending back fewer. Either that, or sending them back without notifying us. It became like a scavenger hunt, and we scoured the globe searching for people like your friends." He said "your friends" like it was a filthy word.

I considered what he was saying, that the aliens were the ones in charge of this so-called relationship. They'd always been the ones with all the power. "So, once you figured it out, why didn't you say something? Try to stop them?"

"What exactly do you think we should've done? Gone to the police? The president? No thank you," he said, waving the idea away. "I've been to those woo-woo conventions. I won't be lumped in with one of those nut jobs passing out pamphlets about how aliens are plotting to take over the planet, even if it's true."

"So you're saying some of those guys are legitimate?"

"Best minds in the world." He said it emphatically. "But no one gives a rat's ass because the second they opened their mouths, they punched their ticket to crazy town. Think about it, what did you think when your old man tried to tell you his theory?" I winced, reinforcing his argument. "Yeah . . . and that was your old man talking. Besides, I realized long ago I could get more accomplished working behind the scenes. The NSA had offered me the perfect hiding place. No one thought to look for a Returned right under their own noses."

I closed my eyes. "Maybe this *is* a mistake." I started toward the door, but Agent Truman blocked me in two long paces.

It was Thom who answered, surprising me. "It probably is, but we don't have a choice. He's already here, and we can't exactly let him go. Besides, maybe he can help."

I shook my head. "We always have a choice. This is too big. We can't afford to make mistakes. We'll figure it out without him."

Agent Truman leaned forward. "Ah hell, don't make me say it." And when I didn't say anything, his face fell. "Fine, goddammit, I wanna help."

"Why?" I asked. "What happened to all this 'they're not my friends' crap?"

"Because, if what you said is true, and they're really coming for us, we could be in a shitload of trouble."

"What do you mean?"

"I mean, if that message you heard is right, then we've done something wrong. We could be facing a war. And if that happens, no one is safe. We could be extinct within a week."

I glanced at Thom, who looked as sick as I felt. "What do we do?" I asked Agent Truman.

"We need to stop them from coming in the first place."

We only stayed at the motel long enough to scrub the room of signs we'd ever been there in the first place. On our way out, we slid two more fifties across the front desk to Mabel, hoping the extra hundred would work like that flashy-thing in *Men in Black*, erase her memory. Then we stopped at the nearest Walmart, where Thom and I ran in and grabbed the first things off the hangers that looked like they might fit. We changed in the car.

Thom now wore a Bob Marley T-shirt and a pair of stiff

new Dockers (khakis, of course), and I'd grabbed a Kiss Me I'm Irish tee off the clearance rack, a garden-variety navy hoodie, and a pair of black stretch pants. I kept Blondie's boots, not just because I didn't want to waste extra time searching for new shoes, but because they were surprisingly comfortable. I did my best to flashy-thing my own memory so I wouldn't have to think about Blondie, and the last time I'd seen her.

Agent Truman said he knew a guy, which I assumed meant someone who might be willing to help us. Thom didn't ask, and neither did I. Mostly because I was so totally focused on that other thing he'd said, back at the motel. You know, the one about a war coming to Earth.

Even if I'd had other questions, which I was sure I did—things like where were my dad and Tyler and the rest of the Returned right now?—our impending doom was enough to shut me up. To consume me. To eat me alive.

War.

Coming to Earth.

And if it did, humans would become extinct.

Was it possible he'd been exaggerating that last part?

I sneaked a sideways glance at the agent who sat stiffly behind the wheel, hands at ten and two. Nothing about this guy struck me as the exaggerating type.

So if he wasn't exaggerating, what did that mean for us?

How would they do it? Would they invade in waves, destroying everyone and everything that stood in their way? Would innocent people be sacrificed because they were incapable of fending for themselves? I imagined my mom and my little brother, ravaged by the perils of war. I imagined starvation, untreated diseases, festering injuries, and people turning on each other just to survive.

Or would the aliens just end it all at once? Destroy everything, the entire planet in one fell swoop?

That would be simpler, it seemed. More efficient.

My eyes slid downward to the watch dangling loosely around my wrist. Even fastened at the shortest notch, Chuck's beefy arms had been giant-sized compared to mine, but that didn't stop its rhythm from settling my rattled nerves.

Blinking about a million times, I tried to focus on the city whirring past in the dark—businesses of all shapes and sizes, some packed together in neat little strip malls and some freestanding with drive-throughs or giant parking lots. We'd driven all day and now neon signs flashed, and billboards and streetlights glared, all backed by hillsides dotted with houses and churches and more businesses, some lit and some not.

Whenever a car pulled alongside us, I'd dropped my head, keeping my chin low so whoever was in the other vehicle wouldn't see me. The last thing we needed was for someone to notice my eyes—eyes that glowed in the dark and could probably be seen even from behind the tinted glass.

It wasn't right to be here, with Agent Truman, when I'd been avoiding this . . . running from him for so long.

We'd stopped once so he could call "his guy" in private. His guy put him in touch with the next guy who knew how to reach a group that was not only unlisted, but was even deeper underground than the Daylight Division.

It didn't surprise me that clandestine was a language Agent Truman was fluent in. But whoever he'd gotten in contact with seemed willing to help.

It was that same willingness that made me uneasy. That and the secrecy. If it weren't for the whole brink of extinction thing, I'd be worried Agent Truman had another agenda . . . maybe planning an auction of his own so he could sell me off and spend the rest of his days on the beaches of Bali sipping mai tais.

But, so far he hadn't taken us into custody, and I couldn't help thinking he was genuinely concerned over the possibility we were facing an alien invasion. I mean, of course he was concerned, right?

Still, every time we asked where we were headed, Agent Truman said our destination was on a need-to-know basis, deeming that neither Thom nor I had that kind of clearance.

He was such a jerk.

I'd tracked our progress anyway . . . as we'd traveled through Oregon into California. I'd noted the names of cities on road signs along the way—places like Portland, Eugene, Medford, then Sacramento. I felt feverish, my limbs trembling, as the number in my head had rolled from eleven to ten somewhere just past Redding.

Now the midmorning sun was high as we veered onto the more isolated roads that led into the California hills.

Ten.

If we were counting down days, did that mean there were only ten left? Just over a week?

I was reluctant to share what I suspected, because what if I was wrong? What if it was something else, this crazy obsession with numbers? What if it had nothing at all to do with a possible impending war?

Being cramped in the car with these two for the past sixteen hours hadn't gone far to getting us better acquainted.

Unlike Simon, Thom had always been the more silent type. He still didn't trust Agent Truman, and I didn't entirely blame him. But there was more to it than that. I figured he was probably still licking his wounds over the whole Natty situation.

As far as Agent Truman, I hadn't tried to have any heart-to-hearts with him or anything, but I'd definitely started to get a feel for subtle shifts in his demeanor. For his part, he'd actually attempted to break the ice with us. Even gone as far as trying to crack a joke or two, which had been nothing short of awkward. The corners of his eyes had gotten squintier than usual, almost as if he wasn't quite sure of the proper procedure for smiling. Like it was a lost skill. But even after hours of traveling together, he hadn't given us a first name so he was still just Agent Truman. Maybe "Agent" for short.

The one time I'd tried to broach the subject of Griffin, he'd frozen over like arctic tundra.

But of course Agent Truman wasn't the buddy-buddy type and we weren't friends. Agent Truman was more the shoot-your-daughter-and-leave-her-for-dead type.

The only reason we were together at all was to stop an alien race from invading the planet.

Message received.

CHAPTER TEN

Days Remaining: Ten

THE STOP SEEMED TO COME OUT OF NOWHERE, maybe because we *were* nowhere. Not just up in the mountains, but parked in front of an actual mountain, facing a wall of jagged stone that would have been imposing if not for the tiny white flowers that sprang from its rocky surface.

I started to open the passenger side door because my legs were killing me, and right now, getting out and stretching them was all I could think of.

Agent Truman's hand shot over and stopped me. "You might wanna hold up a sec."

Without warning, the car plummeted as if it had been suspended by only a taut wire, and that wire had just been cut. My stomach lurched up all the way into my throat. I guessed we'd been parked on some sort of platform, a super high velocity elevator.

Whatever it was, the drop felt endless.

"What . . . the . . ." Thom glared at Agent Truman, who wore an almost-legitimate smile as he watched us from behind the wheel.

"A little warning next time," I accused breathlessly, after my stomach had slipped back into place.

"Where's the fun in that?" Agent Truman asked, switching off the ignition.

When we were parked aboveground, it had been broad daylight, but down here, deep underground, it was pitch-black. "What is this place?"

Agent Truman's sly grin was back. "You'll see." And just when he said it, like he'd issued a command, a series of pale lights switched on all around us, illuminating walls that were carved from the cliffs themselves.

Beyond our car, a wide corridor extended as the walls shifted from rock to steel, the floor from stone that was rough and coarse to granite so polished it gleamed.

A woman emerged from the end of the tunnel. Her white lab coat was stark against her dark skin, and her hair was pulled away from her face in a ponytail that ended in a thick cluster of soft curls. It was clear from her welcoming smile that she'd been expecting us.

"*Now* it's safe to get out," Agent Truman said as he opened his door.

"Welcome to the ISA," the woman greeted us as she approached. "The Interstellar Space Agency," she clarified as she came to a stop in front of us. "I'm Dr. Clarke. So glad you could join us."

The Interstellar Space Agency. She made it sound like I should know who, or what, the Interstellar Space Agency was. Like they were up there with the FBI or NASA, or even the PTA when it came to public awareness, rather than a clandestine organization operating from underneath a mountain.

Before I could ask exactly what it was the ISA did, and how they thought they could help us, Dr. Clarke turned to lead us back down the corridor she'd just come from. "Let me give you the grand tour." Since Agent Truman and Thom were already following her, I wasn't given much of a choice. I supposed I should too.

Even though we were so far beneath ground, the place had a sterile feel about it. When we emerged from the tunnel, we stepped out into a space that didn't look at all like it could possibly be buried beneath a mountain. I remembered the first time I'd seen the Daylighters' Tacoma facility—that blown-away sensation I'd had that I'd just walked onto an elaborate movie set. A science fiction lover's wet dream.

I had that feeling now as I looked around at the enormous operation. Equipment that looked even more state-of-the-art than what I'd seen at the Tacoma facility. Things that looked like they didn't even belong to this world. "What is this place?" I asked again.

"Remember I told you about those brainiacs no one takes seriously?" Agent Truman answered. "Well, these are who I meant."

Dr. Clarke gave Agent Truman a look that reminded me of one my mom used to give my dad, a we'll-come-back-to-that look. A put-a-pin-in-it look.

I sort of hoped I'd be there for that conversation.

Then she launched into her own explanation. "You've heard of SETI?" Dr. Clarke asked.

I shook my head. "I don't think so. Should I have?" I answered vaguely.

Dr. Clarke nodded, like she'd expected as much. "Most people haven't. Stands for the Search for Extraterrestrial Intelligence," Dr. Clarke went on. "It's the collective name given to several organizations using scientific data to establish interstellar communications. To search for life . . . out there."

She moved us through the rest of our tour like we were in a race, zipping through one vast room after another. I'd call them labs, except the word "labs" wasn't quite right because it didn't do any of these places justice.

I wanted her to slow down. I wanted all of this to just . . . *slow down.* I had questions. I wanted *her* to ask questions—about who we were, what we were doing here, what we wanted. But she just kept talking . . . kept shuttling us forward until I'd lost track of where we were.

There were multiple levels with glass elevators on each side. There were chambers running around the perimeter with a giant open area in the center, and walkways that connected one side to the other across each different floor. People worked on different levels, on different projects with names she ticked off like Andromeda One, the Axis Venture, Project Frontline, XtropX. She tried to explain each one, but they blurred together until nothing made sense anymore.

We reached what looked like a nursery—another "lab" filled with plants, some beneath large lighted hoods and some that grew so large they were taller than we were. But all these plants were unusual—their colors and the textures of the leaves and the stems shooting up from the soil—none of it was quite right. Even the soil they were planted in was *off* somehow. Not Earth-like.

Curious, I stepped away from Thom and examined one of the spiky, red-tinged leaves. It was covered in a strange spongy substance that looked like it was expanding and contracting. I reached for it.

Just as my fingertips brushed it, the thing moved. Not the substance covering the leaf, but the plant . . . the entire leaf.

First, it shifted, but then in a swift lunging motion it took a swipe at me.

Thom yanked my hand away before I could even flinch.

"Did you see that?" I cradled my hand to my chest.

Dr. Clarke came up and steered us back expertly. "Oh,

dear, you don't want to touch those." The offhanded way she said it made me think that the delayed nature of the warning wasn't entirely an oversight.

I rubbed my fingertips and my thumb together until they were practically raw, wondering what might have happened if Thom hadn't saved me. I shot him a what-the-hell? look and he just shook his head because he had no idea either.

Dr. Clarke finally began to fill in the blanks about her agency. She barely acknowledged the part where a sentient plant had just tried to—*I don't know*—attack me. "Not everyone realizes what a delicate balance the universe is. NASA has used their Hubble telescope and measured the age of the oldest planet in our galaxy at thirteen billion years," she explained. "That's more than twice as old as Earth. But there are more than one hundred billion galaxies in the observable universe." She flashed a knowing grin. "And that's just what NASA will admit to. There are species—*beings*—far more advanced and complex than us, who've survived millennia. Planets a hundred times older than ours. The Milky Way is just the tip of the iceberg, so to speak." She was specifically looking at me and Thom, and I wondered how much she knew . . . about us. How much Agent Truman had told her when he'd placed his private phone call. "It used to be that everyone had their hands in SETI's research—the Russians, NASA, most major universities. But by the mid-'90s, Congress canceled all government funding. Now it's strictly a private enterprise, mostly through UC Berkeley."

"So . . . you're part of the SETI project?" Thom asked.

"Was," she clarified. "Now I'm here, working with the Interstellar Space Agency. We do a lot of the same stuff, only with much better funding."

We were approaching something that looked vaguely familiar. I froze as I glanced uncomfortably at Agent Truman. Dr. Clarke turned to watch us.

The canisters in question were so similar to the ones I'd seen at the Daylight Division, the human-sized ones they'd had at the Tacoma facility, that my skin went cold and clammy.

The only difference between them was that these weren't empty. Or at least one of them wasn't.

Dr. Clarke gave me a significant look, and then glanced back at the canister. "We've made better contacts as well."

I followed her gaze. "You're not saying . . ." I tilted my head, hesitating. "That's not . . . ?"

I never finished my question, I didn't need to—she knew what I meant.

An alien. I'd meant: *That's not an alien, is it?*

But I was sure it was. As sure as I'd been about anything in my life—Old Kyra's or New Kyra's.

I separated myself from Dr. Clarke and the others to get a better look, and no one told me not to go. My palms hadn't been this sweaty since the first time I'd taken the pitcher's mound and faced my very first batter. I hoped things turned out better this time around.

By the time I reached the canister . . . the one that was occupied, my teeth were chattering like one of those windup toys.

The liquid behind the glass was an odd translucent blue that bubbled in thick sticky swells. But there was something in there, embedded in all that gelatinous fluid. A creature of some sort.

If it truly was an alien, like Dr. Clarke hadn't denied, it didn't feel that way to me.

Something inside me tripped at the sight of it, like a switch or a trigger, and I was drawn closer.

It was human-*ish* but so obviously *not human*. It had a head and four limbs—two arms and two legs—hands, feet, a torso, fingers and toes, although nothing was in exactly the same shape as mine or Thom's or Agent Truman's or Dr. Clarke's. Its skin was thicker, its head larger, its jaw wider, and as I circled around the canister, I noticed its spinal column was raised and thorny.

"What . . . ," I tried. "What do you call it?"

"He's part of a larger group we call the M'alue. Their actual name is unpronounceable, so M'alue is the closest our language can get to it. The meaning itself is totally lost."

Thom moved to stand next to me. "But it's a *him*?"

"Yes," Dr. Clarke acknowledged. "We call him Adam."

"What's wrong with him? Is he . . . *alive*?"

Dr. Clarke's voice was somewhere behind me. "We keep him in stasis. For his health."

I stepped closer to the tube, as close as I could possibly get. There was something about him, about Adam . . . "How did you get him?" I asked. "How did *he* end up here?"

I leaned in, my breath clouding the glass as I pressed

my forehead against it. I raised my hand and let my fingers roam along the cool surface of the cylindrical canister. I felt sorry for him, thinking how easily the roles could have been reversed—me and him. I let myself wonder if that's how *they'd* kept me, during the time they'd taken and held me for all those years. Had I been *up there* in a similar tube, breathing jelly-like blue liquid?

When his eyes opened, I jumped. Behind me, there was a gasp, although who it came from, I wasn't sure.

Adam was looking directly at me. *Into* me.

The eyes that looked out at me were wide and golden and, like my newly transformed ones, they glowed.

Glowed.

But more than that, there was something happening between us. Something I was sure no one else in the room was aware of. I wasn't sure if I heard or felt it. Or maybe it was just a singular awareness coming from inside my veins. But it was him . . . it was definitely him. He was communicating with me. Adam, he was trying to tell me something.

"Do you see that?" It was Thom, right at my back. "Kyra, are you seeing this?"

I nodded, thinking, *How could I miss it?*

"Step back," Dr. Clarke said, but she said it uncertainly. "We need to go." And when I didn't move, I felt her hand on my shoulder, more confident than her voice. She pulled me away as she insisted, "Now."

★ ★ ★

"Okay, so that was something, right?" I whispered to Thom, when the tour abruptly ended and Dr. Clarke ushered us as far away from Adam as she could manage. Her welcoming attitude had vanished and now she was silently leading us down endless corridor after endless corridor.

Agent Truman stayed by her side, but every now and then he'd throw me a frosty look to let me know I'd messed up, even though I couldn't quite figure what *I'd* done wrong.

We went into another of those glass elevators and Dr. Clarke punched a button. I barely noticed as the elevator sank and darkness closed in from all sides as chiseled cavern walls surrounded us. I was stuck on what had just happened back there. About that thing—Adam—trapped inside that tube. The way he'd looked at me.

Dr. Clarke had refused to answer any of my questions about him . . . about why they had him in there, and what was wrong with him. He was hurt I tried to tell her, mostly because it seemed so obvious. He was . . . damaged.

I knew because I'd felt it from him. I'd sensed an intense, unbearable, excruciating pain coming from him.

Her only response was that her team was doing its best for him. That he had the best minds in the world working on him and he was in good hands.

But I wasn't like her. I couldn't so easily brush Adam from my thoughts. . . .

When we emerged from the elevator, Dr. Clarke said, "I thought it was a coincidence, you showing up the way you did." She eyed me, and then looked to Agent Truman. "But after what I just witnessed . . . up there just now, I believe I've been mistaken . . ." Her voice trailed off as we stopped in front of a large metal door. I heard muffled voices coming from the other side of it. "I think your arrival might be connected in some way," she explained, and then stepped aside as she opened the door.

SIMON

WE'D BEEN KEPT WAITING FOR HOURS, TOLD SOMEONE would come for us when, so far, no one had. My restlessness was sharp.

When the door began to open, and I saw who was standing on the other side, that restlessness mutated, becoming sticky and hot as it burned the back of my tongue.

Of all the people it had to be, they'd brought us Thom. A snake might've been better. Or a rabid junkyard pit bull. Anyone but Thom.

After everything he'd done—sending the NSA the coordinates to Blackwater Ranch, putting a tracking device in the watch he'd given Kyra . . . he was seriously the last person I'd expected to find standing there. Facing us.

"What the fu—" I started. But then I narrowed my eyes and bit down hard, clenching my jaw. "You piece of crap!" I bit out, right before I landed the first punch, hard in the face. And then the second. Somewhere along the line there was a third and probably a fourth.

From behind . . . or above us, since I was pretty sure we were on the floor now, I heard that son of a bitch Agent Truman, and realized he was here too. He was laughing. There were shouts and screams, but Agent Truman . . . yeah, he was seriously getting his rocks off.

No matter. I was seeing red—figuratively and literally—as I took everything out on Thom, wondering if he had any intention of fighting back.

TYLER

KYRA WAS HERE.

That's all I could think. All I could focus on, even while Simon was wailing on Thom, and that NSA agent was cracking up. Even as a team of security agents rushed the room.

Kyra was here. As beautiful as ever.

Alive.

I could breathe again.

CHAPTER ELEVEN

AS SECURITY SWARMED PAST, I WONDERED WHY an agency whose sole purpose was research needed their own small army, and why they'd been so readily available. But the thought came and went quickly, swallowed up by my gratitude that they'd been there to break up the fight. My voice was hoarse from screaming at the two of them to stop, even though I doubted either Simon or Thom had heard me.

"Enough!" Dr. Clarke's voice cut through the chaos as the enormous armed men peeled the boys apart.

But it was my dad, who seemed to suddenly be aware I was standing there, whose voice I heard as it echoed off the metal walls and stone floors. "Kyra!" He shoved everyone aside to reach me and I breathed in his scent as he crushed me to his barrel-sized chest. "Kyra, my god . . . Kyra," he repeated, as if he was trying to convince himself it was real. That I was actually there.

I wanted to ask him how he'd gotten here, where he'd been, and how he was. I wanted to know when they'd met up with Simon and to know every detail of every second from the moment we'd been separated, but it would have to wait.

When he let me go, all eyes were on me—curious and questioning. In my periphery I spotted Tyler, and he was watching me back. I tried to decipher his expression, that look on his face. Had he forgiven me? Or did he need more time?

Without thinking, I turned and caught Simon's copper eyes. "Kyra . . ." He sounded like all the wind had just been knocked out of him, and I couldn't remember a time the sound of my own name had been so intimate.

But it was too much, the way he said it, and I forced myself to look away. To look around.

And they were all there, all my friends in one place—Willow, Jett, Simon, even Griffin—and all I could think was how grateful I was they were alive. That my dad and Tyler had found them.

One of the guards was restraining Willow, and I tried to remember if she'd been part of the brawl. Beneath her breath she muttered, "*scumbag*" and I knew it was directed at Thom.

"It's not like that," I said, moving to stand by Thom's side. "It wasn't him."

Griffin's hands settled on her hips. "Don't you dare defend that traitor. If it wasn't for him . . ."

Simon crossed his arms and shot a scathing look at Thom. I had my work cut out for me.

"Seriously, you guys. It was Natty."

My eyes slid to Thom, who wasn't exactly making himself seem innocent by glaring at the lot of them. I guess I couldn't blame him though; I'd be pissed too, if I'd been greeted by a full-scale assault.

Griffin narrowed her brown eyes. "So you're saying Thom was, what? A pawn? That he was innocent. Natty was some kind of mastermind this whole time?"

"Go ahead," I implored Thom. "Tell them. Tell them it was Natty who sent out the message."

He squeezed his eyes shut. "I had no idea who she really was. She used my passwords to send out a message, and when I caught her, she and Eddie Ray took me prisoner. They tortured me to try and get my private code word for Silent Creek, so they could ambush my camp." He shook his head and sighed. "Until Kyra found me, I had no idea Natty and Eddie Ray had kidnapped her too."

"God, I'd love to shake the hand of the person who put that bullet between Natty's eyes," Willow ground out.

"Here's your chance," Agent Truman butted in. "She's right here. She shot all of 'em apparently." He held out a hand all Vanna White-style, offering me up as the grand prize on some game show.

"Christ," Simon breathed.

But it was Tyler, whose eyes landed on mine that I cared about. "You? It was you who . . . *killed* them?"

I wasn't sure what I saw in his expression. Accusation . . . disappointment . . . anger? Or was he disgusted that I'd pulled the trigger on my own friend, even though she'd been planning to sell me off the entire time?

Whatever it was, Griffin didn't have the same qualms. She let out a gusty sigh. "I had no idea you had it in you." But it was clear she approved.

"It was our only way out," I explained, looking at Tyler now, and wishing everyone else would just go away.

I turned to Dr. Clarke, hoping to take the attention off me. "You said you didn't think it was a coincidence when we showed up at the same time," I said. "What did you mean?"

Dr. Clarke ran her hand over the side of her ponytail, making sure every hair was still in place. She signaled for the guards to wait outside.

"Because when I was showing them around," she said, looking to Tyler, who hadn't stopped watching me. "He woke the M'alue too."

Dr. Clarke and Agent Truman had only been gone a few minutes, but already their absence was this thing you could feel, like someone had been sitting on your chest and once they were gone you could catch your breath.

It was like that, like finally breathing again.

Everyone started talking all at once. I asked my dad for a minute alone, and even though I knew he didn't want to leave me again, he reluctantly let me peel away from him.

Willow was just as bad when it came to Simon, staying glued by his side, which wasn't a big surprise or anything, except that Griffin stayed there too, the three of them forming an uneasy truce as they hovered near Thom. But at least they were giving him the chance to tell his side of the story.

I needed to talk to Tyler, and when I turned to find him, he was right there, waiting for me.

"This is it, you know?" he said, before I could say anything. "The place I was telling you about back at the diner, before you were . . ." He dropped his gaze and gave a quick shake of his head before meeting my eyes again. "Before you vanished. The place I thought we needed to be."

"Wait? The one you dreamed about?" I frowned. "How do you know? Are you sure?"

"Jett figured it out—using that map I drew. He used his mad computer skills to trace the coordinates to this exact location."

I tried to make sense of that. The map, the one Tyler had drawn that night in the desert—on the cliff.

"And that's how you ended up here?"

"Pretty much. The weirdest part is, that when we showed up, these guys came out and invited us in, showed us around like they'd been expecting us. Like we were guests or something." He shrugged. "But once I saw that . . . when I saw *Adam* . . . I don't know . . . I just felt . . ." His eyes searched mine, looking for an explanation. "Did *you* feel it?"

I thought about the way I'd wanted to stay there with

him. With Adam. I nodded. "I think so."

"It's the strangest thing though. It's not just Adam." His eyes were so green as they scoured my face, and it was almost as if I could feel his fingers on me. "It's you too. Before you even walked through that door, *I knew* you were here."

I frowned, mesmerized by his voice, his admission. His inspection. "You did?"

He nodded as he contemplated my face. His eyes roving over my nose and each and every one of my freckles.

"Did you tell the others?" I asked quietly.

He shook his head. "I was wrong last time, about the asylum. At least about when you'd be there. I didn't want to be wrong again. So when I felt you, when I sensed you were here, I thought, *What if I'm wrong again? What if it's not her?*" His gaze shifted to my lips. "And then when Thom was standing there instead of you, I was . . ." His face creased. "I was *so confused*. Until I saw you behind him."

His hand started to move toward mine, but then he stopped himself, and I realized what I'd seen in his eyes: disillusionment. "So you really did that? Shot Natty and the others?"

I wanted to explain my reasons. How I'd been forced to look someone in the eyes and pull the trigger, again and again and again. But somehow I just couldn't. Not now. Not when the fate of the planet was at stake.

This . . . us . . . suddenly, it just didn't matter as much. And maybe he was going through the same thing.

I almost couldn't speak. When I found my voice it was

like rusted metal, crumbling and dry. "I'm sorry."

His brow crumpled. "For what?" he finally managed in the softest tone known to man. A heartbroken sort of sound. "Because you forgot to tell me how in love I am with you? Or for shooting your best friend?"

My shrug was microscopic. "For everything."

He waited, thinking it over. "Me too."

And then he left me standing there.

TYLER

GRIFFIN RAISED ONE EYEBROW. IT WAS THE SAME buck-up-soldier look I'd seen her use a thousand times before. "You okay? I'm happy to knock some sense into her, if you don't have the heart." Her tone though was gentler than when she was really giving a get-your-shit-together speech, which meant I must really look bad.

I laughed, or the best I could manage. "I'm fine." I glanced over to where Kyra was still absorbing our conversation. I wasn't sure what I felt.

Bad for not absolving her, sure. But after what Truman had

said, about Kyra being responsible for that bloodbath at the asylum . . .

It was a lot to take in.

If what he said was true, then Kyra had assassinated those people, one of whom was supposedly her best friend. Shot them point-blank.

Maybe I didn't know Kyra as well as I thought I did. I definitely didn't know how I felt about that.

And maybe that was the problem.

I'd stood in front of her telling myself she was a virtual stranger, this girl who could kill in cold blood, and yet, still, I'd wanted her.

I'd wanted to grab her and kiss her and tell her *I* was the one who was sorry.

How messed up was that?

Super messed up.

Griffin leaned back against the wall and crossed her arms over her chest. "It's a standing offer. Let me know if you change your mind." Griffin was a soldier—I knew she'd killed. Griffin never hid that fact. She was a what-you-see-is-what-you-get kind of girl. So why was I holding Kyra to a different standard? Why couldn't I forget what I'd seen at the asylum?

Because Griffin wasn't the one I couldn't keep my eyes off of. Griffin wasn't the one I couldn't stop thinking about.

I wasn't in love with Griffin.

"Thanks, Griff, I'll keep that in my back pocket."

"No you won't," she baited, knowing exactly where my heart was.

I shook my head. "Nope. I won't."

The door opened and Dr. Clarke and Agent Truman—Griffin's crazy ex-scientist-turned-Daylighter dad—came charging in. Griffin's demeanor shifted from relaxed to tense in the blink of an eye.

"What about you?" I asked. "You okay? I'd offer to knock some sense into him, but I'm pretty sure your old man could beat my ass."

She sighed, and let her arms fall to her sides. "Wouldn't do any good anyway. He is smart, but never did have much sense."

She kept her eyes on him as he moved to the center of the room, Dr. Clarke coming to stand directly behind him. Without even trying, the two of them filled all the space and demanded our attention. "All right, kiddos," Agent Truman said, clapping his hands decisively as if he were issuing an edict. "Playtime is over. Let's get down to business."

CHAPTER TWELVE
Days Remaining: Nine

THE CONFERENCE ROOM WHERE DR. CLARKE gathered us was sleek, all glass and metal and shiny surfaces. She never touched a light switch, but the lights went down as if she'd mentally commanded it. And almost on cue, there was a gasp from one of the lab-coated professionals. As if they'd never seen glow-in-the-dark eyes before.

I wanted to reprimand them, something along the lines of, *Grow up already!* Instead, I sank lower in my chair, hating being singled out already.

Behind Dr. Clarke a screen flashed to life, reminding me vaguely of one of those Smart Boards from school. Of course, there were a few minor differences between the technologies here at the ISA and what my old high school was using. First, Dr. Griffin queued up the image of an actual-authentic-*not-animated* alien—Adam. The second was that she only needed her fingertips, which she flipped and waved through thin air, to navigate the representation. Third, and also the most impressive, there was nothing two-dimensional about what we were looking at. The image wasn't only up there, on the screen, like the boards at school. We were staring at some sort of hologram.

So cool.

"How much do you actually know?" Dr. Clarke began. "About how we first came in contact with them—the M'alue?"

"You mean the First Contact meetings?" I asked, referring to the first secret government meeting with the aliens, the one President Eisenhower allegedly attended back in the '50s.

I shot a quick glance at Jett, who hated this particular part of our history. He was rubbing the place on his arm—a place that had healed decades ago—where he'd been tortured by our own government to find out whether he was a Returned or not.

My stomach tensed for a different reason. I couldn't stop thinking about the things Tyler had told me, about how that map he'd drawn had led them here, straight to this underground facility. The whole thing bugged me, considering the messages I'd heard: *The Returned Must Die.*

All with what I had to assume were only nine days remaining.

It wasn't—it couldn't be—a coincidence we'd found Adam here. Had we—the Returned and the Replaced—somehow been corralled here? Had we made the most enormous-gigantic-*monstrous* mistake of our lives by following Tyler's map?

I tried to stay focused on what Dr. Clarke was talking about.

She looked pleased not to have to launch into a detailed explanation of the First Contact Meetings. "So you're up to speed already? Good. It makes things easier. I'm sure you realize then, that, for a time the agreement between us and them was peaceful."

"*Peaceful?*" I interrupted, sounding more than a little skeptical considering where we were standing right now. "Do you mean the part where they were kidnapping kids and experimenting on them, while the government turned a blind eye?" I crossed my arms. "We may have different definitions of peaceful."

"Agent Truman has informed me of . . . of *what* you all are. So I can see why you might not understand the situation." She glanced around at us. Other than my dad, everyone in our group had been taken and returned. "The matter was complex, Kyra. There was more to it than a simple pact. What you might not realize is that it wasn't exactly a *negotiation*."

Griffin shot her a black look. "Are you saying they would

have taken us whether there was an agreement in place or not? I have a hard time believing the president would have just accepted that."

"And what would he have done about it? What would anyone have done about it?" she asked. "Do you know how incredible it is that they found us at all? Of all the planets, in all the solar systems, in all the galaxies, and they just happened to track us down? It's the universal version of a needle in a haystack. If their goal had been to destroy us, then they could and would have. But clearly they had other plans for us. The M'alue are explorers. Scientists in their own right." She made it sound like they impressed her. That she revered rather than feared them. Shrugging, she added, "Cooperating was our best option."

"So what was the point?" I asked. "If you know so much about them? What was their reason for coming here in the first place? Why were they doing this to us?"

Dr. Clarke looked around—not at us, but at her team. "Clear the room."

She didn't say who was supposed to go, and who should stay, but they seemed to know. Only about five of her people remained by the time the evacuation was complete.

Beneath the table, I settled my hands on my knees to stop them from bouncing. This was it. We were finally going to get some answers.

"When they came here, they were dying. That is to say, a large segment of their population was sick, and they were looking for a cure. They thought we might have . . . that we might be the answer they were searching for. Genetics isn't my specialty." She nodded to Agent Truman. "Dr. Arlo Bennett here could probably do a better job explaining the science of this, but I'll give it a shot." The hologram of Adam vanished and was replaced by a large, rotating double helix. "This is our DNA," she explained. "Ours is remarkably similar to that of the M'alue considering how different our species and environments are." She used her fingers to indicate she wanted to ply the strands apart, and the double helix exploded, sending fragments flying into virtual oblivion. All that remained was a single coiled, X-shaped piece. "What it really comes down to is this. They needed one imperceptible, but crucial, chromosome from our genome."

Jett's fingertips drummed on the tabletop. "Why not just ask for it? Couldn't they just get a sample rather than go through all the trouble of abducting us? Experimenting on us?"

Dr. Clarke's lips pursed. "It was more complicated than that. You might have noticed that you age slower now. Well, there's a reason for that. Human DNA is subject to something called the Hayflick limit. Basically, it means that there's a limit to the number of times a human cell can divide before those cells start to ultimately die. Our natural life span." She shrugged. "And ours is significantly shorter than the M'alue. In order for our chromosome—the one they potentially needed—to be useful to them, they first had to make the life spans match, and the only way to do that was to get their *specimens*"—she raised her eyebrows as her gaze swept meaningfully over us, letting us know in no uncertain terms that *we* were the specimens in question—"to live as long as they do before extracting the test samples. Increasing the life spans had other side effects as well—the advanced healing, the slower metabolisms, the need for less sleep."

"You seem to know a lot about us. How come we've never heard of you?" Griffin challenged.

"We've tried to be discreet," Dr. Clarke replied. "But we're not entirely unknown. The government knows we exist, and as long as we don't interfere"—she smiled smugly—"they don't bother us too much—although, sometimes it's a matter of what they don't know won't hurt them. All in all, we do our best to stay off their radar."

Tilting my head, I asked, "So did it work? Did they get what they needed from us?"

Dr. Clarke frowned. "We don't know. Not exactly." She closed her fist and the images vanished, the screen behind her going dark. "There was a breakdown in communication—if you could call it that in the first place—between us and the M'alue. Cooperation ended abruptly, and we no longer know where they are in their experiments." Her lips flattened into a thin line. "I had a chance to meet privately with Ben after his group arrived yesterday, and today with Agent Truman, and I think I'm up to speed on your reasons for coming. I know about the maps and the message. It's not good." She paused. "Hopefully, we can help each other out of this . . . *situation*."

Jett glanced around the table, and I realized not everyone had all the pieces. "What exactly is our situation?"

Agent Truman arched one brow at me. "Go ahead."

"What haven't you told us?" Griffin prodded.

"I can't say for sure, but I think they're coming. And I think we only have nine days until they get here," I said.

"How can you be sure?" my dad asked.

"I can't. I mean, that's the thing. Every morning when I wake up, I get this . . ." I turned to Tyler, thinking maybe he'd know what I was saying. He was the only one who'd witnessed what I'd gone through, while we'd been on the run. Plus, how did I even start to describe this? "Pains. Like intense, stabbing pains." My voice was wobbly. "At first I thought it was nothing . . ." I shrugged. "Just part of this whole Returned/Replaced thing. Over time it got worse, and then while Natty was holding me hostage, one of them mentioned I was some sort of countdown. I started to realize what I was feeling was them . . . getting closer. Somehow I can sense them."

"The same way you felt Adam," Tyler said.

I nodded. "Yeah, like that. It's like I'm tracking them. I mean, I could do without the stabbing part, but . . . yeah, like that."

Jett—as our resident numbers guy—was the first to ask, "So where'd the nine days come from?"

"Same place Tyler's maps came from, I guess."

"So, thin air," Simon said snidely to Tyler.

Tyler shrugged. "If that's what helps you sleep at night."

Simon rolled his eyes. "I wish."

"We've gotten a bit off track," Dr. Clarke interrupted.

"The real question is, what do they want?" When no one answered, Dr. Clarke continued. "Have you ever heard the term extinction level event?"

"Do you mean like the dodo bird?" I asked, wondering where she was going with this.

"I mean," she stressed, "that the Earth has already survived five mass extinction events, including one that wiped out ninety-six percent of all life on this planet."

I wasn't sure how I was supposed to respond to that.

Dr. Clarke straightened the hem of her jacket and fixed her gaze on each of us, one at a time like she was weighing our skills. "This is our chance to play a part in stopping the next one."

"How do you figure?" Willow asked.

"We need to find a way to prevent them from coming. To prevent *them* from exterminating us. And, apparently, we have nine days to figure out how to do that."

CHAPTER THIRTEEN
Days Remaining: Seven

TWO DAYS HAD PASSED AND WE WERE NO CLOSER to figuring out what the M'alue's message meant, or what they wanted from us, than we'd been when we'd first taken the underground plunge into the ISA for help. I also still hadn't figured out where Tyler and I stood. I knew he was avoiding me—using his new ability to sense me to vacate any room before I arrived, or to wait until I was gone to enter. It was frustrating and awkward, because everyone knew what was happening.

And whenever we were forced into the same room, I could feel his eyes on me. It was the same thing my dad had done, that watching-me thing, like I was too blind to notice.

With no news in the two days since Dr. Clarke had given us her "We need to stop them from exterminating us" speech, we'd all started to go a little stir-crazy.

We'd been given limited access to the underground facility, the parts that weren't classified. Griffin and Willow had started making several trips to the gym each day, and then again to the large indoor track, just to burn off steam. I'd gone with them once, but they were hard core. Working out, for the two of them, was something that rivaled the Olympics, each of them jockeying to be the fastest runner, to lift the most weight, to do the most pull-ups, push-ups, chin-ups, or sit-ups. Pushing and challenging the other until I realized I'd gone invisible.

One trip had definitely been enough.

I'd tried on several occasions to convince Dr. Clarke to let me see Adam again, but she'd denied me every time, not even bothering with excuses, just telling me his lab was restricted. I argued we'd seen him once already, and she just repeated that it was a "restricted" area.

I even tried convincing the security guards to give me a tour of the upper floors, hoping to catch another glimpse of the M'alue in his body-sized test tube. It was weird the way I was consumed by thoughts of him, and if Tyler and I had been on better terms I would have asked him if he felt the same. But we weren't.

Then there were the tests. Strange ones.

It had started that first day, just before dawn, when Dr. Clarke had come to me and asked if I wouldn't mind being monitored while the sun came up. If my dad had known what they were planning he would have objected, which was why I didn't tell him.

Normally, I'd never want someone watching while I squirmed in agony. It would be like letting someone watch me pee. *Superweird.*

But with the fate of the world in jeopardy, who was I to deny such a simple request? What if they discovered something that might help, even in some small way?

So I'd agreed, not realizing they were going to turn it into an event. That I'd be on display, like a circus sideshow—*Step right up, ladies and gents, see the freak who counts down to the alien apocalypse! For an extra ticket, you might even be able to touch her.*

I was surrounded by scientists and technicians, then hooked up to conductors and wires and probes.

That was what sent me right over the edge, straight into Panicville. The probes. It was too much like the asylum . . . of everything Natty and Eddie Ray had done while they'd kept me strapped to that rusted metal gurney, monitoring me.

Somehow, though, I'd kept that panic in check, swallowing it down like hunks of sharp cement. It was prickly and it tore up my esophagus, but I reminded myself I was here for mankind's sake . . . for my friends and family. I took one for the team.

At the onset of the pangs, I pretended not to notice them, those first pricks and pinches. But within minutes, tears had been streaming down my face.

Eight . . . eight . . . eight . . .

Eight . . .

The number repeated over and over in my head while I'd broken out in a sweat, holding my breath, struggling against the shooting, stabbing, slicing pains. All these people watching . . . all these intruders. I didn't want to embarrass myself. I didn't want them to see me at my worst.

In the end, though, I was weak. I couldn't help but give in to it, and I let out a low moan. *What difference did it make? Why should I care anyway? I didn't owe these strangers anything, let alone a show of dignity.*

When it was finished, when it was beyond-the-shadow-of-a-doubt over, I opened my eyes at last. The room was empty of everyone except Dr. Clarke, who thanked me for coming. For "participating," she'd said as if I'd just competed in Field Day and earned a blue ribbon in the sack races or the water balloon toss.

The whole thing happened again this morning, the tests. But at least this time I'd known what to expect. The only difference was the number repeating in my head: *Seven, seven, seven, seven . . .*

Simon materialized out of nowhere just as I was ducking out of the track, where I'd taken a quick run before Willow and Griffin decided it was time for another of their marathon sessions. I made a point of acting as if he hadn't caught me off guard, but the truth was he had. I'd been avoiding Simon the same way Tyler had been avoiding me—pretending I didn't notice him while I was acutely aware of his presence at all times.

"So," he said, falling into step beside me. I picked up my pace even though I had nowhere in particular to be. "You and lover boy, back together again . . ." Even from the corner of my eye I could see the way he raised an eyebrow. "I guess congratulations are in order."

I shrugged and kept walking. "You know that's not how it is."

"Isn't it? You got exactly what you wanted. I'm happy for you. Really, I am." He was lying, of course. I could hear the letdown in his voice.

I slowed, looking down at my feet. "I don't think he can forgive me about Natty. About having to kill them. And I don't blame him. Not really." I inhaled, trying to wipe my own memory of what I'd done. Maybe loving me wasn't enough. "Even if he does remember about us, it might not even matter now."

When I realized Simon had stopped walking, I did too. I turned back to him, and he was giving me a look that said what he thought: *I was being stupid.* "What'd you expect, Kyra? You really think you'd drop a bomb like that, and it'd be all happily ever after?" His tone was harsh. "This isn't some fairy tale. Things don't work like that. And even if they did, you two don't have that kind of history."

I clenched my jaw. "For once I wish you'd just say what you mean."

"What I mean is, how well do the two of you really know each other? You were together, what . . . a week, ten days before he got sick? That's less than two weeks during which you fell *madly in love*? Are you kidding me?"

"Shut up," I insisted. "You're wrong." Tyler and I might only have had two weeks together after I'd been returned, but that had been two weeks added to the rest of a lifetime that we'd known each other.

Okay sure, a lifetime where we'd been virtual strangers, where I'd barely given him the time of day because he was younger than me back then . . . but that didn't change the fact we had a history, whether Simon understood or not. We'd gone to the same schools, our families had been close . . . and we'd spent our entire lives across the street from each other.

Those experiences counted for something.

I started to walk away, but Simon reached for me. "Seriously, Kyra, hear me out. Are you just hanging on to Tyler because he's part of your history? Because he reminds you of your past? Is that enough to make a relationship? Is it really about memories—the things you think you shared? Or is it about having a *connection*?" His fingers curled around my wrist, insistent, and I stopped trying to get away from him.

Hadn't I wondered those same things, when I'd first come back . . . and in the weeks since? Not just about the people around me, but about myself. What made me who I was—was it my memories and past experiences? Or the person I was now and my actions going forward?

It was kind of like my old bedroom at my mom's house. After I'd come back it was no longer my room anymore. Sure, it was the exact same space—the same room in the same house—but it wasn't *the same.* Not really. My mom had packed up all the things that had made it mine—all my pictures and posters and trophies, my stuffed animals and clothes, ticket stubs from the movies I'd seen, and my journals and CDs. Everything personal to me. Everything that had given it character.

Everything that made it *feel* like home.

Maybe my body was just a new bedroom where all my old stuff—all the things I'd collected and cherished—had been moved. A new home filled with Old Kyra's memories and feelings. A place where I could start all over again.

"Think about it, isn't it better to really *know* someone . . . to see the other person for who they are, *flaws and all*, and still want to be with them?" Simon's grip loosened but I stayed still, trapped by my swirling emotions, and by eyes that were so vibrantly copper I got lost in them. "You and I," he went on, "we've spent more time together than the two of you ever did." His voice swept over my skin like liquid silk. He inched closer, a playful smile tugging his full lips. "We've survived so much. We can survive this too." He reached underneath my chin and nudged it up. My breath hitched and I wanted to look away, but the only place I could look was there . . . at those molten eyes of his. "You and I might not have history, not yet anyway. But I know you. I *see* you, and that means something. You just have to give me a chance, Kyra." He leaned closer, coming right at me. My brain sent the signal to shake my head, to tell him, *No . . . no way!* But my heart was thumping out of control, and all I could think was, *This isn't happening . . . this isn't happening . . . this isn't happening.*

But it so totally was. Simon was positively-for sure-*without a doubt* going to kiss me. "I can't promise you won't regret it, but I can guarantee we'll have fun along the way." He exhaled then and his breath was there, fusing with mine. His lips, those lips of his that I'd been watching just a moment earlier were right there, and I was helpless . . . hopeless to stop them.

It was the light above us that made me pause. It flickered. Just like that, out of the blue it went on and off, then back on again.

Without realizing what I was doing, my hands flew to Simon's forearms, which were sinewy. I felt stupid when I saw he was grinning down at me. "See? Together, we're electric . . ."

I was about to tell him what an idiot he was for being so cheesy, but then the bulb above us exploded. Tiny shards of glass shattered down on us, landing in my hair and hitting my exposed skin.

Simon's arm clamped around my shoulder as he dragged me out of the way. "What d'you think that was?" I asked as I reached up to brush fragments of glass out of my hair.

Forgetting his whole seduction act, Simon surveyed the

hallway. The rest of the overhead lights flickered but stayed on. He shook his head.

As I followed his gaze I realized something was terribly wrong. We needed to get to the others.

But before I could warn him or take a single step, I was gripped by the sudden knock-me-to-my-knees kind of pain.

I knew what this was.

Simon was at my side, the concern thick in his voice. "Kyra. What is it? What's wrong?"

I wanted to explain, but I couldn't breathe. Each spasm was worse than the one before. It was the same pain that came at dawn, only stronger . . . more intense. And at entirely the wrong time. My body was trying to collapse in on itself, like a can being crushed from the inside out.

I couldn't breathe. Couldn't talk. I couldn't do anything except curl into a ball and wait for it to pass.

Just another two seconds, I told myself, and then two stretched into five . . . and then ten . . .

Sweat broke out over my forehead. It soaked my chest and my back. My skin itched, suddenly not fitting right, like it was being stretched too tight over my bones.

An unwelcome image of Adam flashed through my mind, and suddenly I wondered if his species ever shed their skin. Maybe that's what was happening to me. I was shedding this Kyra-looking skin, and when I did, the real me—the M'alue me—would materialize at last.

If that were the case, what would this next version of Kyra look like? Would I be reptilian and scaly? Or maybe doughy and soft . . . a milky, marshmallowy version of myself?

Just when I thought I'd been stretched too thin . . . when I was wondering if maybe I was going to explode into a million grisly pieces, the whole thing just . . .

Ended.

As quickly as it had begun, it was over.

I waited several beats, several breaths, wondering if it would start again. But there was nothing. Not a single pinch or cramp, or tightening of my skin.

"You okay?" Simon hovered in front of me, anxiously rubbing his hands on his thighs. All traces of cockiness had vanished.

I sighed. It was nowhere near dawn. This . . . whatever I'd just gone through . . . it should never have happened. But it had, and it definitely meant something.

Getting to my feet, I took the hand Simon offered. "I . . . I guess so."

The sound of footsteps echoed down the hallway, causing both Simon and me to look up.

That was how Tyler caught us.

His green eyes dropped to my hand and to Simon's and he frowned uncertainly. Then his lip curled. And, after a heartbeat or two, his face just went . . . *blank*.

He cleared his throat. "I . . . ," he started. "I thought you needed me. I thought you needed help."

He'd sensed me, I realized. He not only knew where to find me, but somehow he'd known what I was going through and he'd come looking for me.

Before I could tell him he was right—that I did need him . . . or explain that this . . . what he'd seen between Simon and me wasn't what he thought . . . or just to say I was glad he'd come, he was already walking away.

TYLER

"TYLER, WAIT. CAN YOU *PLEASE* JUST WAIT A SEC?" Kyra begged.

I didn't want to be that jerk, the one who makes the girl beg. As if she hadn't been through enough already, what with the kidnapping, and being tortured and all.

I'd finally gotten past it, that's what I was on my way to tell her when I felt her . . .

. . . her need . . .

But then I found them together. Apparently I'd waited too long to get over myself. She'd already moved on.

It was just . . .

Whatever. I didn't even know what it was; I just knew there was nothing Kyra could say right now.

She grabbed my arm, and maybe because even though I was pissed, I wasn't a total ass, I stopped. I looked over her head when I told her, "Look, you don't owe me any explanations. We were what we were. But that's the past. I don't blame you, it's not like I remember any of it. I thought you were in trouble, end of story."

For a second, I half expected her to maybe beg some more. To try to make me see her side of things. But Kyra wasn't exactly like that.

I shouldn't have been surprised when she called me out instead.

"Stop acting like a dick. Obviously you think you saw something you didn't. It might've looked bad, but it didn't mean anything."

From behind her, I heard Simon clear his throat. He never could stand to be ignored. "You know I'm right here, don't you?"

"Shut up, Simon," she shot back at him, and it took every ounce of my willpower not to crack a smile. Then she turned on me. "For your information, I *was* in pain. I doubled over and Simon was just helping me up." Her glare said it all: no way was she letting me off the hook. She crossed her arms to add: I'd jumped to conclusions. "You might not remember—about us. But so what? *I* do. I *also* remember that you kissed me when we were on the run." She tapped her foot impatiently. "So don't act like you don't have some feelings for me, even if you can't remember why."

She wasn't wrong. My feelings might be jumbled, but I couldn't exactly pretend they weren't there. And she was making it damn hard to avoid looking at her, standing her ground the way she was.

Simon came up beside her. "She's wrong, by the way. It wasn't nothing," he insisted in a way that made me want to strangle the jerk. "If you hadn't come back she'd've gotten over you eventually." He glanced down at the back of her head, and I recognized the look; it was familiar and possessive. "Maybe she already had and she just can't admit it."

Kyra grumbled, a sound like disbelief.

She would have stormed away from both of us then if Jett hadn't come running up. He was shouting even before he'd reached us. "Something's happening. Dr. Clarke sent me to find you." He jerked his head down the corridor he'd just come from. "We need to go."

Kyra was already running after him, leaving both Simon and me in the dust.

I scowled at Simon, who was watching her with the same confused expression I was. I got the sense if we'd been friends he might've grunted something like, "Girls," all Neanderthal-like.

But the thing was, I couldn't blame him, because . . .

Girls . . .

CHAPTER FOURTEEN

EVEN BEFORE THE GLASS DOORS OF THE ELEVAtor slid open to the main level, it was obvious something serious was going down.

This was not the same tranquil operation we'd toured just two days earlier with Dr. Clarke.

Bedlam had erupted.

Jett strolled right into the strictly off-limits, you-need-high-level-clearance, heart of the operation. There were more people now—some wearing ordinary lab gear or uniforms, some dressed in regular street clothes, and a few fully suited in biohazard gear.

But it was the pace that was unsettling. Frenzied. Hectic. It was the only way to describe the nervous energy—everyone scurrying from one place to the next, almost as if no one was quite sure where they should be. Just that they needed to be *somewhere*. Furtive whispers and agitated shouts filled the air.

The chaos triggered my claustrophobia and, as if I hadn't considered it before, all at once I was keenly aware of our location: beneath about a million or so tons of rock-solid mountain. If this mountain caved in on us, we were dead meat for sure. There'd be no coming back from that.

Dr. Clarke spotted us and waved eagerly from above the turmoil. Whatever she'd been doing before was momentarily forgotten as she sprinted—no kidding, she *sprinted!*—across the lab to meet us.

The entire way up here, I'd been aggressively ignoring both Simon and Tyler. I was annoyed that they'd made me feel like the rope in their stupid tug-of-war.

Tyler wasn't the only one who could play the "I need time" card, and if neither of them could understand that, then it was their loss.

I'd kept as much distance between us as I could manage, even while we'd been crammed into the tiny glass elevator. I went out of my way to avoid looking at them, and when they talked to each other, which, apparently, was a thing they did now, I pretended I was deaf to them.

But Simon was Simon, which meant he couldn't help himself. So he kept up a steady, one-way stream of rambling conversation the entire way. He wasn't the leave-well-enough-alone type. Instead, he mentioned how awkward things were, like it was all one big joke, and he told Tyler if he'd only waited a few seconds longer, he might actually have walked in on something interesting.

Then he elbowed him with a wink.

Awesome.

But Simon also hadn't stopped watching me, and I knew he was worried I might double over again. Him and me both.

Having Jett there had been kind of a relief. His presence eased some of the uncomfortable tension eating away at our small group.

"Where are the others?" Simon asked Jett, when he realized it was just the four of us.

Jett nodded toward Dr. Clarke, who was eyeing Simon as she got closer. "They weren't invited," Jett answered. "Technically, neither were you or I, though. Dr. Clarke asked if she could get a look at the equipment we'd lifted from the asylum, so we were doing a kind of you-show-me-yours . . . That's when the alert went up."

But I had to question Jett's objective in his little sharing game with Dr. Clarke. I'd never been sure which of his assets made him more indispensable to Simon's team, his love of technology or his sticky fingers. Both meant they never lacked for spare computer parts.

"What kind of alert? And what does it have to do with me and Tyler?" I asked Dr. Clarke, glancing at the mayhem.

Dr. Clarke gestured to a nook away from the bustle, where hopefully we could talk in peace. "How certain are you," she asked, "of your countdown?"

From the side of the room I looked around at all the people huddled over complex computer screens, analyzing what looked like graphs and data that went way over my head.

I thought about what Blondie had told me, about me being a countdown, and considered the numbers that continually replayed through my head. Then I thought about the pain I'd felt downstairs, in the hallway with Simon.

Was that what I'd felt? A change in the timeline?

"I . . . I don't know. I thought I knew how long, but . . ." I shook my head, frowning. "I could have been wrong. Why?"

"We've picked up a signal."

"Signal?" Jett asked. "What kind of signal are you talking about?"

"That's the problem," Dr. Clarke explained. "We're not sure yet. We haven't been able to decipher it. If it's some kind of message, it's buried in a narrow band frequency; similar to the ones SETI was transmitting in their search for extraterrestrial life. It's as if whoever . . . or whatever is out there has been using our own signals to communicate back with us. Only this one's been modified beyond recognition. Actually, this isn't the first signal we've received. They've been coming in like clockwork. Each morning. Usually around dawn Pacific time."

I froze as Tyler's head snapped in my direction. Up until

a couple days ago, he was the only other person who knew what I'd been going through each morning, the only one I'd shared that bit of information with.

"So you already knew?" I repeated numbly. "That they were coming?"

"We knew transmissions were coming in, but we didn't know why or what they meant. And that was before we knew about you. That was why we asked to monitor you. To see if the two were synchronized."

"Were they?"

Dr. Clarke nodded, but it was a dismissive nod, like the answer was obvious to anyone paying attention. "Today, though, we received another transmission. This one came in on a different frequency, at any entirely different time of day. And when it did, Adam went crazy." Her eyes narrowed as she studied me. "Almost as if he *sensed* the transmission—"

"When?" Simon interrupted. "*When* did that happen?"

I slid my gaze to him, thinking the same thing he was.

She checked the clock on the wall while I glanced at Chuck's watch on my wrist. "Twenty-three minutes ago," I answered before she could open her mouth.

She looked at me. "So it is them?"

The waver in my voice was 100 percent reasonable under the circumstances. "If it is, why now?"

Jett crossed his arms impatiently. "You said Adam went crazy. He feels them too then?" He faced Dr. Clarke, clearly frustrated by the lack of information. "What aren't you telling us?"

"You saw him," she stated flatly, her expression neutral. "Do you think he's in there because he wants to be?"

She waited for one of us to put two and two together, but it didn't happen, at least not for me.

But Jett . . .

Jett was better at puzzles. At solving complex problems.

Understanding shattered his boyish features. "You think they're here for him. To save him from you."

My eyes widened. "Is Jett right? Is this some sort of rescue mission?" The idea that we might be caught in the middle of an alien hostage standoff was insane.

But Dr. Clarke was shaking her head. "No." And then again she repeated, "*No,*" and I wondered who she was trying to convince—us or herself. "Trust me, Adam being here was strictly accidental." But she was about as convincing as a terrorist. "It wouldn't make sense that they'd come for him now. Not after all this time. If that's all this was, why not come sooner?"

"How long's he been here?" Tyler asked.

"Almost seven years. Not here, in this facility the entire time, but that's how long he's been on Earth."

Seven years. Her words hit me like a jolt from Lucy. How much of that time had he spent in that tube?

I wanted to scream, to ask how something like this happened. To find out why they'd kept him like that. But all I could manage was, "How?"

"A crash," she said, closing her eyes.

"Like at Area 51?" Jett probed. Jett was almost worse

than my dad with his never-ending hunger for conspiracy tales. Probably because he'd lived so many of them firsthand.

Dr. Clarke made a scoffing sound, another dismissal. "Nonsense. Unlike the Area 51 hoax, *this* crash was real. And it was bad." She said it like her account was firsthand, and I wondered if that was possible. Had she been there seven years ago when Adam had crash-landed? "When we pulled Adam from the wreckage, we were sure he was dead. There was no way he could've survived it. It wasn't until later, when we'd taken him back to our lab that we'd realized he was regenerating. Healing. The same way you Returned can." She looked around at the four of us. "Seeing it happen with my own eyes was"—she put a hand to her lips, remembering—"*thrilling.*"

"So, if he healed, why's he still in there?" Tyler asked. "Why not let him leave?"

Dr. Clarke shook her head. "He might have healed after his crash, but something about being here on our planet is killing him."

"You sure that has nothing to do with being kept in that giant test tube?" I contested.

"We saved him. Without our intervention, he wouldn't have made it. Besides, even if he could sustain himself outside the tube, he has nowhere to go; his ship was too badly damaged in the crash."

I wasn't buying it. Maybe I'd spent too much time on the run from the No-Suchers, aware of what they really wanted with us—all the experiments they had planned.

Or maybe it was just her—Dr. Clarke herself. I couldn't say for sure whether I trusted her or not. That was the thing, I didn't know her. And right now, not knowing someone was the same thing as not trusting them in my world. I'd already let myself trust Natty, and look where that had gotten me. I couldn't afford to blindly trust a total stranger.

Besides, would I want to be kept alive if it meant being trapped in that thing indefinitely?

I looked down at my own hand, remembering the way Adam had responded when I'd touched the glass. It occurred to me how similar he and I were. "If he can't survive on our planet—outside the tube—then why can we?" She knew the others were Returned, but I sort of assumed she knew Tyler and I weren't like the rest of them, especially since Adam had only responded to the two of us. "I mean, if they used their DNA to . . . *replace me*, then why aren't I dying? If anything, what they did made me stronger. Healthier. Right?"

She looked around at us, then specifically at Tyler and me, and I realized she definitely knew our secret. "I wish I had an answer. Maybe it's because your original bodies—the ones they duplicated—were human, and accustomed to this environment. Maybe they did something *different* to alter you, so you could survive here." She shrugged. "Or maybe the crash was just too much for him to recover from completely. I wish I had a better answer for you."

Just another nonexplanation to add to the growing list of complications that made up my life.

Dr. Clarke shifted her gaze nervously as she singled Tyler

and me out from the others. "We also think whatever it is that makes you *different* from everyone else is what allows you to share a bond with Adam. A connection none of the others have. That's why we think he woke when the two of you were near him."

I shrugged one shoulder. "We sorta guessed that."

"Except . . ." She seemed to be weighing how much more to disclose to us, and then nodded to herself. "It wasn't only Adam that came to life. Something else happened, and we believe it's all connected—this new signal and the arrival of . . . whatever it is that's out there." I gave her a confused look and she added, "Maybe it's better if I show you."

We could have been standing in any freight elevator in any warehouse in the entire world, except the security code was longer than my social security number.

And when we descended, it felt like we were sinking to the Earth's core—that's how long the trip lasted. After several seconds, my ears began to clog from the pressure.

When the elevator finally came to a shuddering stop, the giant steel doors grated open with the kind of scrape that makes everyone cringe. But the goose bumps were quickly forgotten as we were bathed in a silvery halo of light from a roomful of computers. The enormous space appeared simultaneously space age and low-tech at the exact same time, with floor-to-ceiling industrial grade computer equipment cluttered with more wires and cables and dials than I'd ever seen in one place.

There were several individual terminals stationed throughout the space as well, these ones looking nothing less than the latest and greatest—gleaming chrome, with crystal clear plasma monitors bigger than most televisions.

There were far fewer people down here, but even so, whatever they thought they were tracking had caused enough panic that every eye in the room shot to us the second the elevator doors parted. Dr. Clarke gave a subtle *it's okay* nod and everyone went back to what they were doing. But the air remained brittle with tension.

At the other end of the chamber, there was a giant window, but the view was blocked by some sort of metal panel.

"I give up," I said as quietly as I could, trying not to draw any more attention than we already had. "What is this place?"

As the doors behind us closed, another woman started toward us. There was something unusual about the way she walked, but it took until she'd crossed the entire room for me to realize she had an almost, but not entirely, imperceptible limp.

She was young, though. Much closer to our age than to Dr. Clarke's. Her hair was almost the exact copper color of Simon's eyes, minus the gold flecks, and it hung in soft waves around her shoulders. Even with the limp, she gave off a cheerleader sort of vibe, reminding me of the girls who'd stood outside the doors to greet the incoming freshmen on our first day of high school, passing out maps of the hallways and pointing us in the direction of orientation. Super friendly. Super peppy.

"This is Dr. Atkins," Dr. Clarke introduced her. "I'll let her explain. This undertaking is her baby."

"Welcome," Dr. Atkins gushed, giving us a perky wave that did nothing to chip away at that cheerleader impression. "And, please, call me Molly." She stepped up to one of the individual computer consoles. "This . . ." She laid her hand flat on the panel, which lit up, outlining her fingers and palm with a green glow. When it was finished, the entire display panel surged to life.

"Handprint identification . . . ," Jett breathed. "Sweet!"

Once the computer was powered up, she entered a string of commands and then behind the large glass window I'd noticed on the other side of the room, the metal screen began to lift.

"This," she repeated, drawing our attention to whatever was beyond the glass, "is The Eden Project."

From our vantage point, we were overlooking something that seemed vaguely like an airplane hangar, but only in the way the M'alue floating in the giant test tube looked vaguely like a human.

Past my shoulder, I heard Jett. "I always thought The Eden Project was just rumor. I never believed it really existed."

"Oh, it exists all right." Molly moved in front of the thick pane of glass and gazed down in admiration.

"So what exactly are we looking at?" I asked uncertainly.

"Yeah, I don't get it. Why all the secrets?" Tyler shrugged, moving to stand right beside me. The back of his hand brushed across mine, and I knew it wasn't an accident. My pulse thrummed in my throat, and even while we stood there in a room full of people, I felt my cheeks get hot, and I forgot all about being mad at him.

The plane down in the hangar was impressive enough. Military. Black and wedge-shaped, making it hard to tell where the body ended and the wings began. There was a small, narrow window tinted so dark it was impossible to see inside.

It vaguely reminded me of the drone I'd blown up outside of Blackwater, but as far as I could tell, nothing about it warranted keeping it deep underground like this, or even giving it the badass top-secret name: The Eden Project.

From what I could see, it was just another cool-looking jet.

"I'm with them," Simon protested. "If you have something to show us, get to it already."

"What you're looking at is the first self-launching spacecraft of its kind." She nodded toward the drone-like plane. "A replica of the EVE—that's what we dubbed it, the M'alue's ship. Or at least the parts we were able to recover." She grinned. "This is where science fiction becomes reality."

"As opposed to the thing where most of us are cloned, or at least partially cloned, from alien DNA?" Simon balked. "And really? Adam and Eve? You had to go there?"

But Molly just nodded. "Okay. Yes. The cloning is pretty

impressive. But think about it. Now, at least in theory, the M'alues are no longer the only ones capable of traveling outside the solar system."

I turned away from the glass, considering the implications. "If you have this, why not set Adam free? Why not let him go home?"

A heavy sigh escaped her lips. "Like I said, *in theory*. We've got all the parts right—we know that. We just haven't been able to get it airborne."

"And you're showing us this because . . . ?" Jett asked.

Dr. Clarke answered, "Like I explained upstairs, Adam wasn't the only thing to react to your arrival." She shot a meaningful look at Tyler. "The moment you arrived here at the ISA, that ship reacted as well." She looked to Molly then, who gave an almost imperceptible nod, acknowledging Dr. Clarke's statement. "That ship down there sent out some sort of signal of its own." When she looked back at me, she added, "Then, when you showed up, the exact same message went out again."

Simon locked eyes with Dr. Clarke. "When you say message, what sort of message was it?"

Molly went back to the monitor. "A map," Molly explained, taking over the explanation as she pulled up an image. "See for yourself."

What I saw made me take a step back. It filled the screen.

But it was Jett who confessed what I already knew—that the map on the monitor was the exact one Tyler had drawn the night in the desert. Jett pulled out his cell phone and held it up so everyone could see. "Identical," he said as if everyone hadn't noticed.

"How can *a ship* send out a message?" Tyler asked. "And how did that same image end up in my head?"

Dr. Clarke raised her brows. "We don't know what triggered the ship's comm system. Kind of odd that it coincided with your arrival though, don't you think?" Her voice was bone dry.

"You don't think we're involved, do you? At least not intentionally." I couldn't believe they thought we were somehow in league with the M'alue. That we'd do anything to draw them here on purpose.

I thought about how my dad had worried the aliens had sent those hikers after me, and how Chuck had tried to relay some sort of message to me right before blowing his brains out.

"No. We're buried so far underground, the only signals that can get in or out have to be relayed through our satellites. When you two arrived, the EVE piggybacked onto one of those signals to get its message out," Dr. Clarke agreed. "Whoever the signal was meant for was basically being told how to find us. How to find you." She looked at Tyler, then me. "Any idea why that might be?"

I shook my head. Then something else occurred to me. "The other signal, the one you intercepted. You said you couldn't decipher it. Can we hear it?"

Mutely, she stared at me. I could see her considering it. I wasn't sure she'd agree, but then, as if it was never even an issue, almost like *What difference would it make*, she took Molly's place at the computer. She entered a series of commands—more security codes, passwords, that kind of thing—and then she stood back.

After a moment, static filled the air.

Garbled white noise.

Except it wasn't white noise at all. It was a message . . .

The message.

"Oh crap," Tyler whispered.

"What?" Simon asked from the other side of me. "What is it?"

My stomach dropped. "You can't hear it?" I asked, suddenly realizing Tyler and I were the only ones who understood it.

"I don't get it. It's just static, right?" Jett said, looking at me and then Tyler.

I looked at Tyler too. My throat felt dry when I explained, "They said, 'The Returned must die.'"

CHAPTER FIFTEEN

WHAT THE HECK WAS I THINKING?

This is a mistake. A huge-ginormous-major mistake.

Can a heart actually explode from beating too fast?

The ship was so much bigger up close. So much more intimidating.

How had I let them talk me into this? I was only one person . . . a kid really. I never even passed my driver's test.

There was too much at stake.

I turned around to tell them so, to tell Super Cheerleader Molly she had the wrong person, when a whirring sound came from in front of me. I nearly bolted from the sound alone, but held myself in check as I swung back toward the ship. Instead of telling Molly where she could shove her "test pilot" experiment I found myself face-to-face with an open hatch.

It definitely hadn't been like that before.

There was a small set of steps—not a ladder exactly, but not like stairs either—descending from the spaceship's bottom, as if somehow the aircraft itself had detected my approach and was inviting me on board. Like it *recognized* me.

This thing, this spaceship that had beamed the coordinates of our exact location into outer space was responding to my presence. I should be completely freaked out by that, so why wasn't I?

It was as if being here . . . this close to the machine had done something to me, similar to the way being close to Adam had. It was as if my brain had been rewired—that was the only way I could describe it. Like new synapses had formed and were firing, making me aware of things I'd never noticed before . . . smells were suddenly more intense, sounds clearer, colors more vibrant.

I was no longer overwhelmed by what I was about to do. I no longer believed this was too much for one person. It didn't matter that I had zero experience with things like flying UFOs. Instead my head was buzzing with thoughts about how totally-freaking-*effing* cool this was.

In my ear, Molly's voice reminded me I was wearing a headset. "It's never done that before."

The sensation that the spacecraft had *sensed* my presence intensified.

Without hesitating, I reached for the steps, and my hands closed around the small handrail as I stepped onto the bottom stair. I didn't have time to wonder if I was right to board it, because the moment my foot lifted off the ground, the entire stairway began to rise. My stomach lurched as I was boosted into the ship's belly, but in anticipation, like when you reach the peak of a roller coaster.

As I landed inside, I heard the hatch seal behind me. *You're here to stay*, that sound seemed to signify. *Ready or not*, as if I had no say in the matter.

"Ready," I whispered in response.

"You okay?" Molly asked into the headset, sounding confused.

I nodded mutely, then remembered she couldn't see me, so I answered her out loud, "I'm good."

"Good. Now, go ahead and take the seat," she said back to me. "See how it feels."

There was only one seat, so the *where* was a no-brainer. The cockpit was cramped, and I maneuvered into the seat like it was made from explosives, afraid to touch anything—any one of the buttons or gadgets. I didn't want to accidentally blast myself into outer space. Or worse, what if I hit a button that launched a nuclear strike against another country?

More likely, I'd send the entire ship crashing into one of the steel walls that surrounded us on all sides, killing myself and everyone else in sight.

Just to be sure, I kept my hands safely in my lap.

With so many levers and buttons and gauges and monitors the panel in front of me surpassed high tech. And what I'd thought from the outside was a window, turned out not to be a window at all. It was one enormous screen, and as soon as my weight settled into the chair, the display flashed to life.

I gasped.

From the other end of my earpiece, Molly's voice reached out to me. "Everything all right?"

"I . . . ," I faltered, momentarily spellbound by what spread out before me. What had begun as random start-up commands had now shifted to images, a rotating series of what looked like weather maps or maybe radar screens . . . all blips and rainbow blobs that swelled and shifted with intersecting lines and numbers, none of which meant anything to me. "I . . . I guess so."

"Do you have questions? What are you seeing? What's happening in there?" she fished.

I leaned forward, examining the joystick between my knees and tried to imagine how they possibly thought I'd have the first clue about flying this thing. "How could I not?" I admitted. "Starting with: What is it you think I'm supposed to do in here?"

There was silence, followed by crackling . . . a muffled noise, like she had her hand over the mic. When she came back, she said only, "We were hoping you might know."

"*Me?* You were hoping *I'd* know how to use this thing?"

I would have laughed, and I almost did, because the idea was so . . . out there. Did they really think they'd just . . . throw me in here, and I'd somehow-magically-*cross-their-fingers* figure it out? Was that their big plan? "You people are nuts," I accused, rolling my eyes.

They'd wasted my time, sending me down here. The joke was on them.

I put my hands on the grips at either side of my seat, planning to get the hell out of here before I seriously messed something up. But when I did . . . when I put my hands on those handles . . . something happened.

I wasn't sure it was real at first, the slight, barely unnoticeable shift. It was so very, very subtle.

Except somewhere, deep inside me, I knew the truth because my heart picked up speed, every muscle in my body went still, every synapse started igniting.

Things just got real.

I waited an eternity, then, when I trusted myself enough, when I could actually breathe again, I squeezed my fingers around the grips again . . . just the tiniest bit. Testing it.

This time when the ship moved, it was more than just noticeable, it was staggering. I wanted to be blown away by what I'd just done, because that's what I should be, that's what a normal girl would be, *blown freaking away*. It was the normal response, to be overwhelmed . . . frightened . . . horrified by the fact I'd just managed to move this thing.

"Kyra?" Molly's voice was demanding in my ear. "Kyra, what's happening? Is everything okay? Was that you?"

I couldn't answer because my mouth was stuck in a giant, stupid grin. That was normal, right?

The display in front of me had stopped showing the blobs that made it look like the Weather Channel, and a new series of images were rotating past in rapid succession. They were too fast for me to take in, except here's the weird thing: they weren't going too fast for me.

I understood each and every one of them.

This whole thing . . . all of it was getting more and more bizarre. But I stayed where I was . . . mesmerized.

There were strange patterns, of stars and landmarks with lines of longitude and latitude that crisscrossed them to create maps; similar to the one Tyler had drawn out in the desert. But now I somehow knew where all of these places were. I wasn't afraid or even shocked at how easily the information came to me.

Many of them were places I'd been before—Thom's camp at Silent Creek, Griffin's at Blackwater Ranch, the old Hanford site where Simon and his people had been hiding out when he'd first introduced me to them. There was even a map of the abandoned asylum in Wyoming where Natty and Eddie Ray had been holding me. There were other things in those images as well, not just maps, but information that shouldn't have made any sense at all, that I shouldn't have had the first clue how to comprehend, but that my mind somehow just . . . absorbed. I was a sponge, sucking in all the knowledge being thrown my way.

I was a computer, and this was my download.

By the time it was finished, I knew this ship inside and out. Its schematics were etched in my mind as if I'd engineered the thing myself. I knew which alloys had been used and where they'd been mined. I had a working knowledge of the components—of the spectrometers, nodules, shields, and trusses.

I knew exactly what I needed to do, just like Molly had hoped I would.

I knew how to fly this thing.

"Kyra . . . ," Molly's voice rasped. "Are you seeing this? Are you receiving these transmissions?"

It was the first time I realized that what I was seeing wasn't coming from Molly or the ISA . . . these charts and graphs and diagrams. Maybe, like everything else, that awareness should have freaked me out too, but it didn't. Whoever was out there transmitting signals wanted me to have this information.

"Hell yeah, I am," I answered as I settled back, gearing up for something remarkable. A once-in-a-lifetime experience.

And why not, wasn't that exactly what this was?

"What do you think it means—?" she started to ask, but I cut her off as I reached forward and gripped the joystick. When I did, a harness dropped over my shoulders and locked me in place.

Adrenaline rushed through me.

"Open the bay doors," I said into my mouthpiece.

"The bay . . . *what*? You can't . . . ," she sputtered,

and their voices buzzed and blurred, as whoever was on the other end conferenced about what I'd just commanded them to do.

I tuned them out. They could do like I said or straight up ignore me, but one way or another I was getting this thing outta here.

I concentrated, because that's what this required—I knew because of all the information I'd just absorbed. So I did, just like I had before when I'd moved things with my mind, only this time I wasn't angry or agitated or panicked, I was just . . . *focused.*

"Kyra, are you listening to me?" Molly was yelling into the headset now.

All around me the spaceship rumbled to life. It wasn't loud but I could feel it, its energy vibrating in every muscle and nerve fiber, every cell and every molecule of my body until we were one . . . me and this mind-blowing machine.

"I got this," I responded, infinitely calmer than she had sounded, which was somewhere in the range of: her head might explode. And then I repeated, "Open the bay doors."

Even though she'd never confirmed there actually were bay doors, she knew what I meant, and she knew I knew it. When the aircraft lifted again, it raised up so smoothly you would've thought I'd been flying this thing my entire life. It hovered evenly . . . perfectly beneath me.

I didn't wait for her to agree, I just went for it, and the spaceship did exactly what I wanted it to, gliding the way I meant it to, the way I told it to . . . *with my mind!* I didn't pretend it wasn't the coolest thing ever, because it one thousand percent was.

I was doing this. I had total control. This thing was responding to something inside me. I could think—*just think!*—a command and the spaceship did what I wanted it to.

Up, I'd thought, and it had risen, just the right amount, exactly as I'd imagined.

The area inside the hangar was massive, and the ship navigated smoothly, with room to spare. I couldn't see where I was going, not like in a car or truck, where you watched out the window. But I wasn't flying blind either. I knew from the screen exactly how far off the ground I was, and how much distance there was to the ceiling and to the walls on either side.

Ahead, there was a tunnel carved through the mountain, and even without being told it was the right way to go, that was where I headed.

With a simple: *Forward*. And then *Faster*.

I grinned again as the ship slipped inside the wide channel.

Toward the bay doors, I thought, and stifled the follow-up words: *The ones that are still closed*.

But I couldn't let myself care because that wasn't the point. That was their problem.

"Open them," I said again, this time out loud, more insistently.

"Kyra . . ." There was hesitation in Molly's voice.

"Do it," I demanded, forcing myself not to think about

slowing. I refused to give them the satisfaction. This was their baby . . . *Molly's baby*, this project. I was only the pilot. Hadn't Dr. Clarke said as much? If it crashed, odds were I'd heal.

The truth was, though, I didn't believe they'd let that happen.

On the screen I saw the end of the tunnel fast approaching, and realized I was coming toward them—the bay doors.

They were still sealed shut, and if she didn't open them soon, I'd find out just how resilient my body really was. The first flash of doubt filled me, but I didn't waver.

Faster, I thought again, this time clutching the handles, and the ship did as I commanded, plunging ahead.

The display in front of me showed that we were within one hundred kilometers and closing.

Seventy-five.

The gap was narrowing with each heartbeat.

Fifty.

Just when I thought they'd decided to dismiss my order, I saw the doors begin to part.

Too late, I thought. *They'll never open in time. Not all the way.*

Twenty-five . . .

The crash was inevitable, I was certain. I sucked in my breath and held it.

Just as the nose of the ship edged through and I waited for the wings to collide with the doors on either side, the entire ship flipped to the left, doing a ninety-degree rotation onto its side. The harness at my shoulders tightened as the frame of the craft skimmed through the way-too-narrow opening, and I jolted forward as the underside scraped along the door.

I let out an audible gasp as the ship leveled out again. Open skies stretched before me on the screen. We'd somehow not only cleared the bay doors, but the ISA and the mountain entirely.

"Kyra? Kyra, can you hear me?" It wasn't Molly now, but Dr. Clarke, insistent. I smiled, guessing she was angry too.

"I hear you," I answered, but only because even though the signal wasn't nearly as strong now, Dr. Clarke still intimidated me. But that didn't change the fact that I was flying a freaking spaceship . . . not exactly the kind of thing that happens every day.

"We need you to come back now . . ." I could hear her but she was definitely breaking up. Crackly.

I looked at the screen, and reveled in the weightless feel of the spacecraft beneath and around me. I'd come back . . . I mean, of course I'd come back. "Five minutes," I finally answered. "Just give me five more minutes." And then I tipped forward and did something I knew they wouldn't want me doing—I disabled the ship's tracking device.

She said something back to me, but I couldn't make it out; it was too static-y. And then there was only white noise. *Real* white noise.

I had no plan, no coordinates or destination in mind, so

I leaned back and thought only, *Go*. Plain and simple.

As if on a course of its own, the ship went, ascending higher and higher. My ears were congested, similar to the sensation when we'd plunged underground in the elevator, or the one time I'd flown across the country—to Florida—when my parents had taken me to Disney World when I was in the fourth grade. And like that time, I reached up to plug my nose so I could unblock them.

Then, all at once, before my fingers even reached my nose, there was an explosion of lights—flashes that blinked in and out and all around my periphery. For a moment I thought I was seeing fireflies, that's what my brain told me, how I processed them. But that wasn't what they were at all.

They were small bursts happening inside the ship, like miniature stars that formed and exploded and re-formed, all within a matter of milliseconds. All close enough that if I reached out, I might actually be able to touch them.

The air is too thin, I thought fleetingly. *I've gone too high. I'm not getting enough oxygen.*

But I was. Somehow I knew that what I was witnessing wasn't an optical illusion caused by an oxygen-deprived brain.

When the ship suddenly lurched forward, the shoulder harness locked in place. If I hadn't known better, I would have sworn my entire body had just been turned inside out. My organs exposed, my heart beating right there in the open, my lungs slippery and raw. Everything else, my skin and hair and eyeballs felt like they'd been turned inward, while the force of the journey thrust me so hard against the back of the chair I was immobile.

The whole thing lasted only moments . . . a breath . . . a heartbeat, maybe. And then the ship came to a sudden and complete stop, and everything went still and freakishly silent. My body, this body of mine went back to feeling . . . *normal.*

Even without looking at the monitor I could have guessed where I was: in outer space.

These stars were the stationary kind, unlike the ones I'd seen inside the cockpit. They didn't burst like angry fireworks in the margins of my vision.

But it was what appeared in front of me that got my attention—a giant glowing ball of some sort. The sun, I might have thought, except the shape wasn't uniform, and there were shades of green and gold and even flashes of red bursting throughout it.

A ship, I realized. This, I somehow knew, is where the signals have been coming from.

Maybe I should have been afraid . . . probably terrified. But afraid was the last thing I was. Even curiosity somehow escaped me.

"Go," I said, this time out loud. The ship obeyed, leading me directly into the glowing orb ahead of me.

SIMON

DR. CLARKE'S FACE HIT A SHADE SO FAR PAST RED IT qualified as another color. "Someone tell me what the hell just happened!" She spun around to glare at everyone in the control room, including us, like we were the ones who'd let Kyra slip through those bay doors in the first place.

But it confirmed what I'd suspected. What I saw, up on that screen . . . I hadn't imagined it. The blip we'd been watching, the one we'd all been focused on because it represented Kyra—her ship—it had just . . .

. . . *vanished.*

The guy manning the radar screen was the jumpiest of all.

You could tell he didn't want to answer. "We, um . . . we lost her, ma'am," he admitted at last.

Dr. Clarke's flinty gaze leveled on the poor guy. "Lost her? And how do you suppose that happened?"

His eyes shifted toward the elevator as if he was seriously contemplating making a break for it. He undid the top button of his shirt, his fingers shaking. "She . . . the entire ship . . . they just dropped off the radar."

"Send up a drone," she demanded without missing a beat. "I want the entire grid scanned for signs of that ship. If she crashed it, I want to know, and I want the wreckage recovered ASAP." She turned to Molly, her jaw set. "Tell me you tagged her before you sent her up?"

Molly nodded. "Of course."

Dr. Clarke granted Molly the most restrained smile. "Good. See if you can get a lock on it."

But they all seemed to be forgetting we were talking about Kyra here. "Tagged? What the hell did you do to her? You better not've hurt her." I wished I could back my threat up somehow. Here, I doubted it held any weight.

"It was nothing," Molly reasoned. "Harmless. Nothing she was even aware of. We had to be prepared. Just in case."

"You mean, in case she crashed?" Tyler railed, and at least he had the balls to sound hacked about it, because this whole mess was bullshit.

Dr. Clarke waved to someone at the door. "Get these kids out of here."

"No way!" Tyler insisted. "We're staying." And then, when

one of the guys tried to grab him, he shoved back. "Get your hands off me!"

Another one of the beefy security guards charged at me, and if I hadn't been so worked up I might've pointed out that my guy was built like a bull . . . because—*clearly*—they considered me the bigger threat. I ducked away. "We're not leaving 'til someone tells us what happened to Kyra. Where the hell is she?"

"If we knew we wouldn't be forced to track her, now would we?" Dr. Clarke enunciated, pressing her lips together. "But we *will* find her. We just need to focus. Now, please, just go upstairs and let us do our jobs. I promise, we'll tell you if there's news."

I glanced at Jett, who'd thrown his hands in the air the moment there was a hint things might get physical. *Thanks for nothing*, I told him with my glare.

Sorry, he shrugged in return.

Then Molly's voice interrupted our silent altercation. "I think I've got something." She pointed to the large monitor. "Yes! There! That's her." I saw what she meant, the tiny blip on the radar.

But she had to be mistaken. The place she was indicating was way, *way* too far away, and not just because it was nowhere near us—near the mountains, or even near California. It was nowhere near Earth.

She was implying Kyra was somewhere in space.

"Where is that?" I asked, hoping someone would tell me I'd completely misread her position.

Jett took several steps toward the screen, his hands still raised high above his head. And then he lowered one and pointed at something else. "The question is, what is *that*?"

An enormous oscillating globe had appeared on the screen—one that hadn't been there a moment before. It was like it had come out of nowhere. It pulsed and swelled, looking ominous next to the microscopic speck that was supposed to be Kyra's ship.

He glanced at me and Tyler, and then to Molly and Dr. Clarke and the others, to see if we were all catching this.

I swallowed, wondering what Kyra must be seeing, if that was really her up there. What the hell was she up against?

Just as Jett turned back to the image, just as we all turned back, the giant blob began to break apart. Or rather smaller dots began to erupt out from the larger one. It happened fast, in synchronized bursts. Like the larger thing was releasing hundreds or thousands of smaller ones in rapid-fire succession, until there was an army of them.

A fleet.

"Holy shit," Dr. Clarke breathed.

"What the hell?" I asked, even though I felt like I already knew what I was witnessing.

And before she could answer, the little dot that was supposed to be Kyra was swallowed up by the enormous mass in the center. And like that, we could no longer see her ship on the screen.

"It looks like they've arrived," Dr. Clarke said, shaking her head. "And they just captured Kyra."

CHAPTER SIXTEEN

THERE WAS . . .

Nothing.

Not blackness.

Not light.

Just this strange sense of timelessness, and . . .

Nothing.

CHAPTER SEVENTEEN

Days Remaining: Unknown

COMING BACK.

Again.

I was a million times more terrified than when I'd taken off just a half hour earlier. Everything had changed. I knew things now.

This time as I neared them, the bay doors were open, so at least I wasn't taking my life in my hands. Not just yet anyway.

By the time the ship touched down, there were men in biohazard suits already swarming it. It was definitely overkill for a joyride, but considering I'd told them I'd only be five minutes I was in no position to argue.

Their ship, their rules.

When I disembarked, I walked right into the middle of a plastic decontamination bubble they'd sealed around the steps. It was airtight, and made me wonder what exactly they were worried about.

From the outside of the bubble, a man instructed me to strip down to my underwear—which, *are you kidding me?* The plastic didn't make me invisible. But he was adamant, and he pointed at the jumpsuit he'd left for me—one that matched his own—to let me know he wasn't going anywhere until I put it on.

After realizing I had no choice, I held it up. "Seriously?" I double-checked my watch. "All this because I was gone for less than an hour?"

He didn't answer, just smiled politely while he waited.

"This is crazy," I muttered.

No response.

I stripped while he gave me the courtesy of pretending not to watch, and once I was changed, he said through the plastic, "Hold your breath."

Before I could ask why, the entire tent filled up with a yellow smog-like substance, and I did as he'd instructed, afraid I might choke on the stuff.

When Mr. Personality finally dubbed me cootie-free, I was released from the toxic shower and escorted to some sort of interview room with only a table and two chairs.

Proving worthy of the nickname I'd silently given him,

Mr. Personality told me, "Wait here," in his android-like voice.

"Yes, sir." I would have saluted, but I was worried even that pinch of sarcasm would blow his robot brain.

I was restless during the twenty minute or so wait—I had no way of knowing how long it was exactly, since along with my clothes, my watch had also been confiscated. I tried doing a jumpsuit makeover, rolling and unrolling the sleeves to see if there was any improvement one way or the other. I pulled the zipper all the way to my chin, and then dragged it partway down again, opting for a more casual look.

In the end though, a jumpsuit was a jumpsuit. Besides, there were more important things to worry about.

All I really wanted was to get out of there and back to my friends, but no one would say if or when that might be. So when Dr. Clarke and Molly finally appeared, I practically launched myself at them, knocking over the plastic chair I'd been perched on.

"What's happening?" I asked. "Where are Tyler, Simon, and Jett?" I'd expected to find them waiting for me when I came back.

Dr. Clarke wore a strange expression on her face, and if I didn't know any better, I'd swear she was onto me. Like she somehow knew what had happened up there.

But she couldn't. There was no way she knew the things I'd discovered, I reminded myself.

"Where were you?" she hissed. "What the hell happened?"

I kept my cool, sticking to my plan. "Um, I think the phrase you're trying to come up with is: you're welcome." I took a step back from her. I crossed my arms over my chest, my back rigid. "Not only did I fly your little spaceship, but I brought it back in one piece. Or was that *not* the point?" I challenged.

Dr. Clarke eyed me. "Is there something you want to say to us?"

She was probably waiting for some sort of explanation about the ship's tracking system. I didn't have to admit to shutting it down or anything. For all she knew it was an internal malfunction. How was I supposed to know why it had glitched?

But I could at least *try* to act like I felt bad over how long I'd been gone.

I let out a breath and wrung my hands in front of me. "Sorry, I didn't mean to be gone so long, I just . . . Where are my dad and the others?" I bit my lip. "I want to make sure they're okay. Can I see them?"

Dr. Clarke glanced at Molly, and I got the sense it was a nod. A *Go ahead. You do the talking.*

Molly took an entirely different approach. Her voice was more soothing. *We're friends, you and me*, her tone suggested. She was definitely Good Cop. "Sure. I get it. They're fine. We took your friends back upstairs so they could wait with the others . . ." She glanced at Dr. Clarke. "Until you came back."

"Look, I know I said five minutes, but couldn't they

have just waited a little longer?"

The two exchanged a look I couldn't decipher, and Dr. Clarke's brows raised. "We'll need to debrief you," she stated, all Bad Cop. "We need to go over your timeline, every second of your mission."

My mission, is that what they were calling this? Was that typical, to do a debriefing, just routine stuff?

Good Cop put her arm around my shoulder and led me toward the door. "Come on. We can do that later. For now, let's get you upstairs so you can see for yourself that everything's A-OK. Then when you're feeling better we can do that debrief. Sound good?"

Dr. Clarke wasn't thrilled by Molly's suggestion, but I, for one, was happy to see the door shut behind us. I was in no hurry to be interrogated by Dr. Clarke.

I was already assembling a list. A people-not-to-trust list. After my brief encounter back there, Dr. Clarke was at the very top.

I wondered how much she knew about all this. How deep her involvement ran. How dirty her hands had gotten.

The sooner we got the hell outta here, the better.

But things were never that simple.

I'd learned too much, and we were past the point of just making a run for it and hoping for the best.

The Interstellar Space Agency was nothing they claimed to be—the peace-seeking scientists who worked selflessly to establish interplanetary contact.

We'd been duped.

From here on out, I had to proceed carefully . . . calculate every word that came out of my mouth, watch every step I made. If I didn't, not only would my dad and my friends pay the price . . . but possibly all of mankind.

Blondie had been wrong. It wasn't just a probability they were on their way. They were already here.

And our entire planet, along with every*one* and every-*thing* on it, was at stake.

The Earth.

But there was a way I could stop it. It was a huge burden, and I had no intention of taking that burden lightly.

"Sorry about all that . . . back there," Molly said when we reached the door to where we'd been staying . . . where my dad and the others were assembled now. "Dr. Clarke's not a bad person, just a little *intense*." She shrugged.

She was intense all right.

I waited while Molly entered the code on the keypad, and I wondered when that had been instituted. "What's with the security? I thought we were free to come and go. Are we being kept prisoner now?"

She paused, right before hitting Enter. "This is for your own good." Then she pressed the last button.

I averted my gaze because none of this—the secrets, the security, the debriefings—were for our good. Whether she admitted it or not, I knew the truth. I bit my tongue—it was the smart thing to do, to just shut up. But seriously?

The door clicked open and for a moment I stopped

thinking about Molly and Dr. Clarke, and about whether we were really safe or not. The people I loved, the people I knew I could trust, were all around me.

Simon only said, "*Where the hell . . .*" before Jett added, "*. . . they made us leave . . . locked us in . . .*" and hugged me hard.

It was reassuring to be surrounded by them, even Willow, who wrapped her arms around me. It was kind of like being mauled by a bear and my instinct was to go limp so she'd stop pawing me.

Simon shoved Willow aside, then clung to me in a way that made me feel like he'd just won some huge trophy—something to be treasured, but also something to gloat over.

Tyler came next, and while he was more restrained than Simon, there was something gentle in his touch, something sweet that made me feel cherished. "I have so many things to say to you." He said it so silently it was more like listening to a memory . . . a whisper from the past. The low timbre of his voice, and the feel of him against me, made me wish it were just the two of us . . . alone together, for a very long time.

Griffin sat hunched over a table in the corner, scribbling furiously on a scrap of paper as she poured every ounce of concentration she could muster into whatever she was writing or drawing. Her pen stilled only once, and that was when Tyler reached for me. From where I stood, I couldn't tell if she was concentrating to keep her distance from her dad, or to stay away from me.

"I was worried sick," *my* dad breathed into my hair when he finally got his turn, and suddenly I was seven and hadn't heard him when he'd called me in for dinner. "When they brought the boys back, no one would tell us when you would return. Jesus, Kyr, I don't know how much more my old heart can take."

I wanted to tell them everything, right then and there, but Molly hovered too, watching our every move, hanging on our every word. "Your heart's fine and you know it." I shoved him away playfully, and then glared at Tyler and Simon. "Why didn't you tell him?"

Simon cocked his head to the side. "It's not like you took a quick detour into outer space." He laughed, shrugging it off.

But I frowned at him again. At them. "You heard me when I said five minutes. I mean, yeah, I didn't realize I was in for the full decontamination treatment when I came back. But it didn't take *that* much longer than I'd said."

Simon looked at Tyler, and then glanced warily at Molly, and I couldn't help noticing the way her brow puckered.

"What?" I insisted, feeling out of the loop all over again.

"Kyra, how long do you think you were gone?" Tyler asked.

"I don't know . . ." My eyes shifted to the clock on the wall and I did the math in my head. It had been about 2:45, last I'd checked, right before I'd boarded the spaceship. Now it was right at 4:37. "Even with decontamination, it's only been a couple hours . . ."

But I stopped talking. From the reactions on their faces, I already knew I'd figured wrong. Like . . . *way* wrong.

My heart thumped once, *really* hard. And then about a thousand times more. "Not even close . . . ?" It came out as a question, but I already had my answer. Before anyone could respond, I managed a tight, "How long?"

Tyler grimaced. "Since yesterday." He took a step closer, his forehead creasing. "You really didn't know? No one told you?"

I shook my head because that couldn't be right. "I was only gone"—I looked to where Molly's eyes were fastened to me, and I amended what I almost said—"a few minutes. I only flew that thing a few minutes . . . maybe half an hour."

This time it was Simon who was shaking his head. "No. We waited for you to come back." Still shaking his head, more slowly now. "You fell off the radar, for like, thirty seconds. Then, when they turned your tracking device on . . . they saw you . . ."

"Tracking device?" So even after I'd turned off the ship's radar, they'd still been able to see me?

Molly waved it off. "It was harmless. A fail-safe in case anything happened. We put it in your headset."

My stomach sank. How was I going to explain this—where I'd been and who I'd been with, especially since now I realized I had no idea how long I'd even been gone?

"We saw you up on that screen . . . in space," Jett finished, and I wondered how much more they knew. "Then Dr. Clarke said they took you."

"*They?*" I asked numbly.

Simon looked to Molly. "She and Dr. Clarke wouldn't let us stay. Said they'd keep us posted," he added bitterly. "That was last night. We've been locked in here ever since."

Tyler stood in front of me. "Where were you all this time? Do you remember what happened out there? Anything?"

An entire day . . .

Had I really been up there that long? I searched my memory for the missing piece of time, trying to fill it in with tangible things that made sense—sounds, tastes, colors, anything to plug the gaps.

But they weren't there.

There was just a missing chunk where the time should be.

Except that wasn't exactly right, because in its place there were new things. Information. Crucial facts the ISA had been withholding. Things they all needed to know.

The missing time was worth the trade.

I hesitated for only a second, and then went for it, clinging to the lie my friends had just offered me. I tried to imagine just how I should behave—I mean, what was the protocol for amnesia?

And then told myself I had this . . . I'd done this before.

"I don't . . ." I let myself grieve for the parts of my life I was already missing . . . not just in the past twenty-four hours, but those days Natty and Eddie Ray had taken away from me.

And the years I'd lost . . . those five long years.

Tears burned my eyes, and instead of being ashamed, I let them come. "I can't remember any of it." I didn't have to lie.

Molly watched me for only a second longer, while my dad held me and patted my back. Tyler and Simon and everyone else huddled around me, doing their best to comfort me. To assure me I was safe now.

It was laughable—safe. That was the last thing we were, yet somehow I kept up the façade.

At least until Molly decided there was nothing to be gained from eavesdropping on our reunion and she sneaked out, letting the door lock in place behind her.

"All right, young lady," my dad reprimanded as he set me away from him. He tilted his chin down and crossed his arms as he zeroed in on me. "Mind explaining what all that was about?"

I turned to Jett, and then moved my eyes knowingly around the room as I lowered my voice. "Is this place secure? Can we talk?" I raised my eyebrows, to make sure he understood exactly what I was implying.

I knew Jett well enough to guess he'd already done a security sweep, checking for bugs—cameras and listening devices. Anything they could use to spy on us.

"Secure enough," he answered uncertainly. "From what I can tell there are cameras in most corridors, but only one on this level—out by the elevator."

Jett's assurance was good enough for me.

Jett looked from me to my dad. "Um, does someone wanna clue me in?"

"Yeah, I think I might'a missed something," Willow added, glancing around at Simon and then Griffin.

My dad shook his head. "You didn't miss anything. In fact, you were front and center. Meryl Streep here just put on the performance of a lifetime." He slow clapped theatrically as if they were all part of my audience. "If I wasn't so afraid you might use your skills against me one day, I'd be impressed. Now spill. And don't leave anything out."

"Fine," I said, wiping my crocodile tears and sniffing in a less dramatic way. "It wasn't like I didn't plan on telling you anyway. I just couldn't risk letting Molly"—I nodded toward the closed door—"in on what we're up to."

Griffin got up from her table and joined us, keeping as far from her dad as possible. "So we *are* up to something?" she asked, more interested now than she had been before.

My temporary bout of amnesia magically forgotten, I nodded. "We are . . . or at least we will be. And we don't have a lot of time." I winked at my dad. "So here's the deal. I wasn't totally faking it; I honestly *don't* remember everything about where I was that whole time. There's a serious blank spot for me. But what I do know, is this place is definitely not on the up-and-up. What do you know about them?" I glanced at Agent Truman, who ignored Griffin's cold shoulder routine. "If you thought there might be a war coming, why'd you decide to bring us here? Why not try to mobilize your own people? Call up the Daylighters instead?"

"Because I know my guys. War isn't exactly something our government shies away from, even if it's unwinnable. And they'd never consider you and me allies. First thing they would've done is round up everyone with a hint of alien DNA and held us hostage, or used us as leverage. If you've read your history books, you saw what happened during World War Two . . . the internment camps. The Japs didn't fare so well on US soil." He scowled, looking more human than I'd seen since I met him. "From what I knew of the ISA, these guys're hippie scientists mostly. Do-gooders who want to hug it out with ET. At least that's how we've always pegged them."

"We, meaning the NSA?"

"We, meaning everyone, far as I know. I've never heard otherwise. In government circles they're considered well funded but harmless. I met Dr. Clarke years ago at a conference, when she was giving a talk on Jerry Ehman." When I just stared at him blankly he clarified, "The guy from SETI who intercepted what was thought to be the very first deep space radio signal." He chuckled. "'Course we all knew it was bullshit. We'd been communicating with the little green bastards for years, but at the time Ehman's little message went public it was big news. Ask your dad. He can tell you." He glanced at my dad. "Ben? Wanna share how you know Clarke?"

I stared at my dad. "What's he saying? You knew her. Like before we got here?"

My dad shifted on his feet, suddenly uncomfortable. "I . . ." He cleared his throat and ran his hand through his hair, something he'd already done several times. "Aw, hell." He sighed irritably.

"Maybe you two'd like a minute alone?" Agent Truman goaded my dad.

Pulling a tight smile at the agent, my dad reached for my arm.

When we were as alone as we could get inside the cramped four walls, he cleared his throat. "He's right. Much as I hate to admit it, I need to talk to you, and what I need to say is better left between us."

I hated the way my dad was stretching this out, avoiding eye contact. The way he kept rubbing the thick bristles on his jaw, because I knew it was a nervous habit, and him doing that was making me nervous too.

"Dad. Just say it."

"Kyra," he started. "I should've told you this a long time ago."

I nodded, but the sour taste in the back of my mouth warned me I wouldn't like this, and I considered faking another crying jag just to make him stop . . . before he said something he couldn't take back.

But he was already in it; the words were already out there: "It was my fault you were taken in the first place."

And once you said something like that, there was definitely no going back.

"You . . . *what*?" I fumbled. "Your fault? What does that

even mean? That's ridiculous. It was *no one's* fault. I was in the wrong place, at the wrong time. It was dumb luck. That's all."

But he was shaking his head, and telling me, "No. No, Kyr, you got it all wrong." He reached up and scratched his beard again. "It should have been me. You should never have been taken at all."

I raised my hand, and my voice, to shut him up. "Stop it. Stop right now. I get that you feel guilty, and it must suck to have your daughter carried away by aliens, but all this bad heart crap and trying to take the blame is just . . . We're wasting time." I whirled to go, but my dad grabbed me.

He was stern in a way he'd never been before. "Goddammit, Kyra, I'm not messing around here. Now stop being such a baby, and listen to me, will ya?"

This time I didn't have to force thoughts of stolen memories to make myself cry. I blinked hard, and now I was the one avoiding eye contact. He gave me a curt nod and let go of me. "Good. Okay then." He started talking, and I kept my eyes glued to his feet. But I listened hard. "Remember when you were little and you used to ask if you could go to the office with me? When they'd have Take Our Daughters to Work Day, and your friends would tag along with their folks? You always asked, and I always made excuses—meetings, appointments. Hell, three years in a row I pretended to have the flu just to get out of it." Something heavy settled in my gut.

"The thing was, I couldn't. Bring you, that is. You knew

I worked with computers, but what you didn't know was that I worked for the ISA."

My eyes shot up to his.

"It's true," he admitted. "I gave them almost twenty years. Most'a my adult life. They recruited me right out of college, and I worked out of their Woodinville facilities. Nothing near as intense as this . . ." He spread his arms to indicate this place, and then he dropped them, shrugging halfheartedly. "But definitely not small potatoes either. My security clearance was pretty limited, but I knew they had other operations all over the country." He chuckled ruefully. "Hell, all over the globe."

I felt blindsided. How was I supposed to respond? All this time my dad had been working with the ISA and he hadn't said a single word. I felt like I was talking to a stranger. Suddenly I had to wonder where he fell on my scale of who I could trust.

But he just kept talking. "I was there," he said, his voice like a growl. "The night the ship crashed—the EVE, they called it. It happened right outside Devil's Hole. They tell you that part?"

I shook my head, too dazed to manage anything else.

Simon had told me once that Devil's Hole was a hotbed of alien activity. I thought when he'd said that, he meant abductions and sightings. I hadn't realized that included UFO crashes too.

"I wasn't actually at the crash site, mind you. That was reserved for top-level clearance personnel only. I wasn't even part of the recovery team. But the body—that M'alue—was transported across the mountains, to where we were in Woodinville, and I happened to be in the facility when it arrived." His voice drifted as he closed his eyes, remembering. "I saw it, all gray and broken." When he looked at me again, his eyes were red. "I had no way of knowing how much trouble that thing would cause, but looking back, we probably shoulda let it die. We damn sure shouldn't have kept it . . . not locked inside that capsule." He covered his mouth to stop from choking on his sob. "Jesus, Kyr, I'm so sorry."

"So why did you then?" I asked.

He let out a long, slow, shaky breath before trying again. "When they realized it was healing . . . that it was going to live, someone—I don't know who, but some asshole—decided we should try to communicate with it. To break barriers." He ran his hand through his hair. "No clue who thought that was a good idea. But that's where I came in." He started pacing, his voice no longer low, and I knew the others could hear him too. Everyone was watching us. Listening. "They put me in charge of writing a code—a translating program." He shrugged. "Turns out it wasn't all that complicated, at least to transcribe some of the stuff we recovered from the crash site. It was rudimentary, and like I said, definitely not perfect, but we made progress. That's how we knew what it . . . what *he* was . . . that they called themselves the M'alue." He scrubbed his face with the palm of his hand. "But we never quite got the verbal part right.

I tried. Worked on it for months. Sat outside his tube and tried to communicate with him, and I thought I was making progress—a couple of times I swear he tried to respond to the messages I was transmitting. He would open his mouth and make this"—his gaze drifted as he remembered it—"this sound at me." His eyes met mine. "Like static." Like the hikers, I could practically hear his thoughts. "But I never understood. The program never deciphered it."

I still wasn't sure what all this had to do with me.

"I realized then just how much he was suffering," my dad went on. "I tried to tell my boss, but he refused to listen. So I went to his boss. No matter who I told, no one wanted to hear it." He just kept rubbing his chin, his jaw, his cheek. "But it was preying on my mind."

He dropped his hands and shook his head. "Around that time, the first of our people vanished. At first, no one thought anything of it. The ISA is a big organization, people come and go all the time."

"Then someone came back with a strange story about being whisked away in a strange flash of light, and waking up with no memory of where she'd been. When a second person returned and had an almost identical story, we started to take them seriously. Both were gone almost two days on the dot." He exhaled. "But it wasn't until the blood work came back and we realized they truly were . . . altered . . . that the higher-ups took notice."

"They were Returned," I said, filling in the blank.

He nodded, less comfortable now. "I was working late

one night, when we received a broadcast over a frequency we didn't even use anymore. At first, the guys on duty almost wrote it off as nothing more than a bunch of white noise. But they asked me to take a listen. When I heard it, I realized what I was hearing—it was that same static-y sound I'd heard coming from Adam. Of course, I followed protocol and reported it, and the person who responded was Dr. Clarke."

My eyes leaped to his. "So that's how you knew her? The two of you worked together?"

He glanced over to where the others were clearly eavesdropping. "We weren't friends or anything, but she listened to the message."

I held my breath. "And your code, was it able to translate the message?"

My dad shook his head. "No, but I think they were using my own code against us. I think they were picking up our transmissions to track our location and that's how they'd been able to figure out it was us holding their M'alue."

I frowned, letting all this sink in. "And even then, you never thought you should just set him free?"

"It wasn't up to me. And then it was kids who started to vanish. The first was the son of a man named Alexander Luddy. Luddy was the ISA's head of operations. His boy's disappearance caused a huge uproar, and Luddy demanded we surrender the M'alue. But by then it was too late. Experiments had begun. Ugly experiments, and they'd done way more damage than good. The ISA was afraid that sending him back would only make things worse. The kid was eventually returned, forty-eight hours later and halfway across the country."

The notion that the ISA had done experiments on Adam—ugly experiments, my dad had said—made me ill.

"After that, Dr. Clarke's own son was taken. That was when the M'alue was moved. I never heard where they took him, I only cared he was gone. I didn't want anything to do with him . . . or with the project. I thought that was the end of it." He scratched his jaw.

"Then, another girl went missing, a thirteen-year-old honor student from Arlington, not too far from us. I worked with her dad—he was an IT guy, and I realized: we'd been tapped. This thing, it was never gonna be over, not as long as the ISA had that monster in custody. All I knew was, I couldn't let anything happen to you, so I decided I'd never let you leave my sight.

"I started following you . . . everywhere you went. I started calling in sick so I could sit outside your school; I watched your practices from the parking lot; I stayed up all night just to make sure there was no way you'd be taken.

"The night you were taken, the whole reason I didn't let you ride with your team after the game was because I couldn't take the chance . . ." His voice broke. "I couldn't risk taking my eyes off you, not for a second."

His entire face crumpled. "And then it happened anyway. Despite all my planning and watching. Despite the sleepless nights and the stakeouts . . . they took you anyway.

But I told myself it was okay because you'd come back . . . you were supposed to come back. Two days, that's what it was for everyone else . . . less than two days."

His face went slack, like all the life had been drained from him. "Not you though. *You* didn't return. I lost my job after that, but I would have quit anyway. I hated the ISA. I hated everything they stood for. This was their fault—my baby being stolen. No one believed me, not your mom, not our friends, and definitely not the police. I had no recourse."

He fell to his knees, sobbing. "I wished it had been me. They should have taken me."

CHAPTER EIGHTEEN

I WANTED TO ABSOLVE MY DAD. SAY SOMETHING comforting. Be one of those good daughters who said nice things and could forgive easily. Forget.

Maybe that was Old Kyra.

New Kyra needed time. Maybe Tyler and I had more in common than either of us realized.

I had no idea how I was supposed to feel. I was numb. Shell-shocked maybe, if that was a real thing.

All this time . . . all those years lost . . . could they really be his fault? Maybe not directly, but he'd known me being taken was a possibility. He'd worked for those responsible.

I thought I'd learned everything when the M'alue had downloaded all that information into me, but apparently even that was one-sided. They either didn't know that my dad had worked for the ISA, or they didn't consider it relevant.

But I did.

That was the other thing, the M'alue weren't really the M'alue at all. They called themselves the Maanjaulfgaa.

The name was more a sensation than even a word. A shiver that started with a hum and ended with a vibration. In my head that made perfect sense, but my mouth couldn't wrap itself around it. So, until there was a better option, Dr. Clarke and my dad were right, M'alue was close enough.

The information the M'alue had given me was enough to fill my brain, my dad's brain, and everyone's in this entire room. It was probably enough to fill every computer in the ISA.

Tyler had been right though. It was no accident we'd come here. The M'alue had been using us, leading us, homing in on us and sending messages meant only for us. They wanted us to be here. But not to hurt us. They weren't the ones who couldn't be trusted.

I now knew the full history of the First Contact Meetings, including who was really there, where they met, and the transcripts of each and every conversation they'd had.

I even knew the exact coordinates of the M'alue's home planet, which was so far from Earth, and so outside the realm of human comprehension, that even if I tried to disclose it, I'd have to hand draw star chart after star chart just to get close.

I had the names, dates, and locations of every abductee who had ever been taken, and the information of everyone who was ever returned, which was a far smaller number.

I knew who'd died and who they sent back.

I would've been angry if I hadn't also been given a glimpse at the M'alue and their dying population . . . not hundreds or thousands, but millions of them. As far as they were concerned, we'd been their last hope. Not because they'd believed we held the cure, but because by the time they'd located us, they'd run out of resources to keep searching for other options.

Fortunately for them, it had been us. We *had* been the answer they were seeking. It had taken them decades, and several failed attempts, but ultimately, through their experiments on humans, they'd managed to perfect and extract the one microscopic chromosome they'd needed to save almost an entire population.

Was it worth it? The M'alue believed it was, and who was I to decide whether their entire planet . . . their entire species should have gone extinct without what we—the human race—had to offer.

If only they would have gone about it a different way.

If only the ISA hadn't captured and held Adam.

"Right now we have bigger problems," I told my dad. "I know the real meaning of the message." Suddenly no one was pretending not to listen, and it wasn't just my dad and me having a private conversation. "We got it wrong," I told the others. "It was a warning, but not in the way we thought it was. The meaning . . . the interpretation . . ." I shook my head, and looked at everyone but my dad. I couldn't do it, make things right with him yet. "It wasn't right. And we didn't have the entire message. It wasn't 'The Returned must die,' it was 'The Returned must end.' They were offering us a bargain. An exchange." I hoped I was making sense because I was talking so fast, wanting to make them understand. We didn't have a ton of time. "They were offering to end all this. To stop taking and returning humans if Adam is released."

Tyler came toward me. "So let's do it. Let's tell Dr. Clarke what we know."

I lifted my chin to meet his eyes. "The ISA already knows. They got the full message and rejected them. They're never letting Adam go."

"How can you be so sure?" Jett asked.

"Because something happened when I boarded that spaceship up there."

Jett looked confused. "So . . . wait. Are you saying you weren't taken by force? Because that's what it looked like . . . on the radar screen. That that ship of theirs, or whatever it was, just *engulfed* you."

I shook my head. "They're not hostile. At least, that's not their intention. I can't explain it, but somehow I sensed they were *inviting* me on board. Maybe not in so many words . . . at least not in a way you or I would understand . . ." I chewed my lip trying to think of a way to make it clear. "And they never actually *spoke* to me, but I . . . *knew* what they wanted." I shook my head. "Seriously, I get how crazy this sounds, and I wish I could make it more clear, but the truth is, I don't remember *how* it happened. I honestly thought I was up there for less than an hour." I tried to laugh it off, because that was starting to feel like the story of my life—gaping memory lapses—but the laugh caught on a lump in my throat. I swallowed, trying again. "All I know is we're running out of time."

Simon drew me back to the issue at hand. "When you say 'running out of time' . . . time for what, Kyra?"

I pushed my shoulders back, determined to find a way to make this clear. "We're in trouble. And not just us," I explained, looking around at all of them, even my dad. His eyes were bloodshot, but he was paying attention. "*Everyone* . . . like the entire planet."

Willow eyed me. "You sure you didn't bang your head on something? You said you don't remember all of what happened up there, maybe you got a concussion and you hallucinated the whole thing."

I glanced at Jett. "You saw the radar. Did that look like a hallucination?"

Hanging back 'til this point, Thom spoke up. "If they're not hostile, then what makes you think we're in danger? Did *they* tell you that?"

I started to shake my head and then stopped myself. "Like I said, not in so many words. My memory was blank, but when I snapped out of . . . whatever happened to me . . . I just *understood* things. Like they transferred information straight into my brain."

Griffin wrinkled her nose skeptically. "Like what?"

"Like this." I lifted my hand and drew their attention to the table Griffin had been sitting at a minute ago. I felt the familiar tingle tugging the skin at the back of my neck, only this time I didn't have to concentrate, I just took a breath and . . .

The pen she'd been using was suddenly hovering six inches above the tabletop.

Willow's mouth fell open as she gaped at me. I flashed her a knowing grin and then flicked my fingers at the pen and it shot toward me. I caught it in my fist, and inhaled deeply.

There'd been a part of me that had worried Willow might be right—that I'd suffered some sort of space fever.

When I turned and caught Simon staring at me, I raised my eyebrows. "And I'm barely concentrating. Like I said, I can't explain it. I just knew stuff. And not just how to move objects; other things too. They taught me how to tap into electrical currents." I was more nervous now. At least the thing with the pen was something I'd tried before, something I'd only been perfecting. The electrical thing was all new to me, and if I blew it . . .

I squeezed both hands into fists, closing my eyes as I concentrated on what I wanted to have happen.

Lights out, I thought. And then, desperate to prove I

wasn't delusional, I added, *Please, for the love of God, get this right . . .*

Even though my eyes were shut, I knew the moment the room went dark because I heard the collective gasp. When I opened them again, eight heads shot my way, and I knew they were all seeing my eyes, and only my eyes.

"Whoa," Jett admired.

"That was . . . *wow* . . ." Tyler added.

"I know," I admitted, with almost audible relief. And just to test things out, I popped my fingers wide, feeling like a tacky, second-rate magician when I did.

Still, the lights came back on at once.

There were several light-adjusting blinks before I announced, "See? Not a head injury."

But there was one thing I needed to make very clear, something we all needed to take seriously. I spoke mainly to Tyler, Simon, and Jett since they'd been there. "You know how Dr. Clarke told us the ISA replicated the EVE? What she didn't mention was that they didn't build just one ship. They have an entire fleet of them. I don't even think the M'alue I met were aware of what the ISA was up to." My eyes fell on Tyler. "At least not until you and I arrived."

"You?" my dad interrupted. "How does your being here make a difference?"

"All I know for sure is that we were what the ISA has been missing. Now that they have us, they're one step closer to getting their fleet airborne."

Griffin glanced from Tyler to me, and then snatched her

pen out of my hand. "That . . . *trick* you just did there might be impressive, but there's no way they can expect the two of you to pilot an entire fleet."

"Not pilot," I explained. "*Power up.* Tyler and I . . . we're some sort of power source for these things. Dr. Clarke told us that when we got here, the EVE sent out a signal, but she was wrong. The entire fleet sent out signals. All of the ships. That's how the M'alue knew the ships were here. But the thing is, they need *us*." I looked at Tyler. "The ship I piloted . . . the ISA made . . ." I frowned, trying to pinpoint the right word. "*Modifications* to its original design. They put in manual controls designed to be used by humans. If they can get us . . . or some other Replaced . . ." I thought of Alex Walker and the way I thought he might be like us before the NSA had snatched him away and experimented on him. "All they need is to power up their ships, and then someone else can step in and fly them."

"Why not use Adam? If all they need is a power source?" Jett asked.

I shook my head. "He's too sick. They've done"—bile flooded my throat—"too much to him. He's barely hanging in there."

"So if the ISA rejected their offer, why haven't the M'alue already blown this place sky-high?" It was Agent Truman asking, and I wasn't surprised that his first response was to resort to violence. I also wondered why he wasn't more concerned that this agency that claimed to be peaceful had secretly been amassing an army of spaceships.

"The M'alue don't want war. They want this to end peacefully. But if we can't make that happen . . ." I thought of the other part . . . the other images they'd shown me, of what they could do to us if we couldn't find the ISA's fleet in time. Images of the Earth, scorched and in ruin. Of a world decimated.

It was grim. Brutal.

Hopeless.

"Tyler and I weren't sent here by accident," I went on. "Those maps Tyler was drawing and the messages we heard—the M'alue were trying to contact us. To remind us of our mission, something we'd both apparently forgotten once we were returned."

"What mission?" Tyler asked.

"To find Adam and send him home." I was overwhelmed by how powerful my sense of allegiance was.

Except it wasn't to the M'alue as a whole. It was to Adam.

Even if it hadn't been coded into me to save him, knowing what he'd been through all these years—trapped in that tube and experimented on—I would have wanted to free him from this place . . . from these people who'd spent years torturing him.

I added, "And now that they've discovered the truth about the ships, we need to stop the ISA from getting them into space. If we can do that *and* free Adam, they've promised to retreat. There will be no war. And they will leave us alone." I searched the room, the eyes of the Returned—different from everyone else's because of what had been done to them—and thought of the things we could stop. "For good."

"As in, no more abductions?" Jett asked, scratching his arm.

I nodded, tears filling my eyes. "As in, never again. No more abductions."

I'm not sure Griffin was even aware she was standing by her dad now, her shoulders thrust back defiantly. "How do you know you can trust them? These ships might be the only line of defense we have against them. What if the M'alue are tricking us into destroying the only thing we can use to defend ourselves against an attack?"

"I can't," I answered truthfully, but I couldn't erase the images of what the M'alue had promised to do to us if we didn't destroy the ships. And I couldn't erase the way I felt about Dr. Clarke and the others here. "But we can't trust the ISA either. No good can come from what they've done—holding Adam hostage, stealing the M'alue technology, building spaceships. How could that *not* be seen as hostile? The M'alue believe we want war, and for all we know, that's where this is headed." I swallowed, my throat suddenly raw with the idea of going up against a race that was so much more advanced than we were. "We need to stop this from happening," I said resolutely.

"So, judging by the way you keep looking at the clock, you know we're on a countdown," Simon said. "How much time did they give us?"

I frowned. "Not enough. That's what I was trying to say. Time isn't the same for them. When I was out there, it really felt like only half an hour. I had no idea an entire day had passed, which means we have even less time than I thought we did." I glanced again at the clock on the wall. "As far as I can tell, we have until nine tonight," I said as calmly as I could.

Jett jerked. "Nine? But that's only four hours."

"Not much time," Willow chimed in.

I nodded. "When they attack, they plan to start with this facility."

There were several long seconds while I let everyone absorb what I'd just told them. I gave them that. It was a lot to take in, possible extinction.

"So where are these ships?" Griffin finally asked, squaring her shoulders as she rolled her head from side to side, cracking her neck. "Did the M'alue tell you, or are we going in blind?"

Blind. That was the answer to Griffin's question about whether I knew where this alleged fleet of spaceships had been stashed.

All I knew for sure was that the ships were here somewhere. Somewhere in this huge-vast-*enormous* facility that seemed to extend all the way to the Earth's core and back again. And it was our job to find them.

Not exactly child's play.

On the other hand, Jett had managed to disarm the access keypad in under sixty seconds using just Griffin's pen and a paper clip he'd found tucked in the back of a drawer, forever earning a place in my dad's heart. My dad called him a modern day MacGyver and then clapped him on the shoulder with pride.

I had to bite my tongue. With my new ability I could have disabled the alarm in my sleep, but I let Jett take the win.

Since we'd tried the "team" thing once, back when we'd broken into the Daylight Division in Tacoma—a strategy that had ended with Willow being taken hostage, I decided we should try a more elementary school approach, not exactly the playground buddy system, but something along those lines.

I assigned everyone a partner to keep tabs on. The idea was to watch each other's back. Heck, if it was good enough for kindergarteners it was good enough for saving the world.

My dad got Jett as his "buddy" since the two spoke the same language: computerese, and Simon and Willow were paired up because their partnership went way back. The four of them were in charge of getting Jett to a computer where he could hack into the ISA's security and figure out where the ships were being stored.

Griffin and Thom would go scouting for the ships on foot, floor by floor. It would be time-consuming and risky, but we needed to cover our bases in case the computer search didn't pan out.

That left Tyler and me with Agent Truman, which went against the laws of the buddy system since it forced us into a three-pronged partnership. I didn't care, though. Ours was the most delicate job.

Tyler and I were going after Adam. And, for once, Agent Truman's lack of moral scruples might come in handy.

"Once we leave here"—I looked around at all the *buddies*, hoping beyond hope I hadn't underestimated my friends—"we won't have any way to get in touch with each other. The goal here is to locate the fleet, but we should have a meeting place." I was stumped. I'd been so focused on who to pair up that I hadn't considered all the logistics of our operation.

"In the bio lab," Tyler offered, taking charge when I faltered. "You guys know where it is. Big place on the main level with all the freaky plants."

Thom flashed me a knowing grin. "Kyra loves the place."

"Good," I said, before I had to explain what Thom meant. "Meet in the bio lab when your task is completed."

"What if we get caught?" Jett asked.

Simon looked around. "Then we proceed without you."

I couldn't think like that. "Everyone got it?" I asked.

Every one of them nodded, and I took a deep breath, telling myself this wasn't the last time I'd see them.

Now all that was left was to save the world.

Getting out of there wasn't the hard part.

Maybe they should've stationed a security guy with a harder head outside our door. Or maybe he should've tried harder *not* to look at Griffin's cleavage when she pretended to twist her ankle.

Either way, he dropped like a rock when Willow whacked him on the skull from behind.

He only had himself to blame, but it made me think we should've paired up in Girls versus Boys, just to see which team landed on top.

After watching Willow and Griffin in action, my money would be on the girls.

From there, we parted ways.

Our group—me, Agent Truman, and Tyler—were taking the main level, not just because that's where Adam was, but also because it was the most dangerous place.

As the only one who could manipulate matter and electricity with her mind, it made sense I take on the most risk. That was according to Agent Truman.

Under normal circumstances, I'd say he was just trying to get me out of the way. But considering he was partnered with me, I could only assume he was some sort of adrenaline junkie who got off on this sort of thing.

I wasn't sure how it was going for the other teams, but with Tyler around, we got around surprisingly easily.

Tyler's ability didn't just work to sense me, it seemed. He apparently knew when and where others were located too. He heard voices and footsteps long before Agent Truman and I did, and he would drag us to a stop. And when he didn't hear those things, he listened for heartbeats . . . for breathing.

He *knew* where people were.

He sensed everyone. Everything.

It was uncanny. And he was never wrong.

The hardest part of our operation was steering clear of the cameras. Agent Truman suggested shutting them down with my "electrical skills," but I worried the outages would draw unwanted attention.

Eventually, they'd realize we'd gotten out anyway, no point raising the alarm too early.

So instead, we backtracked and searched for alternate routes—back stairwells and fire evacuation routes—to get us where we needed to be.

When we finally reached the main level, nearly an hour had passed. So much for meeting back up with everyone else at the bio lab. My palms were sweaty with the awareness that the clock was running out.

Only three more hours to go.

Unlike the day before, when everyone had been panicking about the new signal, today the main level was disturbingly quiet. To the point of nearly being deserted.

This should have been a good thing . . . it made getting around remarkably easy. Unfortunately, I didn't buy it as a stroke of good luck, and my worry meter shot through the roof.

Where was everyone? After the chaos of yesterday, I had a hard time believing this was one massive coffee break.

My heart wedged in my throat.

Beside me, Tyler's hand slipped around mine as if he, too, sensed the wrongness of everything being so . . . vacant.

"I'm gonna get a head count. See what we're up against."

Agent Truman's voice was hushed.

"*Buddy system*," I insisted almost silently, even though it sounded childish. "We stick together."

"Oh. You were serious with that?" he asked, already easing away. "I won't be long."

"And Tyler could—" I began, just as Agent Truman disappeared into the shadows. What was the point of having a plan—a *system*—if he was going to throw it out the window the first chance he got? It was a stupid risk. Tyler could do a better job feeling out who was where.

Tyler reached out and tugged my hand. "I've been wanting to tell you something," he whispered.

"What is it?" I asked distractedly. The uneasy feeling that something was wrong deepened as we moved from one lab to the next.

"It's about what you told me . . . before."

"Uh-huh . . ."

My chest went tight all at once as I stabbed Tyler with a wide-eyed warning. *Voices!* I tried to convey.

But Tyler was three steps ahead of me, and was already dragging me out of the way, pushing me through one of the doorways. I gripped his hand with both of mine, until it felt like my knuckles would pop . . . as we waited and listened.

There were two of them. Men wearing lab coats and talking casually, as if this really were a coffee break. They ambled past us, while the entire time my shoulders were knotted and tight.

When they were gone, Tyler and I stayed where we

were . . . still attuned to everything around us, in case they or someone . . . anyone came back.

When I inhaled, I realized I'd been holding my breath the entire time.

Tyler was holding his too, but for a different reason.

Adam.

We were in the lab where they stored all those enormous canisters, including Adam's. Seeing them again gave me goose bumps. But seeing Adam . . .

Tyler eased forward, and I realized this was where he'd been leading us all along. That he felt what I did . . . drawn to the M'alue.

He . . . we . . . the three of us were the same.

Time became irrelevant as we neared him. Adam woke immediately, making me think he sensed us as strongly as we sensed him.

It's okay. We're here now, I thought, fairly convinced he knew what I was trying to suggest to him.

Tyler lifted his hand, the one holding mine and pressed it to the glass. Adam responded in kind, putting his unusual hand there too.

It won't be much longer . . . The words flashed through my head, making me flinch.

It wasn't my thought. Those weren't my words, but I knew whose they were. Tyler's. I was in Tyler's head now too.

Adam's response came next, *Three hands, one mind.*

I momentarily forgot everything else . . . the mission

or being caught. We were doing this. We were absolutely-totally-*100-percent* communicating without exchanging so much as a single sound.

I turned to Tyler and grinned.

I know, he said back to me, clear as day, a huge smile lighting up his face.

"Look what I found."

I dropped my hand from the canister, and from Tyler's, and spun around. Whatever bond we'd been locked in was severed instantly.

It was Agent Truman, and his face was all smug as he held up a gun like it was a trophy.

"You didn't just find that," I accused. "Who'd you take it from?"

"Security guard," he said, pointing the barrel down and inspecting it. "He won't be needing it."

"Dude, what part of *I have superpowers* don't you understand? *You* don't need it." I threw my hands in the air. "I hope you didn't do anything . . ." I scowled. "Permanent."

"If you're asking, did I kill him? Then no, guy's still breathing. But that's about all he's doin' right now." He checked the rounds quickly and then reassembled the gun. "If you're asking me to give this baby up, forget it. *I* don't have superpowers."

I shook my head. "Fine, just don't shoot anyone."

"So what'd you decide? About that . . ." Agent Truman waved the gun toward Adam and my gut clenched. "That thing?"

"That thing is intelligent, and in pain. We need to get him out of there," Tyler said.

"But *how* do you plan to do that?" Agent Truman asked.

I moved over to the control panel and smirked at him. "Try to keep up," I said smugly as I let my hands hover over the instruments in front of me. They were all foreign to me—much more Jett's or my dad's territory than mine. But it didn't matter; I could feel the electricity pulsing beneath my palms. "I've got superpowers."

Above us, the lights surged as if all the power was draining from the room. *It's me*, I thought. *I'm doing that.*

"Wait," Tyler said as he grabbed my arm. "We're not alone."

But it was too late.

Dr. Clarke stepped out from the shadows, right behind Adam's canister. "I knew you wouldn't be able to stay away from him," she told us. In one hand she was clutching one of the rubber tubes that disappeared directly into the blue liquid Adam was suspended in. In the other she held a syringe. She plunged the needle into the tube. Just the slightest nudge from her thumb was all it would take. "Don't make me kill him." Her voice left little doubt whether she was serious or not.

SIMON

"AND . . . WE'RE IN." JETT PUNCHED IN THE FINAL sequence of commands and then cracked his knuckles.

Ben stood back and admired him. "Damn. I'm impressed. They are majorly wired here. I have to keep reminding myself you're not really a kid though."

I leaned against the doorjamb and smirked. He was right, it took some getting used to, the whole youth thing. Especially on someone like Jett, whose face was more kid-like than the rest of us. Sometimes, I even forgot he was older than me.

I wondered how Ben would feel when it was his daughter he was talking about, years from now.

I shook it off. Jett had just worked a minor miracle—hacking into the ISA's mainframe. Kid really was a frickin' genius.

"Can you tell where they're keeping those spaceships yet?" I asked, looking over my shoulder, checking the hallway. So far no one had noticed us. Willow was down there, keeping an eye out.

"Best I can tell, is someplace they call the Basement," he answered, pointing at one of the monitors where he'd accessed a floor plan of the facility. "One level down from where they're keeping the EVE. They got enough space down there to store at least . . ." He was swiveling in his seat to face me, when the words died on his lips. "Aw, crap," he finished.

I snapped my head around, to see what had stolen his attention.

Behind me, just past my shoulder, Dr. Atkins was there, holding a gun to Willow's head. I tried to hide my surprise, but how in the hell had she gotten the jump on us . . . on Willow?

"Nicely done," she told Jett approvingly. "I honestly didn't think you had it in you." Then she nodded toward Ben. "Maybe the big guy there—I've seen his work firsthand. But not yours." She grinned. "Guess I underestimated you."

A sudden iciness settled over me as Jett looked from her to Ben trying to sort it all out. "Guess so," Jett answered coolly.

But it was Ben I questioned. "So I take it Dr. Clarke wasn't the only one you knew from your old life at the ISA?"

Ben sighed. "Dr. Atkins was one of the scientists I told you about. One who was taken and sent back."

"I told you before, call me Molly."

Jett ignored her request. "You're a Returned?"

She shrugged, pointing her gun at Willow to remind us she still had it.

As if we'd forgotten.

Willow rolled her eyes. "Come on, the gun, is it really necessary? We're on the same side here, aren't we?"

But Molly shook her head. "I don't know what you want with those ships, but *we* need them."

"The M'alue are coming," Jett explained. "And if they do come they'll start a war. Why not just destroy the fleet before that can happen?"

"Let them come. I'm ready for them," she snapped. And then her expression shifted. "I was one of the scientists who found the injured M'alue, you know? I brought him back to the lab and ordered the tests on him." She blinked slowly, taking a long breath. "He probably would've been fine if we'd just let him heal, but I was the one who gave the initial order not to release him." When she let out her breath, she gritted her teeth and a muscle bulged along her jaw. "When they took me . . ." She turned to Ben. "You have no idea what it's like to lose everything."

But she'd picked the wrong person to appeal to.

His face turned red as he slammed his fist on the console. "I lost my *daughter*!"

Shaking her head again, she notched her chin upward. "But it wasn't you. They didn't take you. When they took me, they took everything—my chance at a normal life. My future. They destroyed me."

Jett tried to talk some sense into her. "But you're here now. Your life isn't over. We might not be the same, but we still have options," he explained. "You have the chance to do the right thing. To be better than this."

"I don't want to be better. I want them to pay for taking my life away." Her lips twisted into an ugly sneer.

"So, what, you plan to start a war with them?" Ben asked. "How can you expect to win? How can you think that's okay, to risk other people's lives like that?"

"I'll get my revenge," she stated flatly.

The problem was, she was wrong. There was no way she would win this thing.

We'd have to tread carefully.

I lowered my voice, hoping to make her see reason. "You'll get us all killed."

But she was past listening. Her eyes glittered. "If that's what it takes."

She used the nose of the gun to nudge Willow toward us, then indicated we all take a step back from the computers.

We did as she directed. Finally, Ben spoke up. "Why not just let us go? Give us a chance to get away from here?"

She took a breath once we were away from the equipment, her stance sagging. "You, maybe," she told Ben. "But we need your daughter. Her, and the boy."

That was what this was all about. Kyra and Tyler.

Suddenly I wasn't just worried she was going to shoot us or start an intergalactic war. I was terrified of what she had planned for Kyra. "Why not one of us?" I asked. "Can't I take her place?"

"You think we didn't try that? I was one of the first to volunteer. We all emit a certain amount of the kind of power we needed. Problem is, our human side. Our cell membranes absorb too much of that energy, and then our immune system sees it as a threat and breaks it down. The more attempts we made, the weaker I became. It's why I have this." She pointed to her bum leg. "I broke it a couple of years ago, and it never did heal properly, not even by human standards.

"Our only option was getting our hands on a Replaced." She laughed wryly. "Don't you see? Without those two kids, this whole house of cards crumbles." She never said their names—Kyra's or Tyler's—as if naming them would personalize what she was doing. "Funny, I don't think the M'alue realized they were handing us the solution to our problem when they created them." Her smile was tinged with lunacy. "We searched high and low, sending out teams, operatives. We even had people inside the Daylight Division. We set up our own task forces—teams of Returned who worked for us. They infiltrated camps just so we could keep tabs on new abductees. We promised them the world if they could deliver us a Replaced."

"It was you . . . ," I hissed, unable to stop myself from charging her. "You sent Natty after Kyra."

She tensed, raising the gun again, and Jett caught me. He held me back. His fingers gripped my wrist, reminding me it wouldn't do any good to get shot now. To get Willow shot.

We still had to save Kyra . . . and, yes, Tyler too.

"Yeah," Molly chuckled. "And we almost had her. We got word that Eddie Ray's team had her and she'd be ready for transport within the day. They'd figured out how to sedate her and everything was set." She shook her head. "At first when they didn't answer us, we thought they'd changed their minds . . . maybe found another buyer for her."

Buyer. The pulse in my throat picked up when she talked about Kyra that way. Like she was some sort of property, to be traded on the open market.

"Then you guys showed up. Just . . . *showed up*. Out of the blue." She nodded at Ben. "And it no longer mattered that we didn't have the girl. You handed us the boy on a silver platter. The second he entered the building we knew: *he* was the key." Her long sigh oozed satisfaction. I wanted to punch her in the face. "The girl showing up a day later was just a bonus. You know, we've never seen someone emit so much energy, Ben? You should be proud. She's like a walking power plant."

"You're going to hell," he spat at her.

She smirked. "I'm already there."

CHAPTER NINETEEN

"I HAD A SON ONCE," DR. CLARKE SAID, HER FACE masked in the eerie blue glow coming from the gel inside Adam's tube. She stepped around it, so we could see her more clearly, but she never released her grip on the syringe in her hand. It stayed where it was: ready to kill Adam with just the flick of her thumb.

"You don't have to do this," Tyler said, his eyes moving between the needle and her tortured expression. I didn't know how he managed to sound so reasonable.

Dr. Clarke focused on Tyler. "I'm doing this for him," she explained slowly. Softly. "All of it. This project." She blinked against the tears she could no longer hide. "He was taken at the same time the other children were." Her eyes fell on me. "Not long before you were taken." A single tear slipped down her cheek and she used her shoulder to brush it away. "Only *he* never came back. Not even after all these years." Her voice cracked. "Do you know what that does to a parent?"

Agent Truman lowered his gun as I eased past Tyler and stepped in front of her. I swallowed the lump in my throat, but my chest ached. "I do, actually. My dad . . . he's not the same as he was before. It *broke* him."

She jiggled the tubing, letting me know I'd come far enough. "He was fifteen," she whispered, eyeing me desperately. "And if I can find him . . . If we can go up there and bring him back, he'll *still be fifteen*."

From behind me, Tyler reached for my shoulder, maybe trying to tell me not to, but it had to be said. She needed to know. I shook my head. "All you'll do is make things worse," I told her. "Get the rest of us killed too. You don't want that, I know you don't."

It had been painful to admit the truth out loud—how damaged my dad had been by my taking—but looking at Dr. Clarke I couldn't help thinking maybe it wasn't her fault.

And maybe it wasn't my dad's either.

I took a step toward her. "Dr. Clarke, your son—" I faltered; she'd never said his name.

"Nathan," she moaned. "My son's name, it's Nathan. Do you know?" she asked. "Did they tell you . . . ?" She took a shaky breath. "He's not coming back, is he?"

Nathan Clarke.

I didn't want to answer her. How could I?

But I knew the truth. They'd downloaded all that information into my head. I knew who'd survived the experiments. I'd seen his face. I knew what they'd done to him.

A quiver ran along my spine even before I found the strength to shake my head. Dr. Clarke's face . . . her entire bearing crumpled. I turned to Tyler, wishing he could do something, anything to fix this.

But no one could.

Her mouth fell open, and I thought she might scream or howl, but all that came out was an arid gasp. It was like watching someone take her dying breath.

"No," she finally mouthed.

Her head dropped forward, her chin collapsing against her chest. But her fist was still closed around the tubing, and I was worried she might take it out on Adam, exact what small revenge she could. "No, no, no." Her voice was almost nonexistent, in mute denial.

"Please," I whispered. "Nathan wouldn't want this." My gaze fell on Adam and she followed my eyes. "He wouldn't have wanted you to drag others into this because of him. I know because *I* wouldn't have wanted that. None of us would."

I could feel Tyler behind me, silently agreeing with me.

She stood there trapped by uncertainty as she contemplated my plea. I guessed she was thinking of her son and considering what he would, and wouldn't, have wanted.

Finally, she exhaled and dropped the needle.

Everything inside me uncoiled, like a clock's springs wound too tightly.

"Let's get him out of there," she said. "And then I'll do anything you need me to."

TYLER

FREEING ADAM HAD BEEN LIKE FREEING MYSELF—I saw the world more clearly. My senses were boosted.

The moment the three of us touched, it was like a jolt—the connection . . . our connection—sizzling through my veins. Thrumming beneath my skin.

I began to see images, like clips of broken film. A network of light shining over the dark spots of my broken memory, until all at once it came flooding back.

Kyra and me on the swing set the night she was returned . . .

Me, pulling an all-nighter to draw a chalk pathway between our houses . . .

Leaving her a copy of Fahrenheit 451*—my favorite book.*

Our first kiss . . . and then our second.

Kyra's face when she realized she'd cut herself in front of me.

I had no idea if Kyra was seeing this or not.

Agent Truman protested, "Jesus-H. He smells like a rotting corpse."

Okay, so that part wasn't entirely wrong.

True to her word, Dr. Clarke had helped us extract Adam from the canister they'd been keeping him confined in.

"He's been in a sort of stasis for years," she explained while she drained the solution he was suspended in. "We took him out only when Dr. Atkins ordered it." It was shocking to hear her say that Molly was the one in charge. She hadn't struck me as the decision-making type. "She would do things to him"—Dr. Clarke blanched as she stumbled over her words, her hands shaking—"*horrific* things. I'm not sure how he's even survived all this time."

But we had him now. He was safe, even as he slipped in and out of consciousness—shock, most likely, from being outside of his tube, according to Dr. Clarke.

His body was practically weightless, light like a bird's, and Kyra and I carried him as if it was nothing. His skin was no longer moist from the blue gel but it had a sticky feel. Not in the syrupy sense, but like one of those gummy rubber balls from a candy machine outside the grocery store.

And he stunk, just like Agent Truman said he did.

"They won't have to see us on the cameras, they'll smell

that SOB coming from a mile away," Agent Truman muttered.

But then Dr. Clarke put the facility into evacuation mode, entering the codes herself, and overriding every safeguard they had in place. Her access allowed her to declare a state of emergency that required the entire operation to shut down until the facility could be safely cleared.

There was a self-destruct sequence as well, she told us, in the event of a *real* emergency, but her security clearance didn't allow her to initiate that. We'd need someone with higher access codes to do that.

"Find someone with Level Three clearance—Dr. Atkins or someone who works on the EVE project. Then you can blow up the entire fleet . . . the entire facility," she explained. "They'll lose everything. They'll never be able to duplicate the technology."

For now, all she could guarantee was that the building would be clear, giving us at least a chance to save the planet.

"I'll stay here and lock the lab down," she'd told us. "You get to the Basement. That's where you'll find the ships."

Then she handed us her key card and gave us her access codes. Once she was locked inside, I turned to ask where she wanted us to meet her, when she nodded to us once from behind the glass door—a *Farewell* or *Good luck,* or maybe it was an *I'm sorry*—right before she plunged the tip of the needle into her arm.

I wanted to tell her to stop, but it was already done and the words died on my lips.

She collapsed.

I stood there stunned, waiting for something to change. To realize I'd seen wrong. But then she exhaled, a shuddery breath, and foam escaped her lips which were already turning blue.

I heard Kyra inside my head, and even though I could feel her shock as well, she was right. We needed to go. To get Adam out of here.

Back home.

SIMON

I WAS DAYDREAMING ABOUT ALL THE WAYS I COULD snap Molly's neck when the sirens started. There was nothing subtle about what we were hearing.

An automated voice began repeating, *"Attention! Attention! There has been the report of an emergency. All personnel are to evacuate immediately. Please remain calm."*

Each looped message was followed by a jarring siren that would penetrate the most effective earplugs, while red lights flashed continuously up and down the hallways.

Willow flashed me a think-that's-about-us? look.

Suddenly all I could think of was Kyra. I needed to find her, before it was too late.

The sirens were annoying, but I might be able to use them to my advantage.

I started to call Molly's name to create a distraction, but Willow, apparently, was already two moves ahead of me.

"Hey bitch!" she shouted before I had the chance, and at the same time she shouldered me out of her way.

When Molly jerked her head just the barest amount in Willow's direction, Willow swung as hard as she could. Her fist slammed into Molly's cheek—hard, but not quite hard enough. Molly staggered but managed, somehow, to keep her grip on the gun.

She was just getting her balance again, when the fire extinguisher struck her near the base of her skull. I heard the hard *whack* above the shrill sirens, and even I was revolted by the sound.

Ben stood triumphantly, holding the red canister while the rest of us watched to see what would happen.

For a moment it looked like Molly was going to stay on her feet, but then she swayed. And after another second the gun dropped sluggishly from her hand as her eyes rolled back in her head. Then her entire body just went . . . limp, and she dropped to the floor.

It wasn't until I glanced at Jett and saw his face go ashen that I realized something was wrong.

"Damn," Jett breathed, and then he pointed to the blood

that was pooling on the tile floor . . . blood seeping from the wound at the back of Molly's head. "She's a Returned . . ."

I glanced to Ben, who wasn't like us. Who should never have been exposed to Molly's, or any of our, blood.

"Aw, hell." I dropped to my knees and tried to wipe it away, mopping the blood with my hands and Molly's own hair . . . anything that might stop it from going airborne.

But we all knew it was too late. Whatever toxins Molly carried—whatever Code Red he was going to be exposed to—it was already out there.

"None of that matters," Ben said, reaching down and scooping up her gun. "All that matters is we can fix this mess. That we save the Earth from being attacked. I don't care what happens to me."

You will, I thought, remembering the way Tyler had looked after he'd been exposed . . . when his skin had blistered and peeled, and later, when he'd gone blind. *You just don't realize it yet.*

CHAPTER TWENTY

WE USED DR. CLARKE'S KEY CARD TO GO straight to the place she'd called the Basement. The floor had been cleared—not a single soul in sight.

What we found instead was beyond imagination.

When we'd been told there was a fleet, I'd imagined ten, maybe fifteen spaceships like the EVE.

But what we faced was nothing less than an entire squadron . . . hundreds of ships. No wonder the M'alue believed we were preparing for a war.

"Why would they build so many, without even knowing how to power them?" I asked.

Tyler shrugged. "I guess they were confident they'd find the solution." He gave me a sidelong look. "If not a Replaced, then some other way." He lifted his head. "Someone's coming."

"You kids get your asses down there," Agent Truman ordered, pointing to the hangar deck. Behind us, the elevator hummed to life, and he'd already positioned himself in front of the closed doors to cover us. "Figure out how to wake that thing and get him airborne. This whole plan falls apart if we can't get him back to his people so he can let them know we want peace."

We didn't argue. It wasn't just Adam who needed us . . . who needed this to work. The entire world was banking on it.

Like the first time, when I'd approached the EVE, these ships responded to our presence—to mine and Tyler's and to Adam's.

Adam stirred as well, rousing again.

"It's okay," I whispered, when he opened his unusual glowing eyes and looked into first Tyler's and then my own. *You're safe*, I thought when I realized words were unnecessary.

You're going home, Tyler added.

But there was something else there between us as well. Something coming from Tyler.

An awareness of everything he'd been wanting to say to me . . . everything he'd been holding back. Everything he felt.

I looked into his eyes, because he knew I was hearing him, his thoughts.

I forgive you, he said.

I let the sensation surround me. Cocoon me. And then I nodded, because there wasn't time for anything more. Adam was ready.

A staircase descended from the hull of one of the spaceships; as if Adam had already decided which craft he'd fly. But he was weak, and unable to stand on his own, so Tyler and I hoisted him up, carrying him inside.

It took us a moment, but we managed to strap him to the seat. Only, then his head lolled to the side.

Tyler sat back and studied Adam. Even if I hadn't been able to read it in his head, the worry was written all over his face.

"I know," I voiced out of habit, because I was thinking the same thing: I wasn't sure Adam was up to this.

It hadn't only been his body that the ISA and their experiments had damaged, it was his mind too. He was still in there, I could sense and feel and hear him, but he'd withdrawn . . . a self-defense mechanism against all the torture he'd endured. Years and years of torture.

But the M'alue wanted him back. And now that was one of their conditions. Even after all the humans they'd taken and experimented on . . . all the ones who'd never come back . . . they demanded Adam's safe return.

And the thing is, even if they hadn't insisted, I was desperate to send him. He didn't belong here. On Earth. He wasn't like Tyler and me, with a lifetime of human memories and experiences to define him.

He was M'alue, plain and simple. Maybe *they* could undo the damage that had been done to him.

Before I could even form my own conclusion, I *heard* Tyler's, and I shook my head, denying him. "No way, Tyler, it doesn't make sense for you to do it. *I've* flown one of these before. *I've* been to their ship. *I'll* take him."

The truth was—and Tyler knew, even if I didn't say it out loud—I couldn't live with the idea of anything happening to him.

"And you think I don't feel the exact same way?" he said.

"*I'll* do it." The gruff voice came from my dad, and Tyler and I both whirled to face him.

His head was poking up through the opening in the floor.

"Dad, no." I didn't say it the same way I had to Tyler, like his offer was a legitimate solution. Instead I blew him off. "You wouldn't have the first clue." I couldn't keep the skepticism from my voice.

After Dr. Clarke's breakdown, I saw my dad through a different lens. Maybe I'd been too hard on him. He'd already suffered so much . . . lost so much. And here he was, offering to launch himself into space . . . for me.

He came up another step or two. "You said yourself this thing practically flew itself. All it needed was a jump start."

"Not exactly what I said."

"But close enough," he challenged. "I heard you, the thing was intuitive. That it read your mind."

"That's because I'm M'alue."

My dad shook his fist at me. "Don't you say that. *Don't*

you dare . . ." His face had gone all blotchy and red. "You're as human as any of us." I didn't remind him he was the only true human here, everyone else left was at least half M'alue. And after taking a second to collect himself, he blew out a breath and tried again. "You said the ship seemed to know where it was going. Like it was on autopilot."

I had to concede that point at least. I'd only been in control during takeoff. After that, the ship had had a mind of its own, navigating into space without me. "Still—" I started, but my dad cut me off.

"You can't stop me, Kyr."

I wanted to tell him that's exactly what I could do. Didn't he realize how strong I'd grown—ever since I'd gone up there, to that M'alue's ship? Even being in Adam's presence made me feel more . . . *powerful.*

I could, and I would, stop him if that's what it took to keep him safe.

But he wasn't finished just yet. "I've been infected—the Code Red thing. I'll be sick within hours. Dead within days." He just threw it out there—like a bomb . . . like it was nothing.

But it wasn't nothing. It was huge, his news, and I had a million questions about how and when and who, but none of those questions found their way to my lips. I was dizzy and heavy and tangled all at the same time.

Tyler must've been inside my head and realized how disoriented I suddenly felt, because his hand shot over to find mine.

"Listen, kiddo," my dad finally said. "Going up there . . . with them, it might be my only shot. Maybe they'll help me, the way they helped the kid there." My dad nodded at Tyler.

I glanced at Tyler, and could hear what he was saying, that his case was different. They'd come to get him. They'd chosen to take him.

Besides, hadn't they already said: no more Returned?

And even if that wasn't the case, he went on, *Your dad would be forcing himself on them. And he is old. Older than the rest of us.*

But what about Agent Truman? I countered, because they'd taken him when he was around my dad's age.

I had to believe he at least had a shot.

Tyler stopped arguing, probably because he knew he'd lost. I'd already made up my mind.

"And you call me stubborn," I said as I reached for my dad's hand, pulling him the rest of the way into the ship. The two of them helped me move Adam out of the pilot's seat. We did our best to make Adam comfortable on the floor with a cargo blanket we found.

Tyler disembarked then, giving my dad and me a few minutes alone, and because good-bye was too hard, I started showing my dad what he'd need to do, which was almost nothing. I'd already tapped into the ship's systems, or it had tapped into me . . . either way it was already powering up, preparing to launch.

I indicated the ship's control panel, which mostly

consisted of the joystick and was pretty basic, really. From below, I'd navigate the thing myself, if necessary, until he was safely through the bay doors. After that, he could handle it until the M'alue took over.

Then, when I couldn't put it off any longer, I leaned over and kissed him lightly on his whiskered cheek.

Swallowing, because the last thing I wanted was for my voice to wobble, I said, "'Bye, Dad." I said it like he'd be back soon. That everything would be 100 percent fine. "Be safe."

I started to straighten, and then changed my mind. There was no way I could leave things that way. This was no time to pretend this wasn't a total mess.

I dropped back down, over the top of him and wrapped my arms around his neck. I buried my face in his beard, and when I tried to talk, my voice fell apart. "I love you, Dad. And I don't blame you for what happened," I told him, because he needed to know before he went. "I'll never blame you."

He was already strapped in, but my dad managed to reach his arms back up and around me too. "I love you too, Supernova. Don't ever forget who you are. You're my girl. You'll always be my girl."

I didn't have to see him to know he meant it. He wasn't doing this for the world; he was doing this for me.

Watching as the bay doors opened, I was caught in a strange sort of limbo between agony and relief.

My dad had done it. The hardest part was over, the ship was launched and Adam was on his way home.

But my dad . . .

I clamped my eyes shut. *I can't do this now*, I told myself as I checked the clock. *Less than an hour until the M'alue launch their attack.*

We're running out of time.

I didn't know the whole story, only that it had been Molly who'd exposed my dad after she'd pulled a gun on them and he'd hit her with a fire extinguisher. Griffin and Thom had caught up with them shortly afterward, and now everyone was here as my dad's ship cruised away.

If we'd had more time, I would've asked to hear everything, but instead, we had to finish this thing.

"You all need to leave," I said, turning to face them.

Simon scowled. "What are you saying?"

"I'm saying, get as far away from here as possible."

"What about you?" I was surprised to find Griffin's big brown eyes pooled with worry. It wasn't like her.

I tried to explain. "This isn't about me. We don't have the security code we need." I held up Dr. Clarke's key card as I looked around at their faces, people who'd become my friends . . . and Agent Truman. "But even if we did, someone would have to give up their codes, and no one with that level clearance is gonna cooperate willingly. We're running short on options. But, look . . ." I showed my hands as threads of electricity sparked between them. "Whatever *this* is, I can use it. I can bypass their security and blow this place *sky-freaking-high.* And trust me, you won't wanna be anywhere near here when I do." I grinned, but no one was smiling back at me.

Tyler shook his head. "No way. I'm not leaving you," he insisted.

Not to be outdone, Simon stepped up. "Me neither."

But they weren't getting it. "Look, guys. This isn't some Feats of Strength contest where you win the girl in the end. There's no prize for being the bigger hero." I made a face at them. "Think about what you're saying. Staying means you don't walk out of here, and *neither* of you gets the girl. Or any girl, ever. Don't be stupid, I don't need your help."

But Tyler wasn't buying it. I knew as much because I heard it from him. The thing was, though, I only had to convince him to go—he didn't need to understand why.

I glared at both of them. "If I'm being honest, your being here is a distraction, and the last thing I need is to be distracted. I said this isn't about me, but the truth is, it isn't about any of us. We need to stop this whole thing from happening. We need to convince the M'alue we're no threat, and the only way to do that is to blow these ships up. I can't do that with you two breathing down my neck." Silently I begged each of them to trust me on this. I couldn't let myself think about the part where this would be the last time I'd ever see them—any of them—again. "Please, if you care about me at all, just get away from here."

Tyler gave in first, probably because he was inside my

head and could sense how serious I was and how hard this was for me. But that didn't mean he was okay with it, I knew that too.

His only outward answer was a silent nod.

But seeing that nod, Simon finally exhaled loudly. "Yeah. Fine. Okay."

We couldn't afford anything longer than the briefest of good-byes, and I was totally okay with that. Anything more and I might've lost my nerve.

Agent Truman barely nodded before going to wait in the elevator, while Griffin, Thom, Willow, and Jett tried to make it as painless on me as possible. Jett was the only one who cried, and when he did, I punched him in the arm and called him a baby. Comforting him would've pushed me to my breaking point.

Simon made Tyler go ahead of him, needing, as always, to have the last word.

Tyler looked uneasy with Simon standing so close by, which was definitely the point. Simon wouldn't want to make it simple for Tyler and me. He never had.

But then Tyler reached for my hands and our skin connected. Electricity moved back and forth between us. He told me without words the things he'd been trying to say since I'd come back from the M'alue's ship, and he said it all in one simple phrase: *I'll remember you always.*

I blinked in surprise, my breath catching in my throat as I searched his eyes to see if he truly understood what he was telling me. Those were our words, something he'd told me the night I'd first been returned . . . and then he'd written them in chalk on the road between our houses.

And now he was using them again. *I'll remember you always.*

A dimple cut through his cheek, the same dimple I'd traced with my fingertip once upon a time.

I almost couldn't believe it. He'd more than forgiven me, *he remembered*. He remembered us.

And with that, he leaned down and kissed me. His kiss wasn't tentative or exploratory like this was unfamiliar territory, which was what I'd been expecting since for so long he'd had no memory of the two of us. Instead it was the deep-emotional-*memory-laden* kiss of someone who cherishes you. Someone who knows you.

My heart was pounding when Simon cleared his throat, letting Tyler and me know in his less-than-subtle way our time was up. Tyler pulled away gently and stepped back, his eyes never leaving me.

When it was his turn, I thought Simon would say something corny, or give some big speech to convince me he was the right choice all along.

Instead, he whispered, thinking Tyler couldn't hear, "You made up your mind before we ever even met." And then he kissed me . . . a small, sweet kiss that wasn't meant to sway me at all.

It was what it was—a good-bye kiss.

As the elevator doors closed behind them, I silently allowed myself to decide between them, once and for all.

I said the name in my head the one and only time I would say it—Tyler. Tyler, who I would have picked, who I always would have picked if things could have been different.

If I could have survived all this.

And then I shut my feelings down because I had a job to do. One that didn't allow me to think about either of them.

Any of them.

As long as this place was still standing, everyone was at risk.

Dr. Clarke had given us a brief rundown of the systems, on the off chance we found the codes we needed. I gave the others a twenty-minute head start to get as far as they could from here, which was generous. They'd need at least three minutes just to get back to the main level, and then another five to clear the facility altogether.

Beyond that, I couldn't let myself worry about them. I had to hope they'd find Agent Truman's car and would drive as far away as possible.

If not, they'd have to run and hide and hope the blast stayed fairly contained.

If they were hurt, they'd heal.

If they were killed . . .

I refused to let my mind go there.

This wasn't about us.

I pressed my palms to the CPU's fingerprint recognition software and shot a burst of current through the system, hacking into their mainframe.

Overhead, the red lights stopped flashing, blinked once,

and then once again. And then remained on.

A new loop began on the speaker system: *"Destruct sequence activated. All personnel evacuate the building. This is not a drill."*

A new countdown clock had begun.

TYLER

I PRESSED THE BUTTON IMPATIENTLY, SHIFTING anxiously on my feet.

Overhead, the monotone voice echoed off the walls. *"All personnel must now be evacuated. Autodestruct set to commence in two minutes."* That was new, the audio countdown.

This whole ordeal was almost over.

I jammed my thumb at the elevator's button one last time, deciding some kind of security protocol must have overridden the system and I'd missed my chance.

Then, just as I was about to give up, the doors slid open and

I leaped inside. I still had Dr. Clarke's key card, the one Kyra had given us in case we came up against any security measures, and I swiped it, my pulse pounding recklessly.

"All personnel must now be evacuated. Autodestruct set to commence in one minute forty-five seconds." I didn't want that to be the last voice I ever heard.

When the doors slid open again, I was facing a room full of computers. I did a quick survey, all the time I could afford, and an unsettling thought knocked the wind out of me: something had gone wrong. Kyra had made a run for it.

Then . . . I sensed her.

She was still here, just not on this floor. My mouth went dry as I stabbed the button again.

As the doors finally opened, I exited to the main floor, and I felt her presence . . . her awareness that I'd come back . . . her confusion and anger and reluctant pleasure all mixed up, all at once.

"Tyler? What the hell?" Kyra said, wasting no time coming to me. I wondered if she knew her cheeks flushed when she was pissed, and that it only made her more beautiful.

The voice intruded on our reunion. *"All personnel must now be evacuated. Autodestruct set to commence in one minute fifteen seconds."*

"That?" she said, pointing at the ceiling despondently. "You shouldn't be here."

"Shut up," I told her and reached for her. "This isn't the time to tell me what I should or shouldn't be doing." I put my mouth to hers, not a kiss exactly, but the promise of one. Her lips parted and I could taste her breath. I could feel her heart beneath mine. "You said no one wins the girl, but you're wrong."

And with that, I made good on my promise, kissing her so completely, so thoroughly, she didn't have the chance to argue. Her tongue was sweet and familiar, and I couldn't imagine how I'd ever forgotten her. Forgotten this.

I felt whole and alive. *This* was where I wanted to die.

Overhead, the speaker announced two more countdowns, leaving us less than a minute by the time I released her.

"Why'd you come up here?" I asked gently. Softly.

"I knew I couldn't make it out in time, but I thought, maybe . . . maybe I could find a place to see the sky . . . the stars one last time." Her lips were swollen and her eyes were glossy. "You should've gone." But this time when she said it, she gave me a crooked smile and I knew, even without reading her, she didn't mean a single word.

"Liar."

She shrugged, and I pulled her into my arms.

"All personnel must now be evacuated. Autodestruct set to commence in thirty seconds."

Against my chest, she jerked.

"You scared?" I whispered.

"*So* scared," she answered truthfully. "How do you think it'll happen?"

I half shook my head and half shrugged because I had no idea. But I all-the-way held on as tight as I could. I listened to her breathing . . . in and out, in and out, until the voice gave us our fifteen-second warning.

"I'll remember you always," I told her, this time out loud because I wanted the last things we said to each other to be spoken . . . human.

She looked up at me, her eyes fat with tears as she answered back, "*I'll* remember *you* always."

CHAPTER TWENTY-ONE

"THREE . . ." THE VOICE OVERHEAD DRONED ITS final notes.

It was okay. I was okay . . .

"Two . . ."

Tyler was here. We were together.

"One . . ."

The first blast came from several floors below—the Basement most likely, where the ships were. Followed immediately by a second and a third. I didn't even flinch as Tyler's arms closed around me, trying to shield me from whatever was coming.

When the flashes came, they weren't in sync with the explosions, but I felt them all the same . . .

Tiny pinpricks, like holes being cut right through me . . . all over my body. A million, billion, trillion infinitesimal stingers plunging into my skin.

Tyler must have felt them too because I heard him gasp.

From somewhere I smelled burning chemicals and smoke, and the ground and walls around us were rumbling. There were more eruptions now, closer to us.

And right before everything was over . . .

Right before the whole place went up in flames, I heard him say . . .

". . . always."

EPILOGUE

THE STARS OVERHEAD GLOWED IN AN UNNATU-ral way. Beautiful, but unnatural.

It took me several tries to figure out why.

Plastic. They were the plastic glow-in-the-dark kind that parents stick on kids' ceilings.

I stayed where I was, studying them for an eternity, try-ing to decide if they were familiar or not. They gave me the strangest sense of déjà vu, and I felt like I *should* remember them even though I couldn't quite put my finger on the memory.

I rolled over and looked at the clock. It was 4:13, but I

was *awake*-awake so there was no point trying to go back to sleep now. I chucked the covers aside and made my way to the kitchen in search of coffee.

The hallway was dark but I'd been in this house my whole life, I didn't need a light. Still, everything about this was wrong somehow.

I had the strangest sensation I was sneaking around someplace I shouldn't. Trespassing.

I froze when I reached the kitchen and saw Grant standing over the sink, loading dishes in the dishwasher.

Grant.

I knew him—his name, his face . . . and he obviously recognized me, because he grimaced when he saw me. "Sorry. Did I wake ya, slugger?"

Slugger? Was that really his nickname for me?

I tested it out, and the whole déjà vu thing tilted . . . right, but not quite.

"No," I answered, when he just stood there, waiting for my response. "I . . . uh . . . bad dream, I guess." I shrugged.

Was that the truth? It could've been a dream as easily as anything else.

He nodded, his eyebrows tugging downward. "Your dad again? I'm sorry, slugger. It'll get easier." He reached for a dish towel.

My dad . . .

Just the mention of him brought an overwhelming *something* almost into range. A memory I couldn't quite reach, but there was a sharp stab of pain.

Again, I couldn't help thinking none of this was right.

I took a step away from Grant before he could finish drying his hands. I didn't want him to try to hug it out or anything, and for some reason I got the feeling that's where this whole touchy-feely conversation was headed.

"All right," he called after me as I staggered down the hallway to my bedroom. "I'll be here if you wanna talk."

I slammed the door behind me, and did a quick inventory of the room. It was mine, but not mine.

Mine from before, came the thought, hitting me like a freight train the same way the pain had. All these things were things from my past. From another me.

It all came rushing back at me then. The Returned, the camps, the No-Suchers and Agent Truman, the ISA. Adam and my dad.

The explosion.

So how was I here now? Why hadn't I been blasted into smithereens when we'd destroyed the ISA facility and their fleet of spaceships?

And what had Grant meant about my dad? Why was he acting so weird?

I looked around, at the plastic stars and the purple walls. At the stuffed animals and the trophies. Why was my room back the way it had been before I'd been taken all those years ago?

Then, on my nightstand, I saw the program from a memorial service, and I knew whose it was before I even picked it up.

In Loving Memory the heading read, and below that my dad's face stared back at me. Not the way I'd last seen him, with his soft gray beard and bloated cheeks. In the picture, he was clean-shaven and clear-eyed, as if someone had decided an image from the past would better represent him.

But I knew better. I missed my messy dad. The one who'd waited five years for me to come back and then hugged me so hard he'd almost choked me. The dad who'd gone on the run just to keep Tyler and me safe. The dad who'd sacrificed his own life to make amends for what he'd done all those years ago.

I bolted upright. *Tyler.*

If I was here . . . back from . . . *wherever,* was it possible Tyler was too?

Yanking on a pair of sweatpants I found on the floor, I decided to find out. I didn't want to risk another share-your-feelings moment with Grant, so I climbed over my window ledge and bolted across the street to a house I'd once spent as much time in as my own.

The house was dark, but I went straight around the back to Tyler's bedroom window and tapped on it. The entire time my heart was going a hundred miles a minute in my chest. I had no idea what I'd do if he wasn't in there, if I had to go through *this* . . . whatever was happening to me, all alone.

When the bedroom light turned on, I closed my eyes and whispered a silent prayer, and with each footstep that came closer my stomach did a little flip.

Please don't be his mom . . . please don't be his mom . . .

Then, on the other side of the glass, Tyler's face appeared. I waited a second to make sure I wasn't seeing things, and then gave a little wave to say, *It's me.*

His eyebrows squeezed together as his green eyes took me in. It hadn't occurred to me until this very second that the two of us might be back at square one. That he might not remember anything . . . not just about the ISA and the Returned. But about us.

My heart plummeted, I wasn't sure I could do this again.

"Hey," I said, when he opened his window, not sure how to go about testing the waters.

"Hey. What are you doing here so . . ." He leaned back and looked at something—his clock probably. "So *early*?"

"Jeez, Tyler." Suddenly I felt like an idiot. "I'm sorry." I bit my lip. "I . . ." I sighed. "I don't even know what I wanted. I'll let you get back to sleep."

I turned around and started to cross the street, deciding I had to be the most embarrassing person who ever lived. Behind me, I heard his feet land in the gravel. I hesitated.

"I'll remember you always." I almost missed it, he said it so quietly. Less than a whisper.

I closed my eyes, begging myself not to completely lose my shit, before I trusted myself enough to turn around again.

Tyler started grinning, that dimple making an appearance at last when he saw the tears gushing down my cheeks. "I've been waiting almost a week, but I knew you'd eventually figure it out," he told me, sounding even more relieved than I felt. "I knew if I gave you enough time, it'd all come back to you too."

"Shut up," I told him, right before I ran and jumped in his arms and forced him to kiss me.

It took another two days for me to sort it all out.

There were so many details to get straight, like why our parents—my mom and stepdad, who I was now officially calling Grant, and Tyler's folks—had different memories from our own.

"It was the fireflies," Tyler insisted, every time I challenged him on something that didn't make sense, most importantly why we'd survived the explosion at all. "You didn't feel them? You don't remember?"

Except, that's the thing. I sort of did. My memory was still coming together in pieces, but it was coming.

In those last seconds, right before we were completely surrounded by smoke, right before the heat from the flames became too much, I'd felt something on me. Something swarming over me.

I remembered that sensation from before . . . from Devil's Hole when Tyler had been taken. That creepy-crawly feeling of all those fireflies on my arms and legs. In my nose and hair.

I thought the flashes of light I'd seen had been explosions, but the more I thought about it, I was pretty sure Tyler was right. It had been the fireflies after all. The M'alue had rescued us . . . given us an eleventh hour reprieve.

It was the only explanation that made sense, considering we were still alive and all.

And trust me, I wasn't complaining. Things were good for the most part. Tyler and I were back together, and as weird as it was being home again, I didn't mind being with my mom either. She was different now too, but not in a bad way. She was definitely trying.

Simon and the others had made it out in time, and were living in whatever strange alternate reality we'd been thrust into. Agent Truman was still NSA—still Daylighter—although now, considering what we knew, we weren't even sure the Daylighters had a purpose. I definitely no longer lived in fear they'd land on my doorstep. None of us did.

We hadn't quite figured out what this was, our new version of reality. The year hadn't changed—we hadn't gone back in time or anything. But we were definitely not the same as we'd been a week ago. Before the ISA explosion.

So here's what we knew for sure . . .

Fact: I'd been taken and returned. Even my mom and Grant remembered me coming back after a five-year absence, even if they didn't know I'd been abducted. The whole Austin-Cat storyline still existed in whatever dimension we were in.

Fact: I'd infected Tyler when I'd cut myself in front of him. This information however is on a need-to-know basis. Meaning, yes, all of us who were Returned know. Agent Truman knows. My mom, Grant, and Tyler's parents . . . not so much. All they remember is that Tyler and I got into some trouble and took off for a few weeks.

Fact: Tyler and I both landed ourselves under strict lock-down restriction after we'd come back. This makes sense considering our parents think we're moderate delinquents.

Now here's where things got sticky . . .

My dad.

I could end right there and that would be enough. I missed my dad more than I would ever find words for.

As far as my mom and Grant—and pretty much the whole world—are concerned, my dad died in some sort of horrible accident. I try my best not to get all prickly whenever my mom talks about him, about how much he'd changed after I disappeared. How he was never the same.

But it's tough. She didn't know him the way I did. She has no idea he died a hero.

Here's the other really weird thing: none of us—not me or Tyler or Simon or any of the Returned are any different from anyone else anymore. As in, as far as we can tell, we're back to being ordinary humans.

I know!

It started with my eyes. My normal not-glow-in-the-dark eyes, which also happen to *not* see in the dark. That would've been strange enough, except for the part where I could no longer hold my breath super long or control things with my mind.

I could still throw super hard, but that's because I'm a pitcher—I've always had a killer fastball.

The healing thing was up in the air. I was too afraid to

test it. After what happened with Tyler, I couldn't take the chance.

But Simon and some of the others had—cut themselves, I mean. And, sure, they healed. But faster? Maybe. Simon thought so. But definitely not alien-DNA-fast.

We weren't sure what that meant. Was this all part of the M'alue's promise of no more Returned? Had it extended to us as well?

Maybe it didn't matter. Maybe all that mattered is we were here . . . together . . .

Safe.

"Hey, slugger. Your boyfriend's here," Grant teased, tossing me a towel so I could dry my hands.

I caught it, wiped my hands, and kicked the dishwasher door closed. "That's it," I told him. "Final night of KP."

KP—kitchen patrol. Grant's cute name for kitchen duty aside, that last load of dishes signified the official end of my grounding.

Grant held out my phone and the house keys as a reward. "Home by midnight," he instructed, and I wondered when I'd stopped caring that he took such a fatherly tone with me.

I saluted him. "Yes, sir." I snagged the phone, and patted Nancy on the head before rushing out the back door.

I'd wanted a dog for as long as I could remember, but my mom had always had a strict no-dog policy. She almost gave in once, if my dad promised to find a breed that was hypo-allergenic and didn't shed.

Nancy was neither of those things. Plus, she stunk. But according to Grant, after my dad's funeral, Nancy had refused to leave my mom's side. Mom swore the dog was a major annoyance, but whenever she thought no one was around, I caught her slipping Nancy treats and cooing at her in baby talk.

I practically ran into Tyler as he was coming up the drive. "Come on, let's bail before they change their minds." I grinned, and reached for his hand.

I thought he'd have some big date night planned for our first free outing—dinner and a movie or something like that. Instead Tyler pulled his car into a Park 'n' Ride, steering to a spot way near the back, away from the bus garage, where the lot was mostly empty.

I gave him a long silent look before asking. "All right, I give. What are we doing in this super romantic parking lot?"

He grinned, nodding toward the glove box. "I got you something."

Eyeing him skeptically, I popped it open and started laughing. "You're not serious."

"If you could read my mind, you'd know I totally am."

I hit him with the DMV pamphlet.

"Look," he said, defending his actions as he waved his keys at me. "I just think if we're gonna do this whole human thing, it's time you get your own driver's license."

I leaned closer and snatched the keys from his grasp. "Oh, you do, do you?"

Before I could back away, his finger caught me just

underneath the chin. That small action, his simple touch, made my breath catch.

"I do," he said. His voice was low and reached into me, reminding me of a time, not so long ago, when he didn't even have to speak for me to hear him. "And I definitely think we should do this whole human thing. You and me, together."

ACKNOWLEDGMENTS

CONCLUDING THE TAKING TRILOGY WAS BOTH rewarding and bittersweet. I wanted to give Kyra the ending she deserved, while also wrapping up as many threads as possible. I have a lot of people to thank, both those who have guided me through this storytelling journey, and those who stand by me day to day in my civilian (nonwriting) life to keep me sane.

The obvious is my literary agent, Laura Rennert, who never fails to surprise me with her unfailing support of my work. Thanks also to the fabulous Andrea Brown Literary Agency, just for being such an incredible pool of strong and smart women—I'm proud to be part of your crew. Also to my team at WME, Alicia Gordon, Erin Conroy, and Ashley Fox. I love that you have my back in that mystifying Hollywood world!

A huge thank you to HarperTeen, starting with Sarah Landis, who first acquired *The Taking*, and Kari Sutherland who picked up where Sarah left off. To Jen Klonsky and Alice Jerman, thank you for all your hard work and cheerleading, and for getting *The Countdown* to press. To the amazingly talented cover designers who, again, killed it with this cover—it is truly stunning alone or beside its series companions! And again, to Olivia Russo, who is the World's Best Publicist (you can quote me on that!).

I have to thank my critique partner, Shelli Wells, who was in the room when I first brainstormed the idea for *The Taking*, and was there again when I thought I'd backed myself into a corner during *The Countdown*. I hadn't, I just needed her creative perspective to help me see my way out! And the awesome women of Cave Creek, who let me come back to our annual writing retreat every year even though I'm superstitious about sharing my ideas.

In my real life, I want to thank my friends and family for putting up with yoga pants and ugly writing sweaters and for not complaining when I send your calls to voicemail because I'm working out whether there will be an alien invasion or not. But I have to single out a few people, specifically Molly—sorry I decided to kill your character! And don't worry, Madeline, your turn is coming. . . .

Thanks to (Mama) Shawn for keeping the Derting household operational. To my book club ladies for introducing me to characters and worlds I likely wouldn't discover on my own . . . and also for making me laugh. A special thanks to my Amanda, Connor, and Abby, who've learned that "I'm busy" is code for "I'm working" even if it looks like I'm just daydreaming. To my husband, Josh, who constantly amazes me with his brilliant insights and support—thank you times infinity.

And lastly to Hudson, just for being you.